INTRUDERS

JORDAN QUEST FBI THRILLER SERIES BOOK 1

GARY WINSTON BROWN

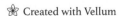 Created with Vellum

Jerry - A new author I found; got his 2nd book too. Disregard underlines in book - too many typos or things I wanted to remember. I wrote the author about typos and he responded. All in all, a good read.

L. A.

As a way of saying thank you for downloading this book (or box set), I'm offering a free book when you sign up for my spam-free newsletter. You'll also be the first to hear about upcoming releases, sales, and insider information.

JORDAN QUEST is the prequel novella to the Jordan Quest FBI thriller series and is available exclusively to newsletter subscribers.

Visit GaryWinstonBrown.com to sign up now and get your FREE book.

This book is dedicated to my beautiful wife, Fiona.
I'm lucky to have you in my life and in my corner.

ILYBBOBKS...ATS

"Out of suffering have emerged the strongest souls; the most massive characters are seared with scars."

— Khalil Gibran

1

J ORDAN QUEST WASN'T CONCERNED. Skeptics came with the territory.

A renowned psychic medium and missing person's consultant to police agencies around the world, Jordan looked out at the group of attendees, all members of the American Association of Police Chiefs. She considered her response to the question posed by the man in the white Stetson. It was one she had been asked dozens of times before, yet it never failed to elicit a small degree of anger within her: "With all due respect Ms. Quest, how can you expect us to take you seriously when what you do has absolutely no basis in science?"

The question brought with it an uncomfortable silence that fell hard over the auditorium. Jordan gripped the microphone. Fifteen hundred faces stared back and awaited her response. Why the hell did it always have to be so hard?

"I appreciate your question, *Chief?*"

"Ballantyne, ma'am. Wayne Ballantyne. Lubbock, Texas."

"Thank you, Chief Ballantyne. I understand your skepticism. I really do. If I were sitting in the audience right now, I might be skeptical too. You're correct. What I do has no basis in science. I don't expect you or anyone else here tonight to believe in me or what I do. That would be an unrealistic expectation. All I can ask of any police agency that reaches out to me for help with their investigation is to agree to suspend their disbelief. If they're not willing to do that, then I'm not interested in working with them. If that sounds harsh, I don't care. I'm not concerned about bruising someone's ego, nor do I see a need to prove myself to anyone. My interest is to bring closure to the family of the victim and help you solve your case. That's it. My track record speaks for itself. I've been involved in over a thousand cases, both missing persons and unsolved homicides since I was twelve years old. I've solved one hundred percent of them. So, if that's not good enough for you or anyone else here there's only one recommendation I can make."

"What's that?" Ballantyne asked.

"Find yourself another girl."

Jordan's straightforward response to Chief Ballantyne's challenging question met with a round of applause from the conventioneers. Jordan raised her hand, called for quiet. Ballantyne glared at her from behind the audience microphone stand. Jordan could tell he wasn't done with her. It had not been her intention to embarrass him in front of his peers, nor had she. But the senior law enforcement officer's body language told her he was not about to let his challenge to her abilities go without a rebuttal. She had to deal with Ballantyne quickly.

Before the Chief could speak Jordan directed her closing comments to the crowd.

"Ladies and gentlemen, Chief Ballantyne is right. There

is no hard science to support or validate my abilities. Some of you may have seen me on television. Others may have read my books and know my story. But for the benefit of those who don't let me explain. When I was twelve years old, I struck my head on the diving board of my family's swimming pool. I was knocked unconscious and drowned. My parents were away on business at the time and I was under the care of our housekeeper, Marissa. I'd been underwater for about thirty minutes when Marissa discovered I was missing. She saw me on the bottom, dove in, pulled me out and called Emergency Services. They began CPR right away and rushed me to the hospital. I died twice while en route. To my knowledge, I'm the only person in history to have survived death-by-drowning for that length of time. The emergency room staff worked on me for thirty minutes. I remember the nurses wrapping me in warm blankets and being surrounded by strange visions and voices. That's when I received brief glimpses into the lives of those entities. When I woke up on the gurney, I had been stabilized. My abilities became much stronger after that. There's not a day that goes by that I don't receive some sort of message or..."

Jordan paused, looked down at the stage, and abruptly disconnected from her conversation with the Chief.

"Ms. Quest..." Ballantyne asked, "are you all right?"

Murmurs rose from the audience.

Jordan didn't reply. Onstage, the striking brunette appeared to be lost in thought.

The Chief took advantage of the moment. "I'm sure all of us can appreciate the horrific tragedy you endured as a child," he said. "But as far as your claim of possessing supernatural gifts is concerned..."

Jordan looked up, cut him off mid-sentence. "Chief

Ballantyne, who is Becky Landry? And what is the significance of the Orono Station Granary?"

Ballantyne felt as though he had just been punched in the gut.

2

LUBBOCK P.D. LAUNCHED their investigation into the disappearance of the missing teenager reluctantly and only after much debate. For most of the town's other young residents, the department would have taken immediate action, issued an Amber Alert and pulled out all the stops. But Becky Landry had proven herself to be the exception to the rule. With her birth mother resting in Peaceful Gardens Cemetery and her father on death row awaiting execution for her murder, Becky became a ward of the state. Three families tried to foster her, none successfully. But Becky's fourth guardians, Joe and Elizabeth Landry, staunchly refused to quit on her. Despite her reputation for being damaged goods, the Landry's adopted the girl, provided her with a loving home, and tried to raise her to their high standards of morality integrity, self-respect, and citizenship. Unfortunately for Becky, her formative years were spent huddled in life's darkest corners, seeking shelter from the constant threat of danger. Hiding in the safety of its shadow made her untrusting, anger worn, and as tough as nails. By the tender age of fifteen she'd proven herself too hard to handle. Becky had become so well known to Lubbock Police that even the patient and understanding Landry's were forced to wash their hands of her. As Joe Landry, a retired apple farmer, once put it after receiving his adopted daughter at their front door from the police officers who drove her home, it had become painfully obvious to him and his wife that in creating the girl her birth father had planted a bad seed in his wife that over the years had destroyed not just the tree but the whole damn orchard that was Becky.

An hour ago, after breaking for lunch, Chief Ballantyne received a call from his office. His officers had found the body of the girl inside a derelict grain processing silo in the neighboring county of Orono Station.

Becky Landry had been brutally raped and murdered.

News of the discovery of Becky's body had not been shared outside the department. Not even the Landry's had been informed.

"How the hell could you have possibly known that?" Ballantyne said.

Audience reaction to Chief Ballantyne's shocked response was swift. Hushed conversation filled the convention hall.

From center stage, in front of the country's most respected men and women in American law enforcement, Jordan had proven her gift.

"I'm sorry for your loss, Chief," Jordan said. Ballantyne left the microphone stand. He returned to his table and sat down. "There's more I can tell you, Chief," Jordan said. "May I?"

Ballantyne nodded and poured himself a glass of water. He'd have preferred it was scotch.

Jordan walked across the stage. She spoke of the crime scene as it unfolded in her mind.

"There's no connection between your victim and her killer," she said. "They don't know one another." Jordan placed her hand against her throat and swallowed hard. "He was behind her when he killed her." She turned, animating her words. "She was garroted."

Dozens of faces flashed through her mind. Keys jangled, secured to a ring by a retractable chain, bits of skin and dried blood embedded in its links: the murder weapon.

"There was a promise of sex," Jordan said.

The crowd quieted as she continued her reading.

Ballantyne replied. "Becky was an attractive girl with little else going for her. We'd heard rumors."

"Of her exchanging sex for money?"

"Yes."

"I believe that's the case here, Chief. Becky solicited her killer, accompanied him to the silo, changed her mind, tried to leave, and paid for that decision with her life. He strangled her using a metal cord from a pull-type key holder."

Now convinced of the legitimacy of her mysterious gift, Ballantyne asked, "Can you see him? Can you tell me what he looks like?"

Jordan closed her eyes. She saw Becky and the stranger in the silo. "She's on her knees, looking up at him, playing with his zipper. He's tracing her cheek with the back of his hand, smoothing the hair away from her face. Three stars."

"Three stars?" Ballantyne asked.

"In a row. Tattoos. Small. A star between each of the knuckles on his right hand. He's angry, impatient. His hands are around the back of her head, trying to pull her closer. He wants her to get on with the act for which she's been paid." Jordan sensed a change in Becky's emotional state.

"She's scared. She knows the situation has escalated beyond her control. She's clawing at his hands, trying to pull them away from her head. Which she does. She's standing now, trying to push him away, but he's too strong." Jordan moved within the vision, circling the girl, attempting to get a better look at her killer. "She's turned her back to him," Jordan reported. "She's bending over, picking up the barrettes he pulled out of her hair." Jordan observed him yank the round silver key holder from his belt and heard the ratcheting sound as the retraction mechanism inside the device released–*zzzzzzzzzip*. In one deft motion he cinched the metal cord tightly around the girl's neck. "He has her," Jordan said. "He's choking her, lifting her off the ground by her neck." Jordan stood in front of Becky. "She's trying to kick free." She watched Becky attempt to drive her fingers beneath the steel lanyard but to no avail. Her arms fell to her side. Her head dropped to her chest.

Becky Landry was dead.

"She's gone," Jordan said. "He's killed her." The stranger pulled Becky up to his face by her neck, to the point of near decapitation. He inhaled deeply. Her hair smelled of coconuts and almond oil with light floral undertones. Jordan watched him shudder with anticipation at the thought of the act to follow.

"White," Jordan said, in answer to the Chief's question. "Six feet tall, mid-thirties, athletic build, handsome. Tattoos on his right hand. He'll have abrasions on the back of both hands. If he's still carrying the key chain when you find him, run it. Something tells me Becky Landry's won't be the only DNA you'll find on it. She's not his only victim, and probably won't be his last."

Chief Ballantyne's cell phone chimed. He read the text: LANDRY GIRL GARROTTED.

He stood. "If it's possible, Mrs. Quest, I'd appreciate it if we could stay in touch."

Jordan nodded. "It would be my pleasure."

3

CHIEF BALLANTYNE WALKED to the front of the conference room and shook Jordan's hand as she left the stage. "Thank you," he said. "I'll be in touch."

Jordan smiled. "Anytime, Chief. I'm glad I could help." She pointed to the back of the room. "My publisher has asked me to stick around for a while, meet the attendees, and sign a few books. I'll be here for the next half hour or so. Stop by."

Ballantyne joked. "After that reading you might want to push that out to at least an hour." A small group had gathered behind him. They appeared eager to speak with Jordan. "Something tells me you're going to be inundated with requests for help."

"That's why I do what I do, Chief."

"And I, for one, will be grateful for it."

Chief Ballantyne stepped aside. Jordan invited the guests to join her at the back of the room as the next speaker, April Searle, a fingerprint identification expert, greeted the audience from the stage.

"Pardon me, Ms. Quest?" A good-looking man stood next to her book signing table. He wore a dark blue suit, his shoes polished to an impeccable shine. Jordan was impressed by the manner with which he carried himself.

"Yes?"

The man removed his identification from his jacket pocket and presented his badge and credentials. "My name is Special Agent Chris Hanover. I'm with the Federal Bureau of Investigation. May I have a moment of your time?"

Jordan nodded. "Is everything all right?"

"Yes, ma'am. Nothing to worry about," the agent replied.

A member of Jordan's support team organized the book signing table. Officers took their place in line, anxious to meet the recognized attorney and psychic medium turned police consultant in person, get their book signed, and snap a picture with the author.

The surrounding area was getting busier and louder.

"Would you mind if we stepped outside for just a moment?" Hanover asked. "It might be a little quieter. The matter is quite sensitive."

"Lead the way," Jordan said. "I'm afraid I can only give you a few minutes, Agent Hanover. I'm needed here."

"No problem," Hanover said. "This won't take long."

The hallway was quiet compared to the boisterous activity taking place at the back of the convention room. Two wingback chairs at the end of the corridor offered the perfect place to sit and talk.

Special Agent Hanover removed a manila envelope from a leather portfolio and passed it to Jordan. It contained graduation photographs of two beautiful young women; the first a blonde, with piercing blue eyes; the second a hazel-eyed brunette. Both women conveyed an air of sophistication and intelligence. Jordan recognized the purple academic regalia.

"Harvard Law. My alma mater," Jordan said. "Although it's been quite a few years since I graduated."

"This is Shannon Dunn," Hanover said, pointing to the blonde. "And her sister, Zoe. They graduated a week ago. I've been asked to speak with you at the behest of her father, Andrew Dunn."

Jordan recognized the name. "As in FBI Director Andrew Dunn?"

Hanover nodded. "Shannon and Zoe are his daughters. The Director hasn't heard from them for a week. They left Cambridge for Los Angeles right after graduation. Said they wanted to enjoy one last big blowout before entering the 'real world.' They wanted to check out Hollywood, Beverly Hills... maybe run into a movie star or two. Communication from both women came to a dead stop a week ago. No calls, texts, emails, social media posts... nothing. For all intents and purposes, they've vanished."

"I assume you pinged their phones?"

"Both stopped transmitting five days ago."

"You said they were *headed* to Los Angeles. Did you confirm that they arrived?"

"They did. Airport security cams show Shannon's Audi entering the parking garage at Logan Airport in Boston. Four hours later they picked up their rental car at Los Angeles International. We tracked them to the condominium the Director had rented for them. Shannon and Zoe called their father to let him know they had arrived. No one has heard from them since. Agents in Los Angeles searched the condo. The girls had unpacked. There was an open bottle of wine sitting on the dining room table along with two empty glasses and a card from the Director congratulating them on their graduation and wishing them a good stay."

"Nice touch," Jordan said.

"It would have been," Chris Hanover said, "except the card and the wine weren't left by the Director. Someone else did that. We printed the bottle. It came back clean, but the contents didn't."

"What did you find?"

"Trace amounts of Rohipnol."

"The date rape drug."

The agent nodded.

"Any signs of a struggle?

Hanover shook his head. "No forced entry to the building or the apartment. We're going over their phone records, talking to friends, acquaintances... trying to connect the dots."

"Does the Director know of anyone who would want to harm his family?"

"No."

"What about Zoe or Shannon? Could one of them been targeted?"

"We're looking into that. Director Dunn adopted Zoe. Mitch Dawson, her father, was his best friend. He retired from the Bureau eight years ago, died six months thereafter. Cancer."

"What did Agent Dawson do when he was with the FBI?"

"Executive Assistant Director, National Security Branch, Counterterrorism Division."

Jordan stared at the pictures. "Both fathers are high profile. Do you think Shannon and Zoe's disappearance might be related to a case?"

"We're not ruling anything out at this stage. Director

Dunn is working with the investigative lead on the case. He also happens to be someone close to you. Special Agent Grant Carnevale, your godfather."

Jordan smiled. "My father has known Agent Carnevale for decades. They're best friends. He should have been my dad's business partner, you know."

Hanover nodded. "Grant never stops talking about it. More accurately, he never lets us forget it."

Jordan laughed. "I'm not surprised. My dad's been trying to recruit him away from the Bureau for the last twenty years."

"It's my understanding they studied together at MIT," the agent said.

Jordan nodded. "That's right. The theories on computerized machine intelligence my father developed there became the foundation for his company, Farrow Industries."

Agent Hanover smiled. "Grant calls being recruited by the Bureau right out of MIT and not going into business with your dad his 'billion-dollar mistake.'"

"Yes," Jordan said, "My father has done very well for himself. There aren't too many companies in the world today that are bigger than Farrow Industries."

Hanover removed a small envelope from his jacket pocket. "You should know when Special Agent Carnevale heard about Shannon and Zoe's disappearance he reached out to the Director personally. He feels no one is better suited to assist with this investigation than you."

Jordan smiled. "I appreciate that. But I must admit I'm a little surprised that the Bureau would even entertain the use of a psychic in this or any case."

"Under normal circumstances, that would be true. But it turns out Director Dunn's late wife, Caitlin, was a fan of yours. She'd read all your books and followed your career.

She'd told the Director about your reputation for helping to solve missing persons cases and that the FBI should enlist your services to help with cold-case investigations." Hanover handed Jordan the envelope. "Director Dunn wanted you to have this. He thought it might help you locate his daughters."

Jordan tore open the envelope. It contained two items: a gold herringbone necklace and silver charm bracelet.

"The necklace belongs to Shannon," Hanover said. "The bracelet is Zoe's."

Jordan held the objects in her hand. The images were powerful, intense, and frightening. She hid her reaction from the agent.

"I can speak to the Director tonight," Jordan said. "I have another speaking engagement to attend tomorrow in Hawaii. My parents will be vacationing there for the next few months. My husband and I are catching a lift on the company jet. We fly out tonight." Jordan jotted down her cellphone number. "Ask Director Dunn to call me after 7:00 P.M. We should be in the air by then. I'll have time to talk."

Special Agent Hanover stood. "I'll relay the message. Thank you for your help, Mrs. Quest."

"My pleasure." Jordan said. She stood, shook hands with the FBI agent, and returned to the conference hall. The impromptu meeting had put her behind schedule. Her fans, books in hand, stood in line to meet her.

Jordan sat behind the table, greeted her first fan, signed her book and smiled for a picture. But her mind was no longer on the conference.

It was on the vision the necklace and bracelet revealed. The damp, dark place where Shannon and Zoe were being held. And the shackles that bound them.

4

JENNIFER BLEEKER, Jordan's publicist, leaned over her shoulder and whispered in her ear. "Limo's arrived, Jordan. Time to wrap up."

Jordan smiled for a photo. Three remaining fans waited to meet her. "Give me ten minutes, Jenny," she replied.

"Your driver wants you to know the traffic's heavy," Jennifer replied. "Says you'll need at least an hour to get to the airport."

"Remind him it's my father's jet," Jordan teased. "I'm sure they won't take off without me."

"Point taken," Jennifer conceded. "For the record, the guy is gorgeous. Looks like he stepped right off the cover of a romance novel. Do you need me to carry your bags to the car? Better yet, I could warm up the back seat for you."

Jordan laughed. "You're bad."

Jennifer winked. "You have *no* idea."

"Thanks for offering, Jen," Jordan said. "I think I've got it covered."

Jennifer smiled. "Trust me, it's no trouble. I'll be happy to take one for the team."

Jordan shook her head. "I'm sure you would. Tell him I'll be along shortly."

The publicist sighed. "If I must." She picked up Jordan's overnight bag and checked her watch. "You now have exactly eight minutes."

"I'll be there soon," Jordan said. "Why don't you go keep Rock company?"

"Rock?" Jennifer asked. "His name is *Rock*?"

Jordan smiled and rolled her eyes. "Dionne. His name is Rock Dionne. He's French-Canadian."

"Mrs. Rock Dionne..." Jennifer mused. "I could get used to that."

"He's married."

"Of course, he is," Jennifer said. "Thanks for ruining a perfectly good fantasy. You're killing me, Jordan."

Jordan laughed. "Get out of here. Now I'm down to what... six minutes?"

"Five and counting."

Jordan saw her last fan in line was getting impatient. "Go!" she said. "I'll be right there."

"Okay." Jennifer called back as she left the room. "Rock and I will be waiting."

Jordan laughed, then apologized to the man. "I'm very sorry for keeping you waiting." She opened his copy of her book to the title page and uncapped her Sharpie marker. "What's your name?"

The man wore an open grey windbreaker, herringbone flat cap, yellow-lens sunglasses, and black leather driving gloves. He was not wearing a convention badge.

"Marsden," he said.

"Nice name," Jordan said. Something about the man

seemed strange. Jordan couldn't put her finger on it. "First or last?" she asked.

"It was my fathers," the man said, failing to answer her question directly. "And his fathers before that. Been that way for five generations."

Jordan looked up. "Amusing answer," she replied.

"Is it?" the man asked. He placed a hand behind his back. "I don't know why. You asked me, so I told you."

Jordan had a bad feeling.

Because of her family's immense wealth and the potential for kidnapping or personal harm that came with it, Jordan's father employed round-the-clock shadow security. The team's job was to keep his family safe whenever they were in public. The highly skilled operatives were experts at maintaining a covert overwatch, blending into crowds and remaining inconspicuous, yet they were never far away. The members of the Farrow family - Jordan, her husband Keith, and her parents - had each been given a special word, a panic word they were to call out if they suspected they were in danger. Jordan's word was *Shortcake*; the playful nickname her father had given to her when she was a child. Growing up, she had been warned of the consequences of using it, and that it was only to be used in an emergency. If she yelled the word right now members of her security team would surround her within seconds and escort her to safety. The threat would be dealt with accordingly.

The strained conversation and odd behavior of the stranger made her uncomfortable.

She had never used her panic word before. She found it on her lips.

A man and woman emerged from the crowd, casualty positioning themselves on either side of the odd man.

Marsden removed his hand from his waist and placed it in his jacket pocket.

The man moved in behind him to his left, the woman to his right. She brushed past him and skimmed her hand across his waist. She smiled at Marsden, apologized for bumping into him, then looked at her partner.

No weapon detected.

Jordan realized the man and woman were members of her shadow detail. Perhaps additional operatives were circulating in the crowd or standing at the adjoining tables. Until their services were needed, she would remain unaware of their presence. All that was important right now was that she was safe.

"What police department are you with?" Jordan asked. She signed the man's book and handed it back to him.

Marsden tucked the book under his arm. "I'm not."

The operative on Marsden's left moved closer. The woman walked to the side of the signing table, opening a direct path between herself and Jordan.

"I knew your father, Michael Farrow. Sonofabitch took everything I had."

Jordan stood up. "Excuse me? Who are you? How the hell did you get in here?"

Marsden removed a pen from his pocket, pointed it at her, then threw it on the table.

"You'll be hearing from me." Marsden glanced at the operatives standing beside him. "Count on it."

The woman looked at her partner. She shook her head as if to say, 'don't engage.'

"Get out!" Jordan yelled.

Marsden touched the brim of his cap and smiled. "Good day, Mrs. Quest."

Jennifer Bleeker returned to the conference room as

Marsden was walking out. She looked at Jordan, then glanced back at the man. Something felt wrong.

"Everything okay, Jordan?"

"It's nothing, Jenn. Is the car ready?"

"Whenever you are."

"Good. Let's get out of here."

Jordan looked at the pen laying on the table. The Farrow Industries logo was printed on the barrel.

She threw it in her purse.

5

JENNIFER WAVED GOODBYE as the limousine pulled out of the parking circle at the front entrance of the convention center.

Rock Dionne glanced in his rearview mirror. "How did it go?" he asked.

"Huh?" Jorden replied.

"The conference. How was it?"

"Oh, that," Jordan said. "Great."

"Good thing you're a psychic," Rock joked. "You'd make a pathetic salesperson."

Jordan was preoccupied with Marsden's threat. *You'll see me again. Count on it.* She removed the pen from her purse.

"Sorry, Rock." Jordan said. "I had a rather weird encounter before I left."

Rock was affable, friendly. Jordan liked and trusted him. "What do you mean, *weird*?"

Jordan rolled the pen between her fingers. "Rock, how long have you been part of my dad's protection detail?" she asked.

"Three years," Rock replied. "Why?"

"Do you ever recall my father mentioning a guy by the name of Marsden?"

Dionne shook his head. "Doesn't ring a bell."

"Seems he had some kind of falling out with my father."

Dionne looked concerned. "Anything serious?"

"I don't know."

"What happened back there, Jordan? This Marsden guy threaten you?"

Jordan hesitated. "Let's say whatever problem he has with my father was motivation enough for him to crash the conference to tell me about it."

"What did he say?"

"That I'd be seeing him again."

"Meaning?"

"I don't know."

"You think he could be a problem?"

"Maybe, maybe not."

Dionne sounded worried. "That's cause enough for concern. Your father needs to know about this. So does his detail."

"I'm a big girl, Rock. I can take care of myself. Besides, when I was in practice, I received dozens of threats. Nothing ever came from them. I'm sure the guy's harmless."

"In my line of work everyone is harmless until they're *not*," Dionne said. "That was different. You were a criminal prosecutor back then. This sounds personal." He picked up his cell phone.

"Who are you calling?"

"Nick Parsons. Maybe he knows what this is about."

"Thanks, Rock," Jordan said.

Rock smiled. "Don't worry about it. We'll take care of it." He checked his watch. "We should be at the gate in forty-five minutes. Grab some shut eye. I'll wake you when we arrive."

Jordan settled into the deep leather seat and closed her eyes. "Sounds good."

Nick Parsons commanded Farrow Industries security team. Several years ago, at his suggestion, Michael Farrow had begun providing him with transcripts of his telephone calls and business meetings, all of which had been recorded. The transcripts were retained to serve as proof of any threats made against him. Farrow knew that on his way to building a computer technology empire he was bound to run into his fair share of tough competitors, and probably make a few enemies along the way. Perhaps Marsden was one of them.

Jordan tried to rest but couldn't. She held the pen in her hand and concentrated. Although Marsden wore gloves, she could read the latent energy signature off the writing instrument from when he had last handled it.

The images came in rapid succession: Marsden using the pen to sketch out the layout of a building. A meeting with a man; black, muscular, intimidating. He hands the man a document... plans... along with several photographs, the first of a steel cabinet stocked with an assortment of items: brass couplings, push-on hoses, rubber O-rings of various sizes. The second photo was the inside of a building. A wall-mounted chemical spill clean-up kit and plastic goggles hung on the wall. Machines and equipment of various types, their purposes unknown to her, were located about the room. The vision also revealed the smell of paint so noxious it forced Jordan to cover her nose to quell the assault of the phantom odor on her senses. The structure was massive. Jordan moved within it and inspected the facility to which the pen had transported her. A tool lay at her feet. As she knelt to pick it up a brilliant white light formed at the end of the structure. Jordan shielded her eyes as the strange light grew brighter, wider, until soon it had become <u>all-encompassing</u>, blinding her, filling the vision. When the sensorial overload finally proved to be too strong Jordan broke the connection.

She dropped the pen. The vision vanished.

Jordan held her hands to her head. The effect of the psychic journey had been <u>short-lived</u>, minor in comparison to past object readings.

Her senses returned to normal. The foul smell was gone. No head pain remained.

"You okay, Jordan?" Rock asked.

Jordan apologized. "I'm fine, Rock. Thanks."

"Another vision?"

"Yes."

"Looks like it was a bad one."

"More unsettling than anything else."

Rock checked his mirrors, executed a lane change. "Mind if I ask you a personal question, Jordan?" he said.

"Sure."

"This gift of yours... to be able to see and feel things the rest of us can't. You can control it, right?"

"Most of the time, yes."

"Do you ever wish you could just turn it off?"

Jordan flashed back to her childhood. Lying at the bottom of the pool. The coldness of the surrounding water. The rising whine of the ambulance defibrillator as it recharged. The shock of the paddles which threw her small body up off the gurney with each electrical jolt. The flurry of activity in the emergency room to save her life.

This was how The Gift had been delivered to her. Not kindly or gently, but violently, and nearly at the cost of her life.

She answered Rock. "No. It's part of me now. To not

accept it would be wrong. It was given to me for a reason. I have a responsibility to pursue the visions wherever they lead me."

Rock smiled. "I'm glad the Man upstairs gave you a second chance. I can't think of anyone more deserving, even if you do freak me out a little."

Jordan laughed. "Try being my husband."

"Keith's a brave man." Rock answered his cellphone, spoke with the caller, hung up. "Jet's on the tarmac ready to go. Keith and your parents just arrived."

"Are you coming with us?"

Rock glanced in his rearview mirror at Jordan. "Do I look like a guy who would turn down a working vacation in Maui? Damn straight I'm going!"

Jordan laughed. "Will you be at my event?"

Rock shook his head. "An operations team is already at the convention center prepping for your appearance. I'll catch up with you again when I return from Hawaii."

"Sounds good," Jordan said. She looked outside. Through the tinted window of the limousine the sunny sky took on a foreboding, ominous appearance. Her thoughts returned to Marsden. The smile fell from her face.

Rock picked up on the sudden change in Jordan's disposition. "Stop thinking about it," he said.

"About what?"

"Whatever happened back there. Don't give that joker another thought. We'll check him out. Okay?"

Jordan smiled. "Thanks, Rock."

The pen lay on the seat beside her. Jordan returned it to her purse. She would read it again on the flight. Perhaps it could tell her more about the stranger and whether he posed a threat to her family.

6

J AMES RIGEL WAS APPALLED by the smell. He
had insisted the desk clerk in the small roadside
motel check him into the most recently cleaned
room and had paid extra for the request. When he
opened the door, he expected to be met with a bouquet so
fragrant and pleasing he would be quite content to spend
the next hour sitting in the room, inhaling its exquisite
aromas, and reflecting upon the exhilarating highlights of
his road trip. Instead, his olfactory senses were assaulted by
a wave of offensive odors: stale cigarette smoke, sickly sweet
air freshener (that smelled nothing like any pine forest he
had ever walked through), lemon-scented furniture spray,
the overpowering stench of ammonia-based bathroom
cleaning compounds, and fabric softener. He considered
marching down to the front desk, pulling the bastard over
the counter, dragging him along the second-floor walkway
back to his room, gagging the sonofabitch, and forcing him
to sit in the stench that his cleaning staff had created. But
the clerk would have to wait. He needed to tend to a matter
of greater importance.

Rigel covered his nose and hurried through the room to the bathroom. He pulled a towel off the metal wall rack, laid it over the scarred cigarette-burned desk, and opened the wooden cigar box in which he kept his most prized possessions. He removed each of the items from the box with great reverence and laid them out in front of him.

The first was a bright-yellow tongue stud. It had belonged to a young lady he had met a couple of days ago at a highway rest stop in Arkansas, west of Hot Springs. She told him her name was Cathy and that she was eighteen-years old. Likely no older than fifteen, she was physically developed beyond her years. Cathy took great pride in telling Rigel she was hitchhiking across the USA to California, that the better part of her last ride had been spent with her head buried in the lap of a long-haul trucker, and that she would be willing to make the next leg of his trip as pleasant for him as it had been for the trucker if he would give her a lift down the highway. Cathy said she preferred the road to home, that Hollywood was calling, and referred to herself as both a free-spirit and mistress of her own destiny. James was impressed by her natural beauty. He agreed that she had the looks to take the entertainment industry by storm. What most enthralled him most about the girl was the enticing smell of her body. The hint of shea butter on her copper skin, the faint honey-almond aroma of her hair, and the slight scent of citrus in her perfume. He accepted her invitation and enjoyed both her company and well-practiced talent for the next five-and-a-half hours from Hot Springs to Norman, Oklahoma. They finished lunch in a diner on the outskirts of town. When Cathy excused herself to use the restroom, James agreed that a pee break was in order. He followed the girl downstairs, pushed her into the ladies' room, snapped her neck, and ripped the stud out of her tongue. He opened the maintenance closet between the men's and woman's washrooms, removed the Closed for Maintenance sign, and hung it on the doorknob. Having left sufficient cash to cover the cost of the meal and a generous gratuity for their waitress he left the restaurant, unnoticed, through a back door.

It had been a wonderful start to the day.

From Oklahoma he journeyed to Texas. This was his first time traveling through the American Southwest and James was anxious to see as much of the region as his busy schedule would permit. He exited the Interstate at Lubbock County, explored the city, then drove through town until he found himself in the quiet town of Slaton. The red brick roadway and wild west mural in the Town Square paid homage to its ranching and railway heritage. It was in Slaton where he met the beautiful teenager with the pink barrettes.

His reason for stopping to talk to her seemed innocent enough– a lost traveler, having wandered off the Interstate, out of his way and in need of directions. The attraction was mutual and immediate. The girl rested her arms on the roof of his car, exposing the bottom of her breasts beneath her pink FCUK crop top. She asked him where he was from, where he was going, and if he would be interested in partying with her for a while before hitting the road. He lied in response to her first two questions but readily agreed to the third. She took a step back from the door, unfastened her belt, unbuttoned her jeans, pulled down her zipper and removed two joints from her G-string. She told him the pot was free. Partying would cost him two hundred. He opened his wallet, pulled out four fifties, stuck them down his pants, and asked if she was ready to play. The girl's eyes brightened. She introduced herself as Becky, promised him the time of his life, hopped into the front seat of his car, and directed him to what she called party central. The abandoned grain storage silo was located on the outskirts of town. He kissed her when she sat beside him. Her skin smelled delicious: lavender and vanilla. He told her if she smelled as good downstairs as he thought she did he'd gladly double the two hundred. She assured him he wouldn't be disappointed. He pushed her to her knees, insisted she go down on him hard. But when she did nothing more than tease him to the point of white-hot frustration, he dealt with her appropriately, nearly severing her head from her body with the retractable metal cord from the keychain he kept clipped to his belt. Professional assassination was his stock in trade. The device was one of his favorite weapons and had become his trademark. He had even given it a name: *Zippy*.

When his rage had subsided, the girl slumped to the ground at his feet. He unwound the garrote from her neck and retracted its steel cable. The cord caught the pink barrettes in her hair, pulled them out. They fell to the ground. He pocketed the souvenirs.

He left the dead girl lying on the dusty floor of the granary.

In contrast to the perfumery of her lifeless body the surrounding air smelled of mold and mildew, and so grossly offended his senses he thought he might retch. He hurried out of the abandoned silo into the fresh air.

Rigel placed the pink hair clips on the towel beside the yellow stud.

From Lubbock he travelled to Roswell, New Mexico and stayed at the Galaxy Motel Inn where he enjoyed a comfortable bed, a quiet room, and one of the most rejuvenating sleeps of his trip.

That afternoon he gassed up in Benson, Arizona. While waiting to pay for fuel, a thirty-something blonde with exceptional legs jumped the line in front of him. He tapped her on the shoulder and pointed to the customers patiently waiting in line behind him. The blonde flashed a perfect smile, explained she was running late for a meeting with her divorce attorney, thanked him for his understanding, but never once apologized for her inconsiderate behavior. She paid for her purchases, strutted out of the store, jumped into a Porsche Boxster and raced out of the gas station, nearly running down a patron as he crossed the lot. Rigel followed her home (so much for the bogus meeting with her attorney) and parked across the street. He watched her house, waited until she drew shut the upstairs bedroom blinds, then walked to her back door. He removed a professional lock pick set from his jacket pocket, worked the lock and deadbolt until they released, then slipped in through the kitchen. Hearing the sound of running water, he ascended the stairs, entered the bathroom, grabbed her hairbrush off the vanity, pulled back the shower curtain, and rammed it down her throat before she could form a scream. Zippy enjoyed itself. Blood streamed down from beneath the steel cord as he pulled it tightly around her neck, the coppery aroma blending with her magnificent grapefruit and lilac soap covered body. He watched as the last glimmer of life left her eyes. The woman made up for her exceptional rudeness with a perfect body and excellent taste in body wash. The steam from the hot shower accentuated the decadent fruit and floral smell and made their special moment together even more intimate and seductive. Rigel carried her out of the bathroom into the master bedroom, threw her corpse on the bed, and raped her. It was the least she could do to make up for his lost travel time. He was glad they met.

Two hours later, he found himself here: a guest of the not-so-accommodating Cactus Court Motor Inn in Gila Bend.

Rigel placed the hairbrush beside the yellow tongue stud and pink barrettes and closed his eyes.

Before long the polluted smell of the motel room faded. His mind was set adrift on an aromatic sea of strawberry, shea butter, honey-almond, grapefruit and lilac that lingered on the treasures that lay before him.

Now late afternoon, Rigel debated whether he should stay the night in Gila Bend. He was only five hours from Los Angeles.

His handlers in New York had negotiated the contract with the client. His ten-million-dollar fee had been accepted. Five million had already been deposited into his Cayman Islands account as a retainer. The balance would be transferred as soon as the conditions of the agreement was met.

The entire family was to be taken out. There were to be no survivors.

James Rigel had been chosen to carry out the Farrow hit for two specific reasons. First, he was unquestionably the best in the business. Second, eliminating high-profile targets was his specialty. And no target was higher profile than Michael Farrow.

Rigel decided he couldn't handle another minute in the stinkpot room, much less the entire night. He placed the precious items back into the wooden box together with the souvenirs he had collected from his previous road trips. An orange sarong taken from a university student enjoying summer break in Daytona Beach, Florida. White lace panties from a high school cheerleader in South Carolina. Cotton sweat bands from a tennis instructor in Virginia. Black silk pantyhose from a stockbroker in Virginia.

He flicked on the lights, turned up the volume on the television, locked the door to the abysmal room, and returned to his car.

The door to the office was open, the lobby deserted. The motel clerk wasn't at his desk.

Rigel considered tracking him down and introducing him to Zippy. Appealing as the thought was, he passed on the idea.

He started the car and pulled out of the parking lot.

He would be in Los Angeles tonight. If all went according to plan, and it always did, he would be five million dollars richer tomorrow.

Not that the money mattered. He was financially independent. A lifetime of conducting professional assassinations had seen to that.

What James Rigel loved more than anything else about his job was the opportunity it provided him to expand on his collection of souvenirs.

And the smell of fresh blood.

7

THE MAN PULLED into the reserved parking space marked EMERGENCY VEHICLES ONLY, stepped out of the maroon fire department sedan, removed an aluminum clipboard from the back seat, and adjusted his cap. The uniform he wore and the credentials he presented to the desk clerk were legitimate, having once belonged to the dead man in the trunk of the car.

The man introduced himself. "Captain Mark Viegas. Aviation Emergency Response. I'm here to inspect the premises."

The clerk looked puzzled. "We were just inspected two weeks ago," he said.

"What can I say?" the fake fire captain said. "You're on the list." He opened the clipboard. "Name?"

"You're kidding me, right?"

"*Name*?" he repeated.

"Pirelli," the clerk replied. "Anthony Pirelli."

"As in Pirelli the tire company?"

"Yeah."

"Any relation?"

The clerk cocked his head. "Seriously? You think I'd be working here if I was?"

The man waited for an answer to his question.

"No, no relation," Pirelli replied.

He motioned to the aircraft hangars. "They all occupied?"

Pirelli shook his head. "Just A and C. It's a slow day."

"Call them," the man said. "Tell the mechanics to clear the floor. I'll need thirty minutes per box."

"*Thirty minutes?*" the clerk complained. "Are you frigging kidding me? You realize we have to pay these guys whether they're working or not, right?"

The man held up his phone. "It's that or I make a call and shut you down for the rest of the day. Your choice."

The clerk fired back. "I have a suggestion. Call your dispatch. I'm sure there's a kitten up a tree somewhere that needs help. Tell them to send you there instead."

"Ah, cat jokes," the man said. "Never heard those before." He leaned over the counter. "Listen to me, son. I strongly suggest that you pick up the phone and clear those hangars right now, 'cause you're real close to getting your ass canned."

"Yeah, yeah, yeah..." Pirelli made the calls. "There," he said. "Happy now?"

"Ecstatic."

"I'm putting you in my log."

"You do that."

"This is a straight up hassle, man."

"I'm sure you'll get over it. I'll be out of here in an hour. I suggest you put that time to good use. Maybe call the tire company. Ask if they're hiring."

"Funny."

"I don't want to see a soul in those hangars when I get there," the man warned. "We clear?"

The clerk pointed to the two teams of aircraft maintenance workers strolling across the tarmac towards the employee lounge. "There you go, boss. All present and accounted for."

"Good. I don't like to be interrupted when I'm working."

"I'll tell the men to try to contain themselves."

"You do that," the man replied as he walked through the sliding automatic doors that led out to the aircraft hangars. "And it's *Captain*, not Chief."

"Whatever," the clerk said. He returned to his paperwork.

THE FAKE FIRE captain entered Hanger A. A business jet, white with blue and red stripes, stood in the middle of the facility, the cowlings of its Pratt & Whitney engines removed for servicing, the engines exposed. He removed a sheet of paper from his pocket and checked the tail number noted in the bottom corner of the sketch: HN-3RN. This was not the aircraft he was looking for.

No match.

Pirelli had mentioned C hangar was also occupied. He opened the door and stepped inside.

Ahead of him stood the jet, tail number HN-3RN.

Match.

He locked the hangar door behind him. Sunlight poured into the room from the open bay doors which faced the runway at the opposite end of the building. Outside, the absence of wind beneath an unlimited ceiling of bright blue sky offered a perfect day for flying.

The man went straight to work. He read the encrypted

text he had received on his phone two hours ago before killing the fire Captain and assuming his identity. The instructions provided by New York were specific. He referred to the sketch, located the tool chest standing against the wall of the hangar, removed the specified tools, walked over to the aircraft, and followed the instructions. He removed a sheet of plastic from within the aluminum clipboard case, handling it carefully so as not to damage the fingerprints which had been transferred to its surface, and applied the prints to the specified tool. He placed the tool on the floor of the hangar several feet from the aircraft. The scene set, he took a picture and emailed it to New York.

His phone chimed a second later. The text read REVISIONS NECESSARY. CHECK IN.

Strange.

He called the number.

"We have a problem," the voice answered.

"Not on my end," the man replied. "We're good here."

"There's been a development. Your contract has been changed."

"You better not be talking about my fee."

"Relax, Tasker. The funds were transferred as soon as your photo was received."

"Good answer. What's the issue?"

"We have another contract. It was closed."

"*Was?*"

"We've discovered a problem with the operator. One that could bring undue attention to us. We've decided to reopen the contract. But there's a contingency."

"And that is?"

"You'll need to eliminate the contractor as well as the target. You interested?"

"Who are we talking about?"

The caller paused. "Check your phone."

Harrison Tasker watched the photo pop up on screen. He recognized the man. "He's good."

"We know."

"You're sure about this?"

"We don't have a choice in the matter. You want the contract or not?"

"How much?"

"Same as the original offer. Five million on retainer, plus another five with proof of termination."

The hitman raised his voice. "Don't screw with me. We both know a contract of that amount covers the target alone. How much more is it worth to you to make your contractor problem go away?"

The caller hesitated. "I'll need approval."

"Then I suggest you get it."

Tasker waited. The caller reconnected seconds later. "We can do another five," he said.

"Ten."

"Not possible."

"Then I guess he's not as big a problem as you think he is."

"I've been authorized to go to six."

"Nine."

"Eight. Not a penny more."

Tasker said nothing.

"You there?" the caller asked.

"Yeah," Tasker replied. "All right. Eight million, in advance, plus the original ten for the target as stipulated. And you re-close the contract. I'm not interested in dealing with competition on this. He's not going to be easy to take down."

"Agreed. You'll have exclusivity for seventy-two hours. If

you can't complete the job by then we go to the next name on the list and the eight million will be rescinded."

"Fair enough. What's his location?"

"Los Angeles."

"I'm here now."

"We know. Stay put. The contractor is on his way to L.A. We'll send you a code. You'll be able to track his location on your phone. Questions?"

"None."

"Remember, Tasker. Seventy-two hours."

"I heard you the first time."

The caller hung up.

Tasker scrolled through the pictures in the file. The family stood beside a private jet on the tarmac at Maui's Kahului Airport terminal building. The aircraft looked familiar. He noted its tail number, HN-3RN, and realized he was standing under the jet.

"I'll be damned." He read the list of names whose immediate termination had now been entrusted to him: Michael Farrow. Mary Farrow. Jordan Quest. Keith Quest. Emma Quest (child). Aiden Quest (child).

He recognized the name. Anyone who was even slightly in the know about advancements in computer technology knew the name Michael Farrow. The next two names were unfamiliar to him until he read the familial relationship: Jordan Quest was Farrow's daughter, Keith Quest her husband. The last two names were those of the Quests kids. Killing children always bothered him, but in his line of work emotional involvement was right up there with second thoughts. Neither were a luxury he could afford. Attachments of any kind led to hesitation and hesitation led to someone dying. He preferred it not be him.

He opened the second dossier, that of the contractor,

and studied the man's face. Though he knew of him by reputation there had always been something about the man he disliked. Something disturbing even to someone in his line of work. Something... off.

No matter. Within a day or two he'd be taken out and no longer of concern to anyone.

He checked his watch. An hour had passed. It was time to leave. It would be just like the smartass desk clerk to return the mechanics to the hangar early even though he'd specifically told him he was not to be disturbed.

For a moment Tasker welcomed an intrusion by the irritating clerk. The weapon under his jacket was equipped with a silencer. No one would hear the gunshot.

The thought made him smile. The trunk of the fire captain's car was generous enough to accommodate two bodies, not just one.

He could make room.

8

THE WINE... something in the wine...

Shannon Dunn tried to push back the mental fog that had rolled in, obscured her ability to concentrate, and left her memory of the past week as scrambled as the mismatched sides of a Rubik's Cube; pieces of a puzzle, twisted, turned; parts of a whole, yet incomplete.

Her last memory was watching Zoe collapse. They had been in Los Angeles for only an hour, unpacked their clothes and put away the few basic groceries they had purchased en route to the condo (milk, eggs, bread, corn chips, a six-pack of Dos Equis beer). She noticed the bottle of wine and accompanying card sitting on the dining room table. Zoe read the note aloud, reminded her sister how fortunate they were to have such a thoughtful father, then picked up the bottle of Lotus California Cabernet Sauvignon and paraded it around the room with theatrical vigor, extolling the wines 'fruity undertones, with just the right hint of spice,' and how it would, in the absence of expertly prepared filet mignon, pair perfectly with Spicy Nacho Doritos.

She remembered pouring the wine and their toast to Harvard. Minutes later she felt lightheaded. Her body had become tremendously heavy. The room had begun to spin. Walls wrapped around her. Her peripheral vision narrowed, faded to black, and caused the room to morph into a tunnel. The strange change in her equilibrium caused the condominium floor to rise and fall as though she were on the deck of a ship being tossed about in foul weather, trying to maintain balance. Before consciousness finally left her and she fell to the floor, she called out for Zoe.

Shannon recalled another side of the jumbled memory cube before riding the swell into darkness. The lobby communication panel had chimed three times, with long pauses between each ring. Minutes later, two figures let themselves into the condo. Both wore reflective vests, work boots, and gloves. They wheeled two large gray bins into the room, dropped two heavy duty vinyl bags on the floor, one beside her, the other beside her sister. They unrolled the bags and pulled down their full-length metal zipper. Even in her impaired state Shannon recognized what it was: a body bag, used to transport the dead. One of the men rolled her into it, then pulled the zipper up past her face.

She recalled being picked up by the men, dropped unceremoniously into the maintenance bin, and rolled out of the condominium. The *ding, ding, ding* sound of the elevator as it traveled from the tenth floor down to the basement. The jostling around of her body in the bin as the container rumbled over a rough concrete surface and down a ramp. The *beep... beep... beep* of a truck's warning system as it backed up, the high-pitched squeal of its brakes as it came to a stop, and the *hissss* of its hydraulics as the driver shifted it into Park. All the while, Shannon treaded water on the ink-black surface of unconsciousness, fighting the urge to surrender to the incapacitating effect of whatever drug was coursing through her bloodstream, desperate not to sink deeper into a place from which she might never resurface. That they had both been drugged and targeted for abduction was clear. But why, and by whom?

A putrid smell seeped out of the back of the truck. Even in her semi-conscious state Shannon felt the gorge rise in her throat. She fought back the urge to vomit, knowing that if she did, she would choke to death on the bitter bile inside the body bag. The man lifted her out of the container, then rolled her into the rear hopper of the truck. She lay on her side in the trash collection basin, surrounded by the stomach-churning smell of rotten food and the stench of diesel fumes, when she heard a sickening *thud*. Zoe fell in beside her. She heard her sister moan. Bags of garbage were thrown on top of them. The brakes released, and the truck shuddered as it jumped into gear. They were moving.

Shannon passed out. When her senses returned, her body ached from head to toe. She had no idea how long they had been in the back of the garbage truck, how far they had traveled, or where they were. All she knew was that she was still alive.

She woke in the corner of a room, lying on a bed of straw, wearing only her bra and panties, and covered with a poncho. Her shoes, jeans and blouse sat on a stool in the corner of the room. Steel shackles separated by a chain link bound her wrists. A plastic-coated steel cable, fashioned into a noose and fitted around her neck, was secured to a metal O-ring in the wooden ceiling. A ceramic heater glowed and provided heat to the damp, musty space.

Shannon pressed her back against the wooden wall and struggled to her feet.

The cable was sufficiently slack to permit her to walk the

perimeter of the room. She recognized her prison: a horse stall. In one corner stood a compostable toilet. The rear and side walls of the stall were made of wood, the front wall a composite framework of vertical steel bars above horizontal wooden planks. The latched gate was locked.

The toilet reeked of feces and urine. Hers?

Shannon called out. "Zoe? You there? Can you hear me?"

In the stable a horse responded with a loud whinny.

"Zoe?"

Her sister answered from a stall across the hallway "Yeah, Shay. I'm here. You okay?"

"I guess so," Shannon replied. "You have water?"

"Yeah."

"Food?"

"If that's what you want to call it."

"Any idea where the hell we are?"

"None," Zoe said.

"We need to get out of here."

"You think?"

"I don't want to die here, Zoe."

"Neither do I. And I'm sure as shit going to make sure you don't either."

"You think anyone's looking for us?"

"Maybe, maybe not."

"Dad hasn't heard from us for a while. He'll suspect something's wrong."

Zoe didn't reply.

Movement at the end of the barn. The *clop-clop-clop* of boots on the rubber mat. The horses stirred and snorted. Mealtime.

Shannon gasped at the sight of their captor. He stared at her from outside the stall, unrecognizable in his red, green, and blue polka-dotted costume and knee-high yellow boots. A clown mask covered his head; a wild-eyed, evil-looking prosthetic with bushy red hair, long protruding jaw, and wickedly sharp teeth. In his hands he carried two buckets, one filled with soapy water, the other with cans of liquid meal replacement and bottles of water.

The Clown didn't speak. He gestured to Shannon, indicated that she was to move to the far corner of her stall.

Shannon hesitated, then stepped back. The Clown unlocked the gate, entered, threw the bucket of soapy water over her, then tossed two cans of meal replacement and a bottle of water at her feet.

"What do you want from us?" Shannon screamed as she wiped the water away from her face with her bound hands.

The Clown raised a finger to his lips. *Shhhhh.*

"Why are you keeping us here?"

He wagged his finger and shook his head. A warning. He removed a rubber-gripped metal rod from inside his boot.

Shannon's voice cracked as she pleaded. She slid down the wall as the Clown walked toward her. "Please... no."

The Clown lifted the chain links between her shackles with the metal rod, cocked his head, and pressed the trigger.

One-hundred-thousand volts of electricity conducted on the wet chain, shot out of the stun stick, and surged through Shannon's body.

A chattering scream escaped her, then faded.

The darkness returned.

9

R OCK PARKED THE LIMOUSINE in the Executive Air gated lot and opened the door for Jordan. During the drive from the conference center to the airport a light drizzle had christened Los Angeles. The tarmac glistened with beads of oily raindrops. Wisps of steam ascended from its hot black surface and drifted lazily across the private runway. Ahead, the engines of Michael Farrow's private jet whined softly.

Rock and Jordan cleared the security counter, gathered their bags, and walked across the tarmac to the jet. Jordan's mother and father greeted her at foot of the stairway. Keith kissed her.

"Shortcake!" Michael Farrow called out to his daughter. "How's my gorgeous girl?"

"Hi dad," Jordan replied.

"Too bad the kids couldn't come along," her mother said. "They would have loved Maui."

"I know," Jordan replied, "But the thought of being away from them for just one week is more than I can handle. Two months? I'd go out of my mind."

"You realize you're denying us our grand-parental right to spoil them rotten," Farrow said. "It's in the handbook, you know."

"There's a handbook?" Jordan laughed. "No, I didn't know."

"The Farrow Guide to Privileged Grandparenting. Chapter I: Hawaiian Vacations. I'll get you a copy."

"You should get right on that."

"Would you prefer the print or eBook edition?"

"You have a wild imagination."

"Hey, they're kids. A couple of months on the island would do them good. There's still time. I can send a car and hold the jet until they arrive."

"Thanks, Dad," Jordan said. "I'm sure they'd love it. But I can't tuck them in when they're twenty-five hundred miles away."

Her father winked. "There's always Skype."

Jordan shook her head. "Maybe next year."

"Fair enough," Farrow replied. "Keith tells me your tour wraps up next week."

Jordan nodded. "The first leg of it, anyway. One week on the road, then two weeks off to spend with Emma and Aiden. That was the agreement I made with my publisher."

Keith added, "After sixteen consecutive weeks on the New York Times and USA Today best seller lists they weren't about to argue with her."

"They didn't try to negotiate a better deal?" her father asked.

"I have a three-book commitment," Jordan replied. "This is the last one. I told them I was giving serious thought to not re-signing and publishing the next book independently."

"What did they say?"

"They told me to enjoy my time with the kids."

Michael laughed. He wrapped his arm around his daughter. "Sounds like you picked up a negotiation tip or two from your old man."

She smiled. "Could be."

Jordan admired the aircraft. The private jet was the epitome of luxury air transportation and positively stunning to behold. Its pearl-white fuselage gleamed in stark contrast to the bruised purple and orange twilight sky.

"She looks beautiful," Jordan said.

"Your father just had her repainted, plus a full interior makeover," her mother replied. She took her daughter by the arm "Come inside, check her out. She'll blow your socks off."

Rock and Keith followed behind as the family boarded the jet. "Anyone else traveling with us today?" Jordan asked.

"Just Rock," her mother replied. "He'll be staying on with us in Maui. And the crew, of course."

"Same gang?"

Farrow answered. "Captain Sanders and First Officer Brentworth have the flight deck. Julie and Gayle will be taking care of us."

"They're so sweet," Jordan said.

"Sure are. Flight attendants don't come any better. I told them you were coming. They'll be disappointed that the kids won't be joining us."

"I sense a conspiracy," Jordan joked.

Farrow laughed. "Nothing like that, Shortcake. They just think the world of them. We all do."

"Next time. I promise."

"Good. I'll hold you to it."

Captain Sanders voice came over the intercom as Julie and Gayle closed and secured the door. "Afternoon, folks," he said. "We just got the thumbs up from the tower, so we're good to go. We'll be in the air in a few minutes so settle in and buckle up. Flight attendants prepare the aircraft for departure."

As Jordan took her seat a strange feeling came over her. She held Keith's hand tightly.

"Damn, girl," Keith said. "You been working out or something? That's one hell of a grip."

"Sorry, hon," Jordan said. "Guess I'm a little nervous."

"Of flying? With all the traveling you've done this past year I'm surprised you haven't gotten your pilots license and bought your own plane. Since when have you been afraid to fly?"

"I'm not," Jordan replied. She thought about her confrontation with Marsden at the convention center. "It's nothing," she lied. "It's been a long day. I'm just tired."

The whine of the jet's engines rose and fell as the aircraft taxied to its assigned runway. The setting sun serrated the horizon in a bright orange glow. Jordan looked out her window at the row of private hangars. Aircraft mechanics were working on a jet in Hangar A. Hangars C and D were vacant. Jordan watched the ground mechanics roll shut the doors to the Farrow Industries hangar. The jet executed a tight turn. Captain Sanders lined up the aircraft for takeoff.

The turn cast the hangar in bright sunlight. Jordan shielded her eyes against the glare.

Suddenly she remembered the pen Marsden had left behind. Segments from the strange vision she received when she read it on the drive to the airport flashed back to her.

A brilliant, blinding light, narrowing to a column... the smell of aircraft paint... the figure alone in the hangar... the tool on the floor...

The jet began to rocket down the runway, its engines screaming as the plane accelerated.

"Something's wrong," Jordan called out.

Keith turned to her. "What are you taking about?"

Jordan unbuckled her lap belt and jumped out of her seat. "It's the jet!" she yelled. "Abort the takeoff! Something's wrong with the jet!"

Julie called out to her. "Jordan, get back in your seat!"

Rock unfastened his seatbelt and hurried toward her, gripping the seat backs for support.

A tremendous *boom!* rocked the underside of the jet.

Captain Sanders yelled over the intercom: "Everyone down! Brace for impact!"

As the aircraft dropped Rock lost his balance, fell backward, and struck his head on the floor.

The jet slammed down hard onto the runway, sliding off the tarmac, out of control, careening across the soft grass on the outskirts of the airport, ripping through the barrier fence and dragging it under its fuselage before coming to rest in the middle of the Interstate.

Jordan had been thrown forward to the front of the plane. She lay at Julie's feet outside the flight deck cabin door. The flight attendant stared at her through lifeless eyes. Her neck had been broken in the crash. Gayle sat in her seat, slumped forward, unconscious.

The rancid stink of burning metal and blistering paint seeped into the cabin. Smoke crept up through invisible joints in the floor and sidewalls of the jet.

Jordan called out. "Mom... Dad... Keith?"

No response.

"Jordan?" Rock said. "Are you okay?"

"I think so."

The bodyguard rose unsteadily to his feet and wiped

away a trickle of blood from his forehead. "The jets on fire," he said. Thick smoke began to pool on the cabin floor. "We've got to get out of here." Rock moved past Jordan to the front door of the jet and pulled the emergency release. The door exploded off its hinges and fell onto the highway below. The escape ramp automatically deployed, folding itself out from the fuselage onto the highway.

"I'm not leaving without my family!" Jordan yelled.

"I'll take care of them," Rock yelled. "You need to get off the aircraft." He pulled Jordan up off the floor. "Go! Now!"

Jordan fought back. "No!"

"Sorry, Jordan," Rock yelled, "but I have to do this." He grabbed her by her shoulders and threw her out the open door. Jordan half slid, half tumbled down the escape ramp and rolled onto the highway. She rose to her feet, tried to run back up the slick vinyl ramp, slipped and fell. Rock stood in the doorway and waved her away. Blood from the laceration to his head flowed freely, obscuring his vision. He was having difficulty seeing her.

"Get as far back you can. I'll get everyone out. I promise... *Oh Jesus!*" Rock pointed past Jordan. "Get on the ground, Jordan! *Now!*"

Vehicles occupying the center and slow traffic lanes had pulled off the Interstate when the luxury jet came smashing through the safety barrier and screeched to rest against the center lane guardrail. Now a tractor trailer, its load too heavy to stop, was barreling down the open highway toward the downed aircraft. From the open door, Rock watched as the driver fought with the steering wheel, tried to regain control of the eighteen-wheeler, attempted to bring the big rig to a stop. Its wheels fully locked, the transport began to turn as it slid across the rain-slick pavement. The rig shuddered and screeched as it bore down on the doomed jet.

"Get down, Jordan!" Rock yelled.

Its course inevitably set beyond any opportunity to avoid crashing into the jet, the massive rig closed in on the dead aircraft. Jordan fell to the ground. She felt a *whoosh* of hot air overhead as the transport jackknifed and its undercarriage passed over her. It fell on the jet, crushed it, pushed it down, down, down the highway in a raging ball of fire.

Jordan clambered to her feet, bewildered by the incomprehensible event that had just taken place. Mind and body succumbed to shattering panic. She screamed, "*Nooooo!*" and stumbled toward the cremating mass of truck and aircraft until she found herself caught in a struggle with strangers. Unfamiliar voices surrounded her.

"Stop, you can't go there..."

"Jesus Christ, did you see that?"

"Someone get her a blanket..."

"Call 9-1-1. This woman needs medical assistance..."

One voice stood out among the others. "What's your name, honey?" the woman said.

"Quest... Jordan Quest."

"Okay, Jordan," the woman said. "You just take it easy. An ambulance is on its..."

The woman's voice trailed off against the sound of distant sirens as Jordan fainted in her arms.

10

_____

THE ER TEAM burst through the standby doors as the LifeAir helicopter touched down on the rooftop of Angel of Mercy Hospital and raced to meet the paramedics. The Burn Unit had been kept up to date on the status of their inbound patient.

"Talk to me," Dr. Scott Lyons yelled above the _swoosh-swoosh-swoosh_ of the slowing rotor blades as the team transferred their patient from the helicopter to the gurney and rushed back into the health center.

"Jet fuel burns to ninety percent of his body," the paramedic replied. "This guy shouldn't even be alive."

The man's face was burned beyond recognition. Shreds of clothing had melted into his skin. The soles of his running shoes had vulcanized to his feet from the intensity of the white-hot fire that erupted when the eighteen-wheeler collided with the jet.

"Respiration?" Lyons asked.

"We kept him on oxygen but he's barely breathing. My guess is cellular hypoxia from the jet fuel smoke. He'd been breathing carbon monoxide and hydrogen cyanide for God knows how long before we touched down."

The man's physical injuries compounded his already grave condition. The radius and ulna of his right arm were broken, as too his left femur. Splintered bone protruded from his body, held in place by a gluey mass of melted fabric and congealed skin. His fingers were skeletonized, nails on both hands gone.

"You check for ID?"

"Couldn't. Clothing's charred to the body." The paramedic shook his head. "I've attended my share of burn victims, doc. But nothing as bad as this. Poor bastard."

"Any other survivors?"

"One. A woman. She was thrown clear of the jet before it was hit by the transport."

"*Transport?*"

"It's all over the news."

"Where is she?"

"En route as we speak."

"Name?"

"A witness said her name is Jordan Quest."

Lyons turned to one of the nurses. "Notify me the minute she arrives." He looked at his patient. "Maybe she can tell us what happened. And who this is."

"Yes, doctor," the nurse replied.

The team wheeled the gurney into the surgical suite. Lyons turned to the paramedic. "You were right."

"What's that, doc?"

"Poor bastard."

THE AMBULANCE SCREAMED to a stop at the Emergency entrance to the hospital. The rear doors crashed open and

Jordan was wheeled past the triage desk into a waiting suite. The nursing team went straight to work, cuffing her arm, checking her blood pressure, clipping a heart rate monitor to her finger, placing her on supplemental oxygen.

Dr. Lyons entered the room. "Ms. Quest, my name is Dr. Lyons. Can you hear me?"

Lyons removed a penlight from his pocket, opened her eyes, checked Jordan's pupillary response.

"Pupils are dilated and unresponsive," Lyons said. "She's in shock." He instructed the nurse. "Draw blood. Send it to the lab right away. And check her sugar. Let's be sure we're not dealing with anything else."

"Right away," the nurse replied.

"Come on, Jordan," Dr. Lyons said, as much to himself as to his patient, "Help me help you." He walked to the foot of the bed, scraped his penlight up the soles of both feet, checked her reflexes: Neutral. To the nurse he said, "Page me when her tests are back."

JORDAN SAW HERSELF IN MAUI, lying on the beach at her parent's vacation home. Emma and Aiden played in the surf at the water's edge. Keith was chasing after them, water gun in hand, first after his daughter, then his son, spraying them as they ran. Emma screamed with delight. Aiden laughed. In the distance she saw her parents returning from their ritualistic hour-long walk, holding hands, kicking water at one another, acting like a couple of teenagers, just as they had for as long as she could remember. Rock strolled behind them, keeping watch from a distance, glancing inland, ever vigilant.

The day was perfect. Sunny and hot. A gentle breeze. Not a cloud in sight.

She returned her attention to her iPad. She had started to read a wonderful review of a new book from a promising up-and-coming author when suddenly the heavens rumbled, the sky turned crimson, and everything around her began to bleed.

Jordan rose from the lounge chair and walked toward the ocean. The water washing over her feet burned her skin. She stepped back. Though the waves lapped gently against the shoreline and the water itself presented no unnatural appearance, it clearly wasn't water. Jordan examined the sea foam on the beach, watched the bubbles as they broke. A hissing sound preceded the pop of each bubble. Blood flowed out of them. The wet sand crackled.

She called out to Keith, tried to warn him of the unknown danger, to tell him to get the children out of the water. The growl from the heavens grew louder, like the threating sound of a fast-approaching thunderstorm. One ferocious thunderclap followed the last with greater anger.

Oblivious both to her and the impending storm, Keith and the children continued to play. Red rain fell, plopped down from the sky in thick viscous drops, and smeared Jordan's skin when she tried to wipe it away. Blood.

Jordan looked up. In the sky, where the sun should have been, a white dot appeared. The object, whatever it was, was hurtling toward them at meteoric speed. Jordan ran along the beach, called out to Keith, Emma and Aiden, her parents, Rock. Her cries went unheard. Her family were oblivious to the object racing earthbound at terminal velocity and the strange environmental changes taking place around them.

The roar of the object had become deafening. Jordan fell to the ground, looked up, watched as it descended, then recognized it too late for what it was.

Her father's corporate jet, fully engulfed, slammed into the sandy beach and exploded on impact. Flames leapt from the wreckage, then morphed into snake-like form and stood beside the *smoking mass of debris, sentries of burning jet fuel, possessed by an otherworldly intelligence. The flames raced along the beach toward, around and past her, as though she was exempt from their rules of engagement; a civilian, not one of the specific targets they sought. Instead they found her husband, her children, her parents, found Rock, and swarmed them, melting them to the ground on which they stood with a heat so intense they liquified right before her eyes.*

An emotional fire burned within Jordan so hot that she had no choice but to feed it, let it out.

She screamed.

11

SPECIAL AGENT'S Chris Hanover, Grant Carnevale and FBI Director Andrew Dunn rushed into Jordan's room upon hearing the scream and found her thrashing in bed. Carnevale grabbed his goddaughter by her arms and held her down. Hanover and Dunn stood at her bedside.

"Jordan, honey. Settle down. It's Uncle Grant. You're having a dream."

Jordan opened her eyes. The nightmarish inferno of her father's corporate jet plummeting from the sky and crashing onto the Maui beach and incinerating her family quickly faded. It was replaced by unfamiliar faces and surroundings. She searched the hospital room in a panic, looked up, and recognized her godfather. Sweat soaked and breathing heavily, she fell back into bed.

"Uncle Grant?"

"I'm right here, honey."

"Where am I?"

"You're in the hospital."

Jordan stared at her godfather. "Hospital? How did I get here?"

"There was an accident. Do you remember anything?"

Jordan hesitated, focused, then answered. "Something happened to the jet."

Carnevale nodded. He held her hand. "You've been in a crash. But your doctor says you're going to be fine."

"Is everyone okay? Mom and Dad... Keith?"

Carnevale's mouth went dry. He tried to look away from his goddaughter, couldn't. "I'm sorry, Jordan."

Jordan gripped the bedrail, tried to pull herself up. "What do you mean, sorry?" she said. A tremendous pain seized her left arm. She lost her grip on the rail and fell back into bed. Jordan looked at her arm. It was wrapped, shoulder to wrist, in white medical gauze. An immobilizer brace had been secured to her left hand to eliminate wrist movement and protect the damaged tendons from unnecessary strain.

"Where's my family?"

Director Dunn placed his hand on Carnevale's shoulder. "We'll be outside, Grant," he said. Hanover closed the door behind him as the two men left the room.

Carnevale watched the door fall shut. The circumstances seemed so surreal, the news he had to deliver to his goddaughter unfathomable. Could this really be happening?

"They're gone, Jordan. Your mother and father, Rock, the flight crew... they didn't make it."

"*No.*"

"If the transport hadn't hit the jet..."

"*God, no...*"

"I'm so sorry, honey."

Jordan was unsure whether to scream or cry.

"It's a lot to process right now…"

No, this was not the time to cry. She would deal with her emotions later. The faces of her children flashed though her mind. "Where's Keith?"

Carnevale didn't reply.

"You said my parents and Rock and the crew were dead. You said nothing about Keith. Is my husband dead or alive, Uncle Grant?"

"He's alive, Jordan."

"Where is he?"

"Here."

"You mean *here*, as in this hospital?"

"Yes."

Jordan once more fought against the pain in her wounded wrist, tried to lift herself out of bed, couldn't. She searched the plastic guardrail for the electronic lowering mechanism. When she couldn't find it, she kicked at the barrier, tried to knock it loose.

"Settle down, Jordan. You're only going to make your injuries worse."

"Get me out of here, Uncle Grant. Take me to Keith. I want to see my husband."

"Jordan, please."

"Now!"

"You can't, honey."

"Why not?"

Carnevale paused. "Keith is on life support."

The words stopped her. "Life support?"

Carnevale nodded. "He'd been exposed to the fire and the fumes for some time before the paramedics could extricate him from the wreckage. The damage to his body is… extensive."

"Is he going to make it?"

"We don't know. His doctor says it's touch and go."

"I have to see him."

Carnevale conceded. "I know."

"Where is he?"

"The burn unit." He sighed. "He's not good, Jordan. Not at all."

"Take me there."

"Honey..."

"I want to see my husband."

"Let's check with your doctor first. See what he has to say."

"I don't give a damn what any doctor has to say!" Jordan yelled. Her voice trembled. Her eyes were wide with fear. "Either help me out of bed or get me someone who will."

Carnevale called out. "Agent Hanover?"

Chris Hanover pushed open the door and entered the room. "Yes?"

"Tell Dr. Lyons we're going to the burn center. Mrs. Quest wants to see her husband."

Hanover nodded. "Right away."

"You sure you're up to this, Jordan?" Carnevale asked.

"No," Jordan replied. "But I have to be."

12

_____

KOST 103.5, KIIS-FM 102.7 and every other radio station James Rigel tuned in on his drive from the Arizona border to Los Angeles were reporting on the story of the hour: the unfathomable aviation disaster that had befallen a private jet during its take-off from LAX.

Speculation abounded as to the cause of the crash which brought down the aircraft and the inevitable collision that followed when it broke through the steel safety barrier at the end of the runway, slid across the highway, and came to rest in the path of a fully loaded eighteen-wheeler. Mechanical malfunction or pilot error were the most widely offered theories for the tragedy, though none of the bystanders knew exactly what had happened, except that the passengers of the ill-fated jet had lost their lives under truly horrific circumstances.

But the most widely reported account relating to the crash was the miraculous survival of a woman who escaped the aircraft seconds after it came to rest against the interstate divider. They had watched as she stood in the middle of the highway and stared helplessly at the jet, oblivious to their cries urging her to get to safety, her back turned to the immense rig barreling towards her at highway speed, a victim itself to the immutable laws of physics and inertia, unable to slow under the weight of its load, brakes hissing, tires stuttering as it tried to stop, couldn't, then jackknifed with her directly in its path. They watched her throw herself to the ground as the out-of-control rig rocketed over her at full highway speed, slammed into the helpless jet, and drove it down the highway in a fiery explosion. They saw her rise to her feet then run toward the roiling inferno until she was intercepted, caught in the arms of Good Samaritans who held her back and escorted her to safety seconds before the gas tank of the eighteen-wheeler erupted, the explosion so intense that the windows of adjacent passenger cars, abandoned by their owners as they ran to safety, exploded from the heat of the blast.

Half an hour later as he approached the city limits, KIIS-FM announced the name of the woman found on the highway: Jordan Quest. The doomed aircraft had belonged to her father, tech billionaire Michael Farrow. Although representatives for Farrow Industries refused to confirm or deny if their founder or any members of his immediate family were among the dead, the rumor mill had already begun to turn. Reports of a second victim, medical status unknown, had been removed from the wreckage and transported by air ambulance to Angel of Mercy Hospital in Los Angeles.

Rigel pulled off the highway. He needed to think. Was Farrow already dead? The contract! New York had already deposited five million into his account with a second five million payable upon its completion. If Farrow was dead, they would know about it by now. Every broadcaster and social media feed in the country, perhaps even the world, was breaking the story at this moment.

He thought about the money. The first five million was guaranteed. That was non-negotiable. But the question that concerned him most right now was whether he would lose the balance.

A text notification dinged on his cellphone. He read the screen: CALL IN.

Dammit!

New York had made the terms of the contract clear. Farrow and his family were to be taken out. There were to be no survivors. The specifics of how it was to be done had been left up to him. He assessed the facts. As far as anyone knew right now, Michael Farrow might not have been on the jet when it crashed. He was a billionaire, for God's sake. Perhaps he had given his daughter the use of the aircraft for a personal trip. Maybe Farrow himself was alive. He had five million reasons to think positively about the situation.

Rigel had always prided himself on his ability to maintain an optimistic disposition, even under the most difficult circumstances. Beyond his exemplary skill at killing, which he had proven repeatedly, he believed his affable nature was one of the reasons why New York enjoyed their relationship with him as much as they did and why he remained in such high demand. Had he not chosen to pursue a career as a professional killer he would have made an excellent movie actor, perhaps sharing the screen with the likes of Morgan Freeman or Anthony Hopkins. He had so much to offer, so much life experience he could to bring to his roles. One day he would give all of this up and star in motion pictures. But for now, he was having too much fun doing what he loved to do most. Which was to kill.

The phone dinged again. The second message read
URGENT YOU REPLY.

He turned off the phone, tossed it into the cup holder
between the seats, and decided to continue to Los Angeles
and investigate Farrow's status firsthand. If he were still
alive, he wouldn't be much longer.

The radio announced an update on the tragedy. *"The
names of two of the survivors of today's catastrophic plane crash
at Los Angeles Airport have been released. The first is Jordan
Quest, celebrated attorney, psychic and daughter of computer
technology magnate Michael Farrow. The second is her husband,
Keith Quest. Mr. Quest was airlifted from the scene to Angel of
Mercy Hospital. He is reported to be in critical condition with life-
threatening injuries."*

Critical. Life-threatening. But not *dead*. And the
daughter was still alive. Rigel strategized the situation. He
would fulfill the Farrow contract in stages if he had to. First
kill the family, then Farrow himself. New York would be
pleased. They would appreciate his ability to adapt so
fluidly to such unusual and exceptional circumstances.

He put the car in gear, turned on his signal light, sped
up, and merged into the flow of traffic.

He checked his watch: 8:30 P.M. Visiting hours at Angel
of Mercy Hospital would be over soon.

As always, his timing couldn't be better.

13

D R. PAUL TREMAINE, MD, chief of Angel of Mercy Hospital's Burn Center Unit, stood beside Jordan and her godfather. Keith lay unconscious before them in the Acute Zone, a room specifically designed to protect its occupants from exposure to bacterial particulate or micro-organisms which could be introduced by staff, thereby increasing the possibility of infection. The door to the room was fitted with a pressurized airlock which provided a secondary barrier against the threat of airborne contaminants.

The ward was quiet, the lights dim. Staff kept their movements around their patients to a minimum.

Grant Carnevale helped his goddaughter out of her wheelchair. Jordan looked in at her husband through the glass walls of the visitor corridor. An involuntary gasp escaped her. Tremaine and Carnevale caught her as she collapsed, then helped her back into the wheelchair. She began to weep.

Keith's fire-ravaged body was unrecognizable.

"I'm very sorry, Mrs. Quest," Dr. Tremaine said. "I can't even imagine how difficult this must be for you."

Jordan stared at her husband. She offered no reply.

"What is Keith's status, doctor?" Carnevale asked.

Respectful of the deep shock Jordan was experiencing at seeing her husband's condition for the first time, Tremaine chose his words carefully. "We have a comprehensive team standing by to help Mr. Quest with everything he'll need, from cardiology and wound care to microvascular and reconstructive surgery."

Jordan wiped the tears from her eyes. "You didn't answer the question, doctor," she said.

Tremaine nodded. "You're right, Mrs. Quest," he said. "I meant no disrespect to you or Agent Carnevale. As I'm sure you can appreciate, situations like these differ from one patient to the next. In your husband's case his injuries are most extreme."

"Tell me what I'm dealing with," Jordan insisted. "I can handle it."

Tremaine gathered his thoughts. "Your husband's situation is dire," he replied. "Perhaps the worst I've seen in my twenty years treating burn victims. To be perfectly honest, it's a miracle he's even breathing. The trauma to his body from the crash is extensive: Broken bones, multiple fractures, contusions, damage to his spinal cord, inhalation burns from prolonged exposure to burning jet fuel and smoke... I could go on."

"Will he recover?" Jordan asked.

"It's too soon to tell. His immune and respiratory systems have been severely compromised. Even the slightest infection could kill him. His prolonged exposure to the burning jet fuel damaged the air collection sacs in his lungs. The alveoli are barely functioning, which means his ability to expel carbon dioxide is impeded. Aside from the obvious external trauma, his wounds are so extensive we can't use hyperbaric treatment to facilitate their closure. Our sole effort right now is keeping him alive, and that's proving to be a challenge. There is one more area of concern you need to know about. Your husband received a penetration injury to his head." Tremaine removed a plastic bottle from the pocket of his lab coat and handed it to Jordan. It contained a twisted metal object measuring an inch in length. "We think it's part of the aircraft. Airborne debris, most likely. It was embedded in the left frontal region of his skull. If the left lobe has been damaged, which I suspect it has, the affect to his brain will be extensive. Motor control, speech, memory... all will be impacted. We don't know if that's the case yet, but it must be considered. My concern is for the cumulative and permanent effects of his injuries, both mental, physical and physiological."

Jordan sat quietly, deep in thought, her mind processing the gut-wrenching information Tremaine had just shared with her. She looked up at the two men. "I'd like to be alone with my husband," she said.

"Of course," Dr. Tremaine said. Carnevale leaned down and hugged her. "Take all the time you need, honey. We'll be down the hall." The men walked to the visitor's lounge.

Not since her experience as a child lying lifeless at the bottom of her parent's pool had Jordan so felt Death's imminent presence. The man lying in the hospital bed in front of her, her wonderful, sweet, incapable-of-harming-a-soul Keith, adoring husband and loving father to their two beautiful children, was slipping away right before her eyes. She had always been a strong woman, capable of taking on whatever punches life threw at her and striking back twice as hard. Yet now she felt utterly destroyed, lost, without hope, mentality and emotionally crushed. She knew in her heart that it was only a matter of time before her husband succumbed to his injuries. No one could survive such terrific physical devastation, not even her soulmate, her rock, the one she always referred to as *the better part of me*; her Keith.

Jordan called out. "Dr. Tremaine?"

Tremaine and Carnevale stood in the doorway of the lounge. "Yes, Mrs. Quest?" Tremaine replied.

"What are my husband's chances for survival over the long term?"

"Are you asking if he'll ever return to his former quality of life?" the physician asked.

"Yes."

"The odds aren't in his favor. Keith has fourth degree burns to ninety-five percent of his body. He's looking at perhaps two hundred skin grafts to repair the damage, plus numerous related surgeries. I suspect there *is* brain damage. If his lungs do manage to repair themselves, he'll be on oxygen for the rest of his life. That's just a cursory evaluation. There are additional health challenges going on inside his body we haven't yet been able to diagnose. The next seventy-two hours are critical."

"And if there's no improvement by then?"

"A decision will have to be made."

"Meaning?"

"For patients with catastrophic injuries like your husband's we may advocate for the withdrawal of life support. But that discussion would only take place if we believe his chances for survival have significantly diminished."

The words slashed at her. The reality of the truth behind them cut even deeper. It was all too much. Unable to take anymore, Jordan broke down. "I don't know what to do," she cried.

"I'm so sorry, Mrs. Quest," Tremaine said. "Trust me when I tell you we're doing everything in our power to help your husband. But right now, his life is in God's hands, not ours."

From a monitor in Keith's room an alarm sounded. The nursing staff rushed to the air lock.

Dr. Tremaine excused himself. "I'm sorry, Mrs. Quest. I have to leave."

Carnevale steadied Jordan as she tried to stand. "What's happening?" she said. "What's wrong with Keith?"

Tremaine hurried out of the visitor's sub-zone. He called back as he entered the airlock leading to Keith's room. "Your husband is going into cardiac arrest."

Jordan held on to her godfather, afraid that if she let go she would most certainly collapse.

Carnevale heard the door to the visitor lounge open behind him. Agent Hanover entered the room. He stopped, intuitively aware of the gravity of the situation.

"Agent Carnevale," he said uncomfortably, "Mr. Quest's parents have arrived. They're asking to see their son."

14

_____

ANDREW DUNN WAS STANDING in the corridor speaking with Keith's parents, David and Paula Quest, when Chris Hanover returned to Jordan's hospital room. The FBI Director was attempting to answer their questions and bring them up to speed on what few details he knew about the plane crash. The Farrow's housekeeper, Marissa DeSola, had also arrived. She had been charged with caring for the Quest's seven-year-old twins, Emma and Aiden, while they traveled. The children stood by her side.

"We're still putting the pieces together," Andrew Dunn said. "All we know for certain is that Mr. Farrow's jet encountered a problem during takeoff and crashed. The Director of the National Transportation and Safety Board is a friend of mine. I've already spoken to him. He's agreed to prioritize the investigation. My agents will be talking to their people as well as investigators from the Federal Aeronautics and Aviation Administration. A hangar has been secured at LAX for NTSB and FAA personnel to piece together the remains of the aircraft and commence their investigation. We should learn the specific cause of the crash very soon."

"Thank you, Director Dunn," David Quest said. "Where are my son- and daughter-in-law now?"

Hanover answered. "Fourth floor, sir. I'll take you there as soon as you're ready."

"I'll stay with the children," Marissa said.

"Go," Dunn said. "Be with your family. I'll let you know the minute we hear anything of importance."

JORDAN and her godfather watched the flurry of activity taking place in the confines of the air-locked room. Under Dr. Tremaine's direction the nursing staff worked as one, performing the same emergency procedures on Keith as they had done dozens of times before on patients in need of their lifesaving skills.

The elevator door opened. The Quests saw Jordan, crying in the arms of her godfather. They rushed to her side.

The activity in Keith's room suddenly stopped. Dr. Tremaine conversed for a few seconds with his team before leaving the room through the primary airlock and exiting the secondary airlock into the visitor corridor. He walked toward Jordan and lowered his surgical mask. The look on his face telegraphed the words Jordan was afraid to hear.

"I'm sorry," Dr. Tremaine said, addressing the family. "The trauma was simply too much for him. Keith's heart couldn't take it. There was nothing more we could do."

Jordan collapsed. Carnevale eased her into the wheelchair.

Paula Quest fell to her knees. "*No, no, no...*" David Quest held his emotions in check.

"Your husband tried to hold on, Mrs. Quest," Tremaine

said. "He put up one hell of a fight. But his injuries were far too great. You have my sympathy. My staff will help you with anything you need." The doctor excused himself and left the family to grieve.

Jordan's tears turned to anger. "Someone was in the hangar, Uncle Grant," she said. "They tampered with the jet. I saw it."

Carnevale tried to calm her. "No, Jordan. This was just an accident. A terrible, tragic accident."

Jordan shook her head. "This was no accident. I tried to stop the jet from taking off, to warn them, but no one would listen. This is all my fault."

Carnevale kneeled beside his goddaughter and looked into her eyes. "Now listen to me, Jordan. None of this was your fault. You hear me? You had nothing to do with any of this."

"I know what I saw, Uncle Grant. I'm going to find out who was responsible for this. And when I do, I'm going to kill him."

"There will be an investigation into the crash, Jordan. We'll learn the truth soon enough. If it turns out there's more to this than meets the eye, I assure you we'll get to the bottom of it."

"I won't need the Bureau's help. I'll take care of it myself."

Considering Jordan's raw emotional state Carnevale tempered his response. "I know how much pain you're in right now, honey. So are Paula and David. And me. Your father was my best friend, so I'm going to talk for him right now. Before you set off on some wild path of revenge, keep in mind you have two small children who will need their mother now more than ever. I know it seems like you won't, but eventually you *will* get through this. Grieve for as long as you need to, then move on. Because as deeply as you loved Keith, Emma and Aiden loved their father just as much. And their world just imploded."

RETURNING TO HER ROOM, Grant Carnevale lifted the children into his arms and carried them down the hall to the waiting room while Jordan broke the news of the death of her husband and parents to their housekeeper, Marissa DeSola. Jordan had never known a woman as caring and loving as Marissa; the same woman who two decades earlier had dove into the pool, pulled her to safety, and saved her life as a child. Marissa had practically raised her in her parent's absence when the demands of her father's position as Chairman of Farrow Industries required him to travel the world, and her mother, a celebrated sculptor, put in long hours in her studio to meet the deadline for her latest commission. Marissa fell into Jordan's arms and sobbed. Jordan wrapped her arms around her friend, held her tight.

"The children..." Marissa said.

Jordan brushed away Marissa's tears. "I know," she said.

"Do you want me to be with you when you tell them?"

Jordan shook her head. "I'll be fine."

Marissa nodded. "I'm here if you need me."

Jordan smiled. She held Marissa's beautiful face in her hands. "I know you will. Just like you've been my whole life. There when I need you the most."

Marissa composed herself. "This is so hard," she said.

"I know."

"Your parents and husband were three of the kindest people God ever put on this planet, Jordan. They will be missed."

"Thank you."

Marissa looked around. "Where are the children?"

"Uncle Grant is watching them."

Carnevale sat with Emma and Aiden in the waiting room.

"He was a good friend to your father," Marissa said.

Jordan nodded. "Dad said he was one of the few people in this world he could trust with his life."

"The children need to know what's happened."

"I know."

EMMA AND AIDEN hopped up on the bed as Jordan closed her hospital room door. She sat beside them, drew them close.

Aiden pointed to the Immobilizer on his mother's arm. "You okay, mom?" Emma nestled into her side.

"Yes, honey. I'm fine."

"Why are we here?"

How am I going to do this? Jordan thought. She took a deep breath, let it out.

"Can we go home soon?" Emma added. Aiden said, "Uncle Grant said those other men are FBI agents just like him. Why are they here?"

"To help us, honey."

"Why?" Emma said.

God, this was so hard.

"Something's happened to Dad, hasn't it?" Emma asked.

Jordan pulled her children closer. "You know the plane ride we were supposed to take while you guys stayed with Marissa?"

"Yeah," Aiden said.

"There was an accident."

Jordan could see the panic in her son's eyes. "Mom, where's dad?"

"Your father and your grandparents..."

Aiden's eyes welled. "They're dead, aren't they?"

"Yes, babies," Jordan replied. "I'm so sorry."

15

S HANNON SCREAMED. Zoe scrambled to her feet and banged her shackles against the metal gate of the stable. She yelled. "Touch her again and I swear to God I'll kill you!"

The Clown turned slowly, hissed, stepped out of Shannon's stall, walked across the common hallway, and stood outside her stable door.

Zoe stepped back. She called out. "Shannon, you okay? Talk to me!"

No reply.

Zoe summoned her courage, walked back to the gate, challenged the Clown's wicked stare, and shook the bars. "What did you do to her, asshole?"

The Clown unfastened the latch, threw open the gate, clamped his hand around her throat, walked her backwards, slammed her head against the back wall of the stall, and drew his face to hers. Zoe smelled the foulness of his breath as it escaped the mouth slit of the rubber prosthetic. He hissed again, louder this time. Part of her was terrified of him now, not knowing what he would do next. Was the man

behind the mask truly as insane as he portrayed himself to
be? Would he prove his dominance over her by ending her
life, as he may already have done with Shannon?

Zoe swallowed the rising fear, let it sink. She flashed
back to the nightmare years of her adolescence and that
fateful day when she emancipated herself from the living
hell that was life with her birth father. The visits in the
middle of the night when he would perform unspeakable
acts on her... the beatings he would deliver daily, without
warning or provocation... the mental and emotional abuse
that should have left her forever unsalvageable, a damaged
teenager, broken beyond repair, had it not been for her
relentless determination and resilience.

The stench of tobacco on the Clown's breath –the same
putrid stink that had once belonged to the man who called
himself her father– triggered a psychological break in Zoe.
This time however there was no nearby brass lamp to grab
hold of and slam against the side of his skull, no .44
Magnum handgun hidden under the sink to scamper to
on hands and knees, racked with terror, retrieve, and *fire!*
fire! fire! fire! fire! fire! into him, until the last round had
been expended, and all she could hear was the *click-click-*
click of the empty cylinders rotating with every additional
pull of the trigger, long after she had liberated herself
from him.

Fight or flight.

Life or death.

Never again, she thought. Not in this fucking lifetime.
And sure as shit not like this.

Life.

Zoe struggled against the Clown's powerful grip and
raised her head. Curious, he removed his hand from her
neck.

Zoe gasped, sucked in the air, coughed, waited for the light-headedness to subside.

The Clown turned his head from side-to-side, examining her with great interest, as though in her act of defiance he had discovered a new and rare species of human.

Zoe whispered. "Closer..."

The Clown hissed loudly, grabbed her neck once more. When Zoe again began to choke, he relented and released his hand from her throat. Cat and mouse. Zoe coughed again. The Clown jumped up and down, laughing, denoting his approval of the game. He permitted her to raise her shackled hands to her neck and massage her damaged throat.

Zoe spoke again, her words barely audible. "Come... closer."

The Clown hesitated, then brought his head to hers, turned his ear to her mouth, and listened.

"Is my sister all right?"

The Clown nodded slowly.

"Thank you," Zoe said. She lifted her head, forced herself to meet his eyes. "I'm sorry for what I said to you before. That was wrong."

The Clown dropped his head, nodded.

"You don't really want to hurt me, do you?"

The Clown shook his head.

"I didn't think so," Zoe replied. She lowered her voice. "I have a secret that no one else knows. Would it be okay if I told you?"

The Clown stood back. He clapped his hands together gleefully, nodded.

Zoe cleared her throat. "Hard to talk," she said. "Lean in."

The Clown rested his head on her shoulder, put his ear to her mouth.

"Much better. Ready?"

The Clown nodded.

"When I was a little girl," Zoe said, "my father bought me a doll. It was a clown, just like you." She forced a smile into her voice. "And you know what?"

He shook his head.

"I hated that thing!"

Before the Clown could react, Zoe wrapped her chain-bound wrists around his neck and jumped twice in the air, delivering two brutal knee strikes to the Clown's ribs. Her captor let out a cry and fell against her. Zoe spun around and pulled the chain link around his neck as tightly as she could. She listened to him gag, felt him struggle, strain, and kick out against her back as he tried unsuccessfully to fight back. She interlocked her wrists, gained an even greater advantage over him, then pulled down with all her might.

Snap.

Zoe heard his cervical vertebrae break. The Clown's body fell slack and slid to the ground behind her.

The key.

She turned, rummaged through his pockets, found the skeleton key, fiddled with the locks, removed the shackles from her wrists, and slipped her head out of the noose.

Free at last.

Zoe looked down at the man lying at her feet on the dusty floor. Even in death the hooded figure remained a menacing sight. She kneeled and pulled off the Clown's mask.

He was a youth, seventeen years old at the most, but physically a man by anyone's definition. Zoe had no idea who he was, nor did she care that she had killed him. Instead, she took consolation in the hope that his plans for them, whatever they might have been, had likely died with him.

Zoe patted down the Clown's body and found the stun stick hidden in his boot. She pressed the trigger and held it against the metal shackles laying on the floor. Sparks danced on the surface of the chain.

She kept the weapon. Perhaps it would prove useful to them in their escape.

Across the hall, Shannon moaned.

16

ARRIVING IN DOWNTOWN Los Angeles, James Rigel parked on a side street half a block from Angel of Mercy Hospital, opened the trunk of his car, unclipped the emergency road safety kit from its mounting brackets, dumped the contents of the plastic case on the floor of the car, returned the flashlight and flares to the case, opened his overnight bag, removed a lightweight windbreaker embroidered with the name 'Walter,' slipped it on, and slammed the trunk shut.

At nine o'clock in the evening, the back entrance to the hospital was as quiet as he expected it would be at this relatively late hour. He held open the door for a pretty young nurse as she left the building. She smelled of bergamot. Rigel breathed in the sweet essence as she walked past. He couldn't help but wonder what trophies lay hidden beneath her clothes. Were it not so late he would have taken her to a secluded area at the back of the parking lot where they could become better acquainted, enjoy a little time with her, introduce her to Zippy, and add another treasure to his collection. But there was important work to be done, and he took his work very seriously. He suppressed the urge to ravage her. Instead, he bid her a good night and entered the building.

The corridor had been freshly sanitized and positively reeked of cheap citrus-smelling floor cleaner. Disgusted, Rigel covered his nose. How could any place tasked with the responsibility of prolonging the lives of its patients expose them to such olfactory filth? Senses offended but undaunted, he pressed on. At the end of the hallway he saw the sign he was looking for: LAUNDRY SERVICES. He entered the room.

The fresh, clean smells within this room were much more appealing. Dozens of pairs of medical scrubs were stacked neatly on metal racks, ordered by size. Rigel helped himself to a pair, opened his plastic case, rubbed a safety flare against the garment, re-locked the case, and wandered into the main area of the facility.

A voice called out from behind him. "Can I help you?"

Rigel turned and smiled. An elderly woman stood a few feet away. He held up his case. "Facilities Management, ma'am," he replied. "Which one's causing the problem?"

"Problem?" the woman asked. "What problem?"

Rigel held up the garment he had just intentionally soiled and pointed to the red mark on the pants. "This is the third complaint we've had tonight," he said. "Which machine is acting up?"

The woman looked baffled. "I haven't received any complaints."

"Which is why they call me and not you, my dear. You run the machines; I fix them." Rigel looked at her name tag. "Who's in charge here, Agnes?"

"I am," Agnes replied. "Have been for ten years."

"And you're telling me you weren't aware your scrubs

were leaving here looking like... *this*?" Rigel feigned disgust. He held up the pants with two fingers.

"Absolutely not!" Agnes said. "I run a spotless shop. My staff and I would never allow a garment to leave here with even the smallest mark on it. We inspect every one of them before they're shelved. I have no idea how this happened." The woman looked mortified at the thought that such an oversight could have occurred in her department.

"Don't worry, Agnes," Rigel said. "I'll find out what the problem is." He winked. "No one needs to

know about this besides us."

"Thank you," Agnes said. The woman looked like she was on the verge of having a heart attack. "You scared the life out of me."

"Let me take care of it," Rigel said. "I'll slip in behind the machines and take a look. I'm sure it's nothing major. Probably just a simple fluid leak. If it's a machine problem, I'll find the culprit, lickety-split."

"Do you want me to wait?"

"No, my dear. Not at all," Rigel said. He checked his watch. "It's after nine. When does your shift end?"

"It was over a few minutes ago."

"*What?* Oh, that's just not right. I'm sure you've had a very long day, Agnes. Go home, put your feet up, make yourself a nice cup of Earl Grey and leave this with me."

"Are you sure?"

"Is the Queen British?"

Agnes laughed.

Rigel smiled. "Now scoot. When you come in tomorrow morning everything will be good as new. You'll see."

"Thank you," Agnes said.

"My pleasure, dear."

Agnes gathered her belongings. Rigel walked her to the door. "Have a pleasant evening," he said.

The old woman smiled. She looked at the name on his jacket. "You as well, Walter."

Rigel closed the door behind her, walked behind the commercial washing machine, removed his street clothes, folded them neatly, put on the scrubs, removed the flare from the case, shoved it into his waistband, and hid the case and his clothes under the machine.

After locating Agnes' office, he turned on her computer, accessed the patient registry, and soon found the information he was looking for: QUEST, JORDAN. EAST WING. Room 604, Bed 2.

Rigel left the department, walked down the hallway, rode the service elevator to the sixth floor. The lobby ahead was busy. He turned left, kept his back to the crowd, and walked over to a portable blood-pressure machine standing in the hallway. He fiddled with the device, listening intently as a doctor addressed the group.

"I wanted to check in and see how everyone is doing," Dr. Tremaine said. "Once again, please accept my deepest condolences for your loss."

Andrew Dunn spoke. "How is Jordan doing, doctor?"

"To be honest, she's one very strong lady. As you can imagine, in the last few hours she's been to hell and back. I'm going to insist she stay for the night. It would be prudent to keep her under observation for a little while. She appears to be all right. But considering the circumstances I have my concerns."

"About?" Grant Carnevale asked.

Tremaine hesitated. "Suicide."

Carnevale shook his head. "Not Jordan, doctor," he replied. "No way. Not a chance."

"I know how irrational that might sound," Tremaine replied. "But in the last few hours Mrs. Quest has lost her parents, her husband, and from my understanding of the accident, several close friends. That totality of loss, experienced in such a short period of time, can be overwhelming."

"You don't understand, doc," Carnevale said. "Jordan lives for her kids. She would never think of leaving them without a mother. Especially after all of this."

"I'm glad to hear that," Tremaine said. "Unfortunately, I've seen it happen. Some individuals simply aren't strong enough to cope with the loss."

"Jordan *is*," Carnevale snapped.

Sensing he had struck a nerve with the man, Tremaine said nothing.

Andrew Dunn put his hand on Carnevale's shoulder. "The doctor's right, Grant. Perhaps the best thing for Jordan right now is rest and time alone to process all that's happened."

Carnevale reluctantly agreed.

"I'll arrange for her to receive a mild sedative," Dr. Tremaine said. "Something to help her sleep."

Marissa DeSola spoke, "Mr. and Mrs. Quest can stay at the estate with me and the children. We can come back and see Jordan first thing in the morning."

Director Dunn nodded. "I'll arrange for your transportation as soon as you're ready to leave."

"You too," Maria said, addressing Dunn, Carnevale, and Hanover. "Please stay with us. There's plenty of room."

"Thank you," the agents said, accepting her offer.

Dr. Tremaine's pager beeped. He looked at the display. "Sorry," he said. "I have to go."

"You'll let us know if there's any change in Jordan's condition?" Marissa asked.

"Of course," Tremaine answered.

"Thank you, doctor."

Tremaine nodded, walked to the nurse's station, picked up the phone, and answered the page.

Carnevale spoke to his colleagues. "I'll bring the car around. Meet me at the main entrance."

"I'll be along in a minute," Chris Hanover replied. He watched the nurse enter Jordan's room. She was carrying the sedative Dr. Tremaine had requested.

RIGEL GLANCED up from the monitor and watched as the nurse entered Jordan's room. He too had heard the conversation.

Soon his target would be fast asleep, alone, and utterly defenseless.

His timing couldn't have been better.

He wondered what she would smell like.

17

ZOE STEPPED OVER the body of the dead teenager, rushed across the hallway, and found Shannon laying in a puddle of soapy water in the corner of her stall. She was shivering, arms and legs drawn into the fetal position, rocking back and forth, talking to herself. *"Want to go home... no more... leave now... promise to be good... promise... promise..."*

Zoe had experienced this behavior twice in her lifetime. The first time was when she had been found by the police in her home, gun in hand. The second time was when she had collapsed in the courtroom after hearing the jury foreman read aloud her verdict, finding in her favor, acquitting her of all charges in the State's case against her pursuant to the murder of her birth father. Following the trial, she was sent to a halfway house which became her post-exoneration home. Sheltered under its roof were children like her, so troubled, lost and without hope for the future that they sought peace in the only place they could trust: the confines of their mind. Zoe recognized the post-traumatic indicators of her sister's impending mental breakdown. She had to pull

Shannon back to reality to save her. If she failed, she would be gone forever.

Zoe entered the stall, approached her sister slowly, called her by her nickname. "Shay?"

Shannon continued to rock. She stopped talking.

"It's me, Shay. It's Zoe." She kneeled, touched her lightly on her shoulder. "Can I sit with you?"

Shannon stopped talking. She pulled away, pressed herself tightly into the corner of the stable.

Zoe sat down. "It's over, Shay. Time to go home. We're getting out of here. You hear me?"

Shannon looked up. "Home?"

"Yes, sweetie."

"No," Shannon replied. She turned away. The rocking resumed. "Promise to be good... good..."

Zoe had to be firm with her sister. She was about to fall mind-first into a psychological abyss from which there would be no ascent. She had to snap her out of it. She took her by the hand. "Let's go. On your feet."

Shannon leaned into her arms.

"That's my girl. Up we go."

Shannon stood. Zoe wiped strands of soapy wet hair from her face and eyes. "Look at you," she said. "Beautiful as ever. No worse for wear."

Standing helped. Shannon began to regain the use of her faculties. Her speech became more coherent. "Zoe?" she said.

"Well, would you look at that," Zoe replied. "Sleeping Beauty awakens."

"Where are we?"

"I don't know, Shay. Doesn't matter. What matters is that we're getting out of here, right now. Can you walk?"

Shannon took a tentative step. "Yes, I'm fine."

"Good," Zoe teased, "because the thought of carrying you out of here wasn't really working for me."

Shannon looked across into Zoe's stall and saw the body of the Clown laying on the ground. "Is he…"

"Dead?" Zoe answered. "He fucking-well better be."

"How did you…"

"Don't ask. I took care of it. That's all that matters."

"Did he hurt you?"

"He tried."

"I'm sorry."

"For what?"

"I couldn't help you." Tears welled in Shannon's eyes.

Zoe cupped her sisters face in her hands. "Forget about it. Now come on. We need to get our asses in gear before someone comes to check on him."

Horses whinnied at the far end of the stable.

"Wait here," Zoe said.

"Where are you going?"

"To look around."

"Not without me you're not!"

"I'll only be a second," Zoe said. She handed Shannon the stun stick "Hang on to this. Don't be afraid to use it. Not for a second."

A strange sound came from the end of the stables. "You hear that?" Shannon said.

"You mean the horses? Yeah, Shay, I heard them. Horses… stable… one kind of goes with the other."

"No, not horses. Something else." Shannon stepped out of the stall and listened intently.

Zoe examined the stalls as Shannon ventured down the central corridor in search of the sound.

"Holy shit," Zoe said.

"What?"

"Check this out."

"What?"

"*This.*"

Zoe stared at the wall of the stall adjoining the one in which had been kept prisoner. The left side was papered with dozens of black and white photographs taken of them on the Harvard campus. The right side featured grainy surveillance photos of their father, Andrew Dunn. Interspersed between the pictures were photos depicting the hellish carnage delivered by terrorist attacks in Madrid, London, Boston and New York City.

"Jesus," Zoe said. "You know what this means?"

Shannon nodded. "Whoever took us wants Dad, too."

A whimpering sound came from the end of the stables, not equine. Human.

Shannon whispered to Zoe. "You heard it too?"

Zoe nodded. She took the stun stick from Shannon's hand. "Stay with me," she said. "Don't leave my side."

The women walked to the end of the stable. Disturbed by their presence, the horses neighed.

They inspected the stalls. All but one was empty.

A tattered horse blanket lay on the ground in the last stall. It moved.

Zoe gripped the stun stick tightly, then threw back the straw-covered blanket.

A young girl sat on the ground. She tried unsuccessfully to grab the blanket back from Zoe, then curled into a ball, covered her head, and began to sob. "Please don't hurt me," she cried. "I'll be good. I promise I'll be good."

18

THE NURSE ADMINISTERED the sedative, lifted Jordan's head, and adjusted her pillow. "There you go, dear," she said. "Get some rest. Lord knows you need it."

"Thank you," Jordan said. She soon began to feel the effect of the drug. Her body became light, as though she were floating above the bed, not laying in it, her mind a tsunami of thoughts, each crashing into the last until finally, mentally and emotionally drained, the tumultuous dream-waters became calm and she fell fast asleep.

The nurse stood watching her patient, monitoring her vitals. Satisfied she was stable she dimmed the lights and left the room.

James Rigel watched the nurse close the door and return to the central station. With visiting hours now over, she returned to her paperwork. The floor was quiet. An elderly man in a nearby room talked in his sleep with such vigor that Rigel was sure he could be heard on the opposite side of the ward. Hospitals were supposed to be places of peace and tranquility, and this man's unconscious inconsideration for those suffering around him troubled him. Perhaps after he had taken care of his target, he would return the man's room and put a permanent end to the incessant chatter. The nursing staff would applaud him for his effort. Their job was challenging enough without having to deal with such a discourteous patient.

A warning tone emanated from the central station. The nurse responded and entered a room located a few doors down the hall from Jordan.

Time to move.

Rigel walked down the corridor and glanced into each room, looking for any staff members he had not yet seen on the floor. All clear. He opened the door to Jordan's room and slipped inside.

The target was sleeping peacefully. Rigel stood at the end of her bed. For a moment he felt a pang of regret for what he was about to do. It seemed like such a waste. Even in her incapacitated state she was unquestionably beautiful. She appeared less like a patient in need of medical attention than an actress, waiting for the director to say 'Action' and for the cameras to begin to roll.

Rigel moved closer. He wanted to pull down her blankets, explore her body, and discover the treasures that lay beneath. Instead he reeled in his emotions and harnessed his desire. Jordan lay on her back with one arm beneath the covers, the other atop. Rigel leaned over and smelled her, traveling from her wrist to her shoulder, inhaling her perfume: Indian jasmine, Rosa centifolia, cardamom, carnation and benzoin, with a light balance of citrus fruits; a custom blend, exquisite. He considered searching the room for a sharp object, something with the capacity to cut. He wanted a piece of her. Hers was the finest scent he had ever encountered on a woman by far. Although he had never considered adding a body part to his souvenir collection, the temptation to do so in this woman's case was hard to ignore.

Jordan stirred in her sleep. The act reminded Rigel of the true purpose of his mission and the matter at hand: the completion of his contract with New York. Had the circumstances been different, had he met Jordan in a bar and seduced her with his movie-star charm, he could have taken her somewhere private, a place of his choosing, and enjoyed her for as long as he liked. But the confines of a hospital room were not conducive to satisfying both his curiosity and animal needs, and not nearly suitable enough for the romantic and mutually satisfying seductive encounter he knew a woman so perfect would expect from him. Had it been another time, another place...

Zippy would not do here. This woman was the exception to his rule. Even in death her beauty must be preserved.

Rigel lifted Jordan's pillow, slipped it out from beneath her head, and pressed it down over her face.

PRIOR TO THE administration of the sedative, Jordan experienced an unexplainable shift in the energy of the room. It felt as if the air had become charged and now teemed with electricity. In the psychic intervention which preceded the injection she had sensed a malevolent presence. The Gift thrust her back to her earlier discussion with Chief Ballantyne and her vision of Becky Landry, the young girl whom she had witnessed locked in a losing battle for her life with the man with the three-star tattoo. Somehow, he was here now, with her. She tried to fight the effect of the sedative and call out to her nurse, to her godfather, to Special Agents Hanover or Dunn, *anyone*, to warn them of the evil in their midst.

The pressure of the pillow on her face and the sudden elimination of her air supply shocked Jordan back to consciousness. She thrashed under the force of her attacker, punched and clawed at him, turned her head away, just enough to draw in a quick breath and replenish her aching lungs with a brief supply of life-giving oxygen, then grabbed his wrists.

Three stars...

Years of training under the expert tutelage of her late friend and bodyguard suddenly kicked in. In her mind, Jordan saw Rock standing over her, coaching her through the attack, how best to apply the martial arts defense techniques he had taught her, all the while fighting the effect of the sedative. With her free hand Jordan drove her thumb deep into the nerve collection at the base of her attacker's wrist. She heard him scream, felt his grip weaken. As his hand fell from her neck, she repositioned her thumb behind his wrist, grabbed the man's fingers and twisted them as hard as she could, folding them back, forcing him to straighten his arm. Jordan then thrust her knee hard into his bent elbow. The man cried out. The pillow fell away from her face. She pushed it aside, stared up at the man with the three-star tattoo cradling his injured arm, and watched him run for the door.

Still dazed from the drug and the temporary lack of oxygen to her brain, Jordan tried to give chase. She fell out of bed, held fast to a visitor's chair, forced herself to her feet, slumped along the wall, threw open the door to the room as it fell shut behind her fleeing attacker, watched the man race past the nurse's station, past the parting elevator doors, down the corridor and though the doors leading to the stairwell.

Special Agent Chris Hanover stepped out of the elevator.

Puzzled, he saw Jordan leaning against the door to her room, out of breath. He ran to her aid. "Mrs. Quest?" he said. "What happened? What's wrong?"

Jordan fell into his arms. "He tried... to kill me," Jordan replied. She gasped, drew a breath, and pointed to the stairwell at the end of the hall.

"Will you be all right?" Hanover asked.

Jordan nodded.

Hanover drew his weapon and yelled for the nursing staff. Two nurses came running. "Mrs. Quest has been attacked. Call security. Tell them to lock down the hospital."

Hanover ran to the stairwell, threw open the door, cleared the landing. Below, heavy footfalls descended the stairs. He looked over the railing and met the assailant's stare.

"FBI!" he yelled.

Running again.

Faster now.

Pauses between the footfalls as the man took the stairs two at a time.

"Sonofabitch!" Hanover said.

He gave chase.

19

THE FRIGHTENED GIRL grabbed the blanket from the ground, pulled it around her, tried once more to hide beneath it.

Shannon knelt beside her. "It's okay, honey," she said. "We're not going to hurt you."

"What's your name, sweetie?" Zoe asked as she lowered the blanket.

The girl hesitated. "Lily," she answered, wiping her face. She wore a pink Pokemon T-shirt and matching shorts. Her clothes were wet and clung to her tiny frame. She shivered. The bastard had doused her with water too.

"What are you doing here?" Shannon asked.

Lily chewed her lip, said nothing.

Shannon pressed. "Where are your parents, hon?"

The child stared up at the two women. "Gone," she replied.

"What do you mean?" Zoe asked.

Lily stared at the floor. "They're dead."

Shannon asked, "Then who is taking care of you?"

"Me."

"You're telling us you're on your own?"

"Jesus," Zoe said, dumbfounded to hear Lily had been left to fend for herself at such a young age. "What kind of place is this?"

Shannon gave her a *watch your language* kind of look.

"Sorry," Zoe acknowledged. "Forgot about the kid." She looked around the stall. A pair of jockey racing silks hung on a wooden hook. The clothing was clean and dry. "Here, Lily," Zoe said. "Put these on."

Lily held tight to the blanket, pulled it up to her eyes, refused to move.

"It's okay," Shannon said. She winked. "My sisters got quite a potty-mouth on her, doesn't she?"

Lily half-smiled.

Zoe appreciated the girl's apprehension. "Hey Lily," she said, "check this out." She held the silks up against her and posed like a high-fashion model. "Could you imagine trying to find a decent pair of shoes to match this?" She puckered her lips and made a funny face.

Lily snickered.

Shannon partnered with her sister to gain Lily's trust. "It would be hard."

Zoe nodded. "What do you think, Shay? Flats or pumps?" She bounced up and down on the balls of her feet for full effect.

"Pumps all the way. The only way to rock an outfit as ugly as that is in a great pair of pumps."

"Gucci?"

Shannon shook her head. "Christian Louboutin. Goes better with silk. Lily could totally pull off a pair of Loubou's."

"Then again," Zoe said, "there's always Prada."

"Correction," Shannon said. "There's *always* Prada."

Lily pointed to her muddy running shoes. "I wear Nike's."

"Excellent choice!" Shannon said. "What do you say we see how well your Nike's go with this flashy little number?"

Lily hesitated, then agreed. "Okay."

"Perfect," Zoe said. "But if we're gonna do this right, and by that, I mean *fashion model* right, we'll need a change room."

"Coming right up," Shannon said. She lifted the blanket off the little girl, held it up. "Ta da! Instant change room."

Zoe handed Lily the silks. "Garments fit for a supermodel."

Lily smiled. "You two are ridiculous," she said. "I'm no model." She took the silks from Zoe, hid behind the raised blanket, removed her wet top and shorts, and slipped into the fresh, dry clothes. The girl stepped out from behind the blanket. The outfit, tailored for a small person, fit her well.

"Well, look at you," Zoe said. "Positively gorgeous!"

"Can I have your autograph?" Shannon teased.

Feeling they had come a little closer to gaining the girl's trust, wanting to know more about her, Shannon asked, "How long have you been here, sweetie?"

Lily shrugged her shoulders. "I don't know."

"Do you sleep here?"

"Most of the time."

"So not *all* the time."

Lily shook her head. "Sometimes Uncle Emmett lets me stay with him."

Shannon and Zoe exchanged glances. "Where does Uncle Emmett live, Lily?" Zoe asked.

Lily pointed outside. "The main house."

"Did Uncle Emmett put you out here?" Zoe said.

Lily nodded.

"Why?" Shannon asked.

Lily kicked the straw at her feet, stared at the ground. "Because..."

"Because why?" Zoe asked. She was afraid of what the young girl was about to say. *Live or die.*

"I was bad."

"Bad... *how?*"

Lily shook her head. "I don't want to say."

Shannon leaned over. "Tell you what," she said. "Let's sister-swear on the answer. You whisper it to me, and I'll whisper it to Zoe. It'll be our secret. No one else will ever know, not even the horses. We promise. Deal?"

Lily relented. "Okay."

"Good," Shannon said. "Now tell me, sweetie. Why did your Uncle Emmett lock you in here?"

Lily cupped her hand to Shannon's ear and shared her secret.

Shannon looked at Zoe. The anger in her eyes spoke for her.

Zoe understood. She clenched her fists at her side. *Live or die... Live.*

"Come on, honey," Shannon said. "We're going to get you out of here."

"Where are we going?" Lily asked.

"Someplace safe," Zoe said.

Lily pulled back. "No! I can't leave!"

Shannon tried to reason with the young girl. "You can't stay here, Lily. It's too dangerous."

"I won't leave my parents!"

Shannon kneeled down. "Honey, you told me your parents were dead, remember?"

Lily nodded. "They are. But they're here, too."

Zoe asked, "What do you mean, your parents are *here*?"

The girl walked into the adjoining stall, stood in the middle of the floor, pointed at the dirt floor. "They wouldn't do what Uncle Emmett wanted," she said.

"Jesus," Zoe said. "Are your parents buried here?"

Lily nodded.

Shannon took Lily's hand. "We'll come back for your mom and dad, Lily. I promise."

"Sister-swear?"

"More than that," Zoe said. "We promise you on our lives."

The entrance door to the stables was ajar. Zoe eased it open, looked outside. The ground was a blanket of fog, the night black, the moon eclipsed between wisps of passing clouds. In the faint lunar light Zoe saw the tree line of a forest several hundred yards beyond the stables.

"Woods," she said. "Not far. We can make it, but we'll need to move fast." She turned to Shannon. "You ready?"

"One-hundred percent," Shannon replied.

"Then let's get the hell out of here."

Under the dark cloak of night, Zoe, Shannon, and Lily fled the stables for the woods.

20

REACHING THE BOTTOM of the stairwell, Hanover cleared the door, raced along the corridor, rattled door handles, found all but one of the rooms locked. He peered through the mesh-glass windows of the MECHANICAL ROOM doors and listened. Inside, the room hissed with the sound of pipes carrying pressurized steam. He swung open the door, slipped inside, dropped low, took cover against the iron handrails on the landing and surveyed the room.

A maintenance worker lay at the foot of the stairs, his yellow safety hat and clipboard several feet away from his body.

Hanover descended the metal stairs. He held the Glock 9mm handgun tight to his chest, his eyes following the red dot of the weapons laser sight as it glanced off the massive boilers, heat exchangers, generators and ceiling pipes which filled the room. He reached the floor, checked the man's carotid artery for a pulse.

Dead.

He drew his fingers back. They were wet, tacky to the touch. A deep laceration circled the man's neck. Blood seeped from the wound. His final expression in life was one of bewilderment; a vacant stare, born of surprise, cast by fear.

Hanover looked around the massive room. On his left, six gas-fired high-pressure boilers stood shoulder to shoulder, above them a network of pipes - the source of the hissing sound. Gauges on the wall indicated their respective purposes to the hospital: steam sterilization, heating, water, kitchen, laundry. Ductwork for heating and ventilation, plus unmarked supply lines and piping for the hospitals fire sprinkler water distribution system crisscrossed the ceiling. A ladder at the end of the room led to a narrow second-floor catwalk. A metal sign, normally suspended between two chains which warned of restricted access to the service way, turned lazily on a single chain. Hanover read the swinging sign: Authorized Personnel Only Beyond This Point. He surveyed the catwalk. The structure had been erected to create an immense second floor within the room. The facility itself was immaculate, the equipment and floor spotless. Logic dictated that in a room so well maintained there was no way a member of the mechanical staff would have crossed the yellow and black warning markings on the floor and accessed the ladder without first ensuring the warning sign had been rehung behind him. Hanover trained his weapon on the top of the ladder and slowly began his ascent. At the top of the catwalk he stopped and looked down. At the opposite end of the room, down on the ground floor, the hospital orderly stepped out from between the boilers and ran for the exit. Hanover aimed and fired but the round missed its mark. Unfazed by the gunshot, the man dropped to the ground and shoulder rolled across the polished concrete floor. Hanover tried to re-establish a line of sight, couldn't. The orderly reached the wall and bolted to his feet.

"Not very smart, firing a weapon in a room full of pressurized pipes," the man called out. His voice echoed in the room.

Whoever this guy is, Hanover thought, he sure as hell was no amateur. Only a professional could remain this calm under fire.

"You're right," Hanover yelled, stalking the service way, peering down through the slits in the metal floor grates as he made his way towards the boilers in search of the man. "I guess there's no point in getting blown up, is there?"

"Got any suggestions on how we should handle this?"

"Yeah, one," Hanover replied. "Walk your ass into the middle of the room and get down on your knees. I'll come down and cuff you. We'll call it a day."

"That doesn't really work for me," the orderly replied. The voice had moved to another location in the room. The man was somewhere under the catwalk to Hanover's left, heard but unseen.

"Why kill the engineer?" Hanover said.

"I don't know," the man answered. "Force of habit, maybe."

"That a question or a statement?" Hanover replied. On his right now. But where?

Around him, steam hissed and crackled in the pipes. Ducts cooled, contracted, popped. Drops of condensation from a pressure relief valve above dripped on his head. The trapped air between the ceiling and the catwalk was oppressively hot. Hanover wiped beads of perspiration from his face.

"The guy wanted to be a hero and got in my way," the orderly said. "I don't do heroes."

"So you slit his throat?"

"*Slit?* The man laughed. "That wouldn't be very artistic now, would it?"

Keep him talking, engaged. Let him give away his location, then take him out. "That how you see yourself?" Hanover asked. "Some kind of artist?"

"Come on down," the man called out. "You can experience my work first-hand."

There! Hanover saw him standing beside an electrical panel.

The agent took aim, but before he could take the shot he heard a click. The master circuit breaker on the electrical control panel had been thrown. The windowless room fell into darkness.

Disoriented in the now pitch-black room, Hanover waited for the emergency lighting system to engage, then looked at the electrical panel where seconds earlier he had seen the man.

Gone.

Hanover called out. "I'm not surprised you like the dark. Most rodents do."

No response.

Hanover slowly retraced his steps. Sections of the metal catwalk creaked under his weight. He cursed the sound. The beam of the Glock's laser sight illuminated airborne dust particles, sliced through the darkness, and danced off the walls and heavy equipment in the room. He switched off the device.

"Why try to kill Mrs. Quest?" Hanover yelled.

No reply.

Movement in the shadows, behind the bank of boilers.

Hanover reached the top of the ladder. He knew the descent would leave him exposed, temporarily vulnerable. He had no choice. If the orderly were to choose this moment to flee through the far exit doors it would be impossible for him to race down the ladder, run across the room, make his way up the stairs and out the door in time to see in which direction he had escaped. He would lose Jordan's attacker and the engineer's murderer. The man would be free to kill again. He wasn't about to let that happen.

Hanover descended the service ladder, one hand on the rung, the other on the Glock, until he reached the ground. Anticipating an attack, he swept the weapon left to right, then stopped and listened to the room for sounds of movement, heard none.

Had he missed something? Perhaps throwing the breaker was a calculated act of misdirection intended to provide the killer an opportunity to escape. The man had already established himself to be a professional, and no self-respecting pro would ever put himself in a position for which an exfiltration plan had not already been considered.

Hanover inspected the room for an alternate exit.

On the floor behind the boiler he found what he feared: a raised metal hatch. He unclipped his flashlight from his belt, cradled it under his weapon, clicked it on. The bright beam illuminated the entrance to a sub-basement. He turned off the light, holstered the weapon, and descended into the darkness.

No sooner had he placed his foot on the first rung of the ladder when from behind him came a strange sound –zzzzip– followed by the sensation of a metal wire looping around his neck, cutting deep into his throat. The assailant pulled him up and out of the hatch. Hanover kicked furiously at the floor as the man dragged him backwards into the middle of the room. The open hatch had been a decoy, a trap, and he had fallen for it.

White hot pain seized him by the throat, cut off his airway. He was growing weaker by the second, his vitality leaving his body.

He was losing consciousness.

21

WITHIN FEET OF REACHING the tree line Zoe stumbled, fell hard, grabbed her ankle, and cried out. Shannon ran back for her sister.

"Are you out of your mind?" Zoe yelled. "Don't stop! Go!"

Shannon kneeled, placed one arm around her neck, the other her waist. "You think for a second I'm leaving you behind? Not happening."

Lily pointed at the main house. "Hurry," she cried. "They're coming!"

Minutes ago, the only light emanating from inside the house came from the ever-changing glow of the television screen. Now, both the back porch and perimeter security lights were on, casting the grounds and stables in harsh, fluorescent light.

An elderly man, heavy-set, dressed in a T-shirt and overalls, walked out the back door. He stepped down the stairs and surveyed the grounds, his attention drawn to the open stable door. "Denny?" he yelled. "Where you at, boy?"

"That's Uncle Emmett!" Lily cried. Shannon pulled her to

the ground and covered her mouth, hushing her, fearing the girl's voice would carry on the dense mist. Though a thousand feet away, Shannon could hear the man's voice clearly. He called out once more. Not receiving a response, he returned to the house, then reappeared a few seconds later, shotgun in hand. He was accompanied by two younger men.

Shannon whispered to Zoe. "Can you walk?"

Zoe held her ankle. "Not sure."

"What happened?"

"Fucking tree root."

"Potty mouth," Lily whispered.

Zoe stared at girl. "Yes, that would be true," she said, massaging her ankle. "I indeed have a potty mouth."

"You shouldn't swear," Lily said.

"Why not? It fucking hurts."

"Swearing shows a lack of intelligence and is a verbal indication of an underdeveloped mind," the girl said.

"Is that so?" Zoe replied. "And who might I ask told you that?"

"My parents."

Zoe relented and accepted the chastising she had just received from the young girl. "Sorry, Lily. My bad. Your parents were right. Swearing is wrong."

Lily grinned triumphantly.

"It's a habit of mine. Terrible. You shouldn't do it."

"That's right," Shannon added.

"However," Zoe whispered, "with all due respect to your parents, you should know that there will be times in your life when swearing up a storm will feel like the most appropriate response to a given situation. Especially a highly stressful one."

"Really?" Lily asked. "Like when?"

"Oh, let me think," Zoe said. "How about when you're running from a *fucking* death house, trip on a *fucking* tree root, and almost break your *fucking* ankle. Yep, that qualifies."

Lily stared at her, speechless.

"I think you made your point," Shannon said. "How's the ankle?"

"Hurts like a sonofabitch. But I'll be okay."

Shannon watched the men walk down the steps, cross the yard, enter the stables, and turn on the lights. Seconds later, the sound of screaming and yelling rose above the cries of the horses.

"Sounds like they found Denny," Zoe said.

Shannon nodded. "We have to get out of here. They'll come looking for us any second."

"You better help me up," Zoe said. Shannon pulled her sister to her feet. Zoe tested the ankle.

"How is it?" Shannon asked.

"I'll survive."

"That's the plan."

"Damn straight."

Lily said, "I know a place in the woods where we can hide. Dad called it the secret place."

"Secret?" Zoe said. She looked toward the stables. Flashlight beams escaped through slits in the walls of the building. "Do they know about it?"

Lily shook her head. "I don't think so. Dad was very careful. He warned Mom and I never to tell anyone else about it."

"Think you can find it in the dark?" Zoe asked.

"I can try."

"Good enough. Which way are we going?"

Lily pointed into the forest, east of where they were standing. "That way."

"All right," Zoe said. "Let's go." Using Shannon for support, she shuffled for a few steps then stood on her own and retested the ankle. "Resting it helped," she said. "Must have just rolled it a little." She took another tentative step. "No pain," she said. "I'm good."

Commotion behind them.

Cloaked in the ethereal forest fog, they watched the two men run out of the stable. Uncle Emmett lumbered behind, shifting his weight as he stepped through the door in order to accommodate his large frame. He stopped, stared at the woods, then yelled into the night: "You're dead, you hear me? All of you. Dead!"

From around the back of the stable the sound of revving engines broke the stillness of the night. The men re-appeared on ATV's, raced them around to the backyard of the house. One man stayed with the idling all-terrain vehicles while the other ran inside, then returned a few seconds later. Zoe watched him shove something into his waistband and toss an object to the other man. *Guns.* They were armed now, coming after them, and no doubt would kill them when they found them. Apparently, they hadn't taken too well to the discovery of Denny's corpse.

This was their property, their woods, and no doubt they knew every square inch of the land. True, they had home field advantage. But what they didn't have was *them.* Zoe intended to keep it that way for as long as she could.

She remembered her life of horror with her birth father and the six-word mantra she created to help her navigate the turbulent waters of her young life: *Never again. Live or die. Live.*

"Show us the way, Lily," Zoe said. "We're running out of time."

Behind them, outside the stables, Zoe watched the ATV's lighting systems flash on, casting an amber glow over the moonlit fog. The men raced the machines engines, dropped the vehicles into gear, and raced toward the forest.

Lily panicked and screamed. The men heard her, looked in their direction.

"Run!" Shannon yelled. "Wherever this secret place is Lily, you'd better find it... now!"

22

FIFTEEN MINUTES LATE for the start of his shift, Abe Carmichael jogged along the hospital corridor and burst through the double doors into the Mechanical Room. He expected to encounter one very miffed John Skelton cooling his heels as he waited for him, unable to leave the sensitive equipment unattended until his arrival. Carmichael had recently made a habit of being late for work, due to his inability to limit his late-night consumption of cheap Scotch to just one or two shots, opting instead to kill half the bottle. Passing out and waking up well past his alarm had lately become the norm. This morning, looking down from the top of the landing, he encountered John Skelton, his friend and co-worker of the past ten years, lying in a pool of blood at the bottom of the stairs. A man was being dragged into the center of the room by a hospital orderly Abe did not recognize. He was clawing at his neck. It was clear the orderly was trying to choke him to death.

"Hey!" Abe yelled. He jumped over the metal railing to the ground, landed squarely on his feet, and dropped his six-foot four, two-hundred and fifty-pound frame into gear. He ran at the orderly like the former college linebacker that he was, hellbent on a sacking the man's attacker.

Rigel saw the man enter the room, heard him call out. Dammit! All he had needed was another few seconds and Zippy would have taken care of the fed. Now he had another hero to deal with. Reluctantly, he released the FBI agent. Hanover slid to the ground, gasping for air. Rigel kept his back to the human freight train barreling towards him, listening to his footsteps, timing his defense. At the last second, he turned, grabbed the man by his outstretched hand, wrenched his wrist tightly, and heard him cry out as he drove the man's arm under him in a smooth, circular motion.

Carmichael flew through the air and hit the ground hard, landing several yards away.

Rigel heard the man's clavicle break as it met the concrete floor.

Carmichael lay on the ground, disoriented, trying to comprehend what had just happened. A second earlier he had the man in his sights, ready not just to tackle him but to career right through him, pick him up, run him the length of the room, if necessary, slam him hard into the wall, knock him unconscious, call hospital security, tend to the wounded man, then check on his friend. Instead he lay on the ground, staring up at the metal catwalk. He'd experienced his share of football injuries in his day and knew one thing was certain: his shoulder was broken. The man, though smaller than him but stocky and athletic in his own right, was obviously a highly skilled martial artist. He had taken advantage of his powerful momentum, turned it deftly against him, evaded the attack like nothing he had experienced before, and done so with little effort.

Carmichael fought against the white-hot pain, rolled on his uninjured side and struggled to his knees. He tried to fend off the man's offensive attack, a brutal kick to his ribs, couldn't, and fell to the floor. He pulled his legs up to his chest, protecting his vital organs, tasted blood, then heard a strange sound above him- *zzzippp*. He looked up. The orderly was standing over him, a braided metal cord stretched between his hands. "Fucking hero," the orderly said as he straddled his back. "I really, really, *really* hate heroes." Carmichael felt the cold steel loop around his neck.

The gunshot narrowly missed Rigel. He dove to the side, used the big man for cover, watched Hanover's arm drop and the weapon fall to the ground, and used the opportunity to escape. He scrambled away from the maintenance engineer as the cop retrieved his weapon, raised it again, and squeezed off a second round. The bullet whizzed across his cheek, grazed his skin, and *pinged* off the metal boiler under which he had taken cover. He slipped out from beneath the boiler, ran toward the open floor hatch, pulled the safety flare from his waistband, cracked its safety seal, and threw it into the center of the room beyond the reach of the cop.

Chris Hanover struggled to his feet, choking on the acrid smoke billowing from the flare which had quickly begun to fill the room.

A voice called out from the other side of the caustic cloud. "Are you nuts? This room is filled with high pressure equipment. You want to blow us the hell up? *Stop firing!*"

Carmichael emerged from the smoke. He was in obvious pain and struggled to walk. Slowly, he made his way to Hanover.

"FBI!" Hanover yelled. "Stop where you are!"

"Hey man," Carmichael said. "I just got a broken

shoulder and probably a few broken ribs trying to save your ass. Least you could do is not shoot me."

Hanover lowered the Glock and headed in the direction of the orderlies last known position. "Did you see where he went?"

"Hell, no!" Carmichael replied. "I was too busy trying not to die."

"Call security," Hanover commanded. "I need to find him before he leaves the hospital."

"And tell them what?" Carmichael said. "That you're looking for an orderly... in a *hospital*?"

Hanover spied an open hatch in the floor, saw the orderly lower the cover. He ran, stumbled, reached the cover, tried to pry it open, couldn't. Locked. He heard shuffling beneath the concrete floor, moving away from him.

Carmichael had caught up to him. "Where does this lead?" Hanover asked.

"Everywhere," the engineer replied. "It's a subterranean service level, mostly for electrical gear."

"Is there an exit point?"

"*An* exit point? Try dozens of them, all over the hospital."

The smoke from the burning flare had risen to the ceiling, reached the fire detection system and activated the emergency sprinkler valves. Water sprayed down upon the two men.

Carmichael tried to raise his hand and shield his face from the water, but his broken ribs restricted his mobility. "You're FBI?" he asked.

Hanover nodded. "Yeah."

Carmichael winced as he raised his shirt and inspected his damaged ribs.

"You saved my life back there," Hanover said. "Thanks."

"Don't mention it."

"How're the ribs?"

"Better than your neck by the look of it. Who the hell is that guy?"

In the melee, Hanover had forgotten about the laceration he sustained from the metal cord. He massaged his neck, checked his fingers for blood, found none, shook his head. "I don't know. But I'm going to find out." He pointed to the hatch. "I need to know the termination points for this network. Can you get me a set of blueprints?"

"You bet."

"I need them yesterday."

Carmichael nodded, then shuffled toward the staircase. "On it."

"You sure you're okay?" Hanover asked. "That was a pretty bad spill you took."

Carmichael played down the near-incapacitating pain in his shoulder and wrist. "Don't worry about me," he said, opening the door at the top of the landing. "I'll get checked out later. Right now, I want this prick as badly as you do."

"Special Agent Chris Hanover," Chris said, identifying himself to the big man. "Have the hospital page me when you get those blueprints."

"Abe Carmichael. Will do."

Hanover waited until Carmichael had left the room, then called Dunn. "Sir, you need to get the family out of here and lock down the hospital," he said. "Someone just tried to kill Mrs. Quest."

"Is she all right?" Dunn replied.

"I think so. I'm heading back to her room now."

"Carnevale and I will meet you there. Where are you?"

"Basement, mechanical room. Whoever tried to take out Mrs. Quest just tried to kill me too."

"You okay?"

"Yes, sir."

"Do you have him in custody?"

"No, sir. He's still somewhere in the facility. He killed one civilian, tried to kill another."

"Jesus Christ."

"Sir, under the circumstances, I think Mrs. Quest and her family should be placed into protective custody immediately. It's starting to look like that plane crash was no accident."

"I agree," Dunn said. "You stay with Jordan. I'll assign a team to the estate. We're on our way."

Chris returned to the sixth floor. Jordan's nurse stood outside her room talking to the security guard.

"How's she doing?" Chris asked. He stepped inside, checked on Jordan, saw she was sleeping.

"Stable," the nurse replied, "and scared to death."

Hanover turned to the guard and pointed to the security cameras mounted in the ceiling. "I need to see the footage from those cameras right away."

"Yes, sir," the guard replied.

23

_____

HARRISON TASKER LEFT the aircraft hangar and drove the sedan containing the body of the dead fire captain in its trunk to the Runway 69 Gentleman's Club located on the outskirts of LAX airport. He parked beside his black Mustang GT, popped the trunk, removed a leather travel bag, and entered the club. A heavily tattooed biker nicknamed 'Grease,' stood guard at the front door. Tasker tossed him the keys and motioned to the fire captain's car. "One to go," he said. The biker understood, nodded, removed his microphone from the clip on his shoulder and radioed for assistance. A second biker soon appeared, took the keys from Grease, hopped into the maroon sedan, and drove off. The biker would make sure the fire captain and his vehicle were never seen again.

Tasker changed out of the captain's uniform into his own clothes, bagged the garments, handed them to Grease for destruction, fired up the Mustang, and followed the GPS tracking signal his New York handlers had provided him to locate and eliminate the contractor. Traveling from the club to downtown Los Angeles, he reached Angel of Mercy

Hospital, slowed the vehicle, and watched the flashing dot on the screen begin to flicker, then turn solid blue, placing the contractor, James Rigel, his target, somewhere inside the medical facility. He pulled the car into a short-term parking lot across the street from the hospital, overfed the meter, crossed the street, and entered the building through the main lobby, at which point he was promptly stopped by hospital security.

The guard raised his hand as he walked through the automatic doors. "I'm sorry, sir. Visitor hours ended half an hour ago."

Harrison Tasker checked his watch and removed his glasses. He squinted at the guard, fumbled for a cleaning cloth inside the breast pocket of his sport jacket and polished the lenses. Tall, black, powerfully built, with a broad chest, square jaw and tree-trunk neck, he could easily have been mistaken for a professional athlete. He had, in fact, in his early twenties, enjoyed a brief stint with the Oakland A's baseball club until ending the career of the club's in-development pitcher, Wayne Flynn. The A's saw a stellar future for Flynn in the majors. But when an argument about the attention being paid to Tasker by the man's wife concluded with Tasker clamping his hand around the arrogant SOB's throat, pinning him against the dugout wall and smashing his pitching hand to jelly with a baseball bat, Oakland promptly fired him, Tasker kept the bat as a souvenir. Over the next two years he gained a reputation for knocking out more teeth in bar room brawls than he had ever hit baseballs out of ballparks. With his pro-sport career in the dust and his only resume an arrest record more impressive than his baseball stats had ever been, he soon came to the attention of New York. When they offered him the opportunity to put his sociopathic proclivities to more professional use, Harrison Tasker soon transitioned from bone cruncher to full-time contract killer.

Tasker watched as an LAPD police car screeched to a halt outside the main entrance to the hospital, followed quickly by a second cruiser and undercover sedan. The LAPD officers stepped out of their vehicles and conferred. The plainclothes officers exited their car and ordered the uniforms to take up positions elsewhere on the grounds. One of the black-and-whites blocked the main entrance to Angel of Mercy from the road while the second rounded the corner and headed for the rear exit to the building. The undercover cops walked into the hospital. Tasker heard them identify themselves as FBI agents and give the security guard explicit instructions. Under no circumstances was anyone to leave the facility until further notice. He watched the agents board the elevator. The lobby display panel indicated the cab stopped on the sixth floor.

Professional instinct told him why the police were there and why the place was in lockdown. On his way to the hospital, local radio stations frequently retold the story of the day– the horrific jet crash at LAX. Speculation about the reason for the crash ranged from being nothing more than a tragic accident to an act of domestic terrorism. Tasker recalled his assignment. He had followed his instructions to the letter and tampered with the aircraft exactly as specified. New York wanted the crash to look like an accident: a tire blowout during takeoff, the result of a mechanical oversight, missed in the pre-flight inspection. Tasker had found the log, altered the PSI number as correctly recorded by the mechanic, over-inflated the tires by thirty percent, placed several key tools on the floor of the hangar, and wiped down the tires with jet fuel. The prints on the tools and equipment belonged to the lead mechanic responsible for the aircraft's final inspection. The balance of the assignment was watch and wait. Experts in New York had calculated the aircraft's speed required for takeoff, time of day, outside temperature, the heat of the tarmac, and distance to the concrete marker located at the end of the runway. As predicted, when the tires blew the jet immediately dropped, clipped the berm, and struck the ground, assuring catastrophic consequences. But New York failed to take into consideration the near impossible: that someone might actually *survive* the crash. Evidently Rigel had heard the news, disregarded all attempts by New York to contact him, and taken it upon himself to find and terminate the survivors in order to fulfill the terms and conditions of his contract. He had no idea that his agreement with New York had already been rescinded and that *he* had now become as much a target as the individuals which he sought to kill.

Tasker feigned surprise at the police activity. He placed his glasses on his face and adjusted the frames so that they sat more comfortably on the bridge of his nose. "What's going on?" he asked the guard.

"An FBI agent was attacked tonight."

"Here?" Tasker asked. "In the hospital?"

The guard nodded. "Not more than twenty minutes ago."

Rigel, Tasker thought. Had to be. No other operative would be foolish enough to take on the FBI in a facility as secure as this.

"You been following the news?" the guard asked.

"Not really," Tasker lied.

"You don't know about the jet crash at LAX?"

Tasker shrugged.

"You know who Michael Farrow is, right?"

"Name sounds familiar."

"The tech billionaire. It was his plane that crashed. Guy's dead. So's his family, except for his daughter. She's upstairs. Got a few bumps and bruises from what I hear. Other than that, she's all right."

"Holy shit."

The guard nodded, then checked himself and shook his head. "I probably shouldn't have told you that."

Tasker returned the cleaning cloth to his pocket and brought his finger to his lips. "Mums the word."

"Thanks, man," the guard said. "Sorry, but with the place in lockdown I can't let you in. Can I relay a message? Did you come to visit someone?"

"No."

The guard looked puzzled.

"Lost my wallet this afternoon," Tasker lied. "Could have been here, maybe someplace else, I don't know. I thought I'd retrace my steps, ask around, see if maybe somebody found it and turned it in. You hear of anything?"

"Not to my knowledge," the guard replied. "Best thing would be to check with Lost and Found in the morning."

"I suppose," Tasker agreed.

The men watched a third LAPD unit roll to a stop at the front entrance. "Tell you what," the guard said. "Give me a sec. I'll put it over the radio and ask around. But I better talk to these guys first, let 'em know the FBI's here."

"Do your thing," Tasker said. He pointed to a bench outside the gift shop. "Mind if I wait over there?"

"Not at all," the guard said. He looked Tasker up and down. "Man, you are one *big* dude," he said. "Ever play football?"

"Nah," Tasker replied. "Never really been much into sports. I'm more of a bookworm."

"What a waste," the guard said. He shook his head. "You could have broken a few bones out on the field."

Tasker smiled. "Yeah, and with my luck they'd all be mine."

The guard laughed. "Sit tight, okay? I'll be right back."

Tasker nodded. He watched the guard walk to the front entrance to greet the arriving officers. He waited until he was alone in the empty lobby then headed down the corridor, found an exit door, left the hospital, returned to his car, and checked Rigel's GPS coordinates.

No signal flashed on the screen.

The ghost app New York had covertly installed on the contractor's cellphone had stopped transmitting his location. Rigel's signal was gone.

Tasker slammed his fist against the steering wheel. "Sonofabitch!"

24

R IGEL HURRIED THROUGH the narrow service space beneath the mechanical room floor, negotiating his way between pipes and around electrical cables. After his failed attempt to kill both the FBI agent and Jordan Quest, he needed to find a way out of the hospital as soon as possible. If the facility wasn't already crawling with local cops and federal agents, it soon would be.

No operation had ever gone so wrong, so fast.

He turned on his phone. Sandwiched between two concrete floors the device provided no cellular signal but offered a useful solution to his predicament. In the dark confined space, the bright screen illuminated the passageway. He could see well enough to find a suitable exit, preferably one that led back to the Laundry Services department where he had stashed his clothing and belongings behind the commercial clothes dryer.

Rigel followed a circuitous path through the service space, first turning left, then right, left again for another fifty feet, then right. Ahead, light seeped through the edges of a second-floor hatch, eclipsing the access point to the room in which it was located. The scent of clean clothes confirmed he had found Laundry Services. Rigel ascended the ladder, tried to lift the hatch cover, couldn't. He tried again, pushing it up with greater force than his previous attempt. The hatch refused to open. Although free within the facility, here in the bowels of the hospital he was, for all intents and purposes, trapped.

He heard voices above, followed by footsteps, coming towards the hatch. Had his attempt to lift the hatch been seen and aroused the curiosity of the employees in the room? Worse yet, had he somehow been tracked? Post 9/11, most major institutions had become hypervigilant and tightened their security. Angel of Mercy was the largest hospital in downtown Los Angeles. It wouldn't have surprised him to learn that the institution had installed security cameras throughout the facility, including this subterranean service passageway. Perhaps the authorities were waiting for him on the other side of the hatch, weapons drawn, prepared to take him into custody the second he raised the cover and poked his head up from beneath the floor. Rigel steadied himself. If he was about to come face to face with police in his attempt to escape, he would fight his way out. At the very least he would take a few of them with him before he died.

More commotion from above, then the *clack-clack* of wheel locks being released. Wheels rolled over the access cover, first one set, then another. Rigel visualized the room, then understood why he could not lift the hatch: a service cart had been resting on top of it. Heavy with garments, the weight of the cart had made the cover impossible to lift. The wheels of the cart squeaked as it rolled away. Relieved of the pressure of the cart, the hatch's metal hinges creaked. Rigel waited, then tried the hatch once again. It lifted with ease. He raised it high enough to permit him to see into the room and judge the timing of his ascent into Laundry Services. He couldn't afford to be seen. There was no time to make up a viable story which would convince the staff of the reason for his sudden appearance. He needed to get to the dryer, change his clothes, and leave the hospital while he still could.

The time had come.

Rigel lifted the cover.

All clear.

He scrambled up the ladder and gently lowered the steel cover behind him.

On the opposite side of the room he saw the bank of commercial clothes dryers and identified the one behind which he had stashed his belongings. He ran to the unit, changed out of the scrubs and back into his street clothes. He picked up the plastic box that served as a prop for his charade and walked through the department, faking his inspection of the machines, affably engaging the staff in small talk, apologizing for the intrusion, assuring them that all the machines were now operating exactly as they should, and made his way through the exit door into the hallway.

Two men in business suits walked in his direction: plain-clothes cops or federal agents judging by their body language. Rigel spotted a floor cleaning cart across the hall-way. He walked to the trolley, removed a yellow A-frame sign labelled SLIPPERY WHEN WET and placed it in the middle of the floor. He wrung out the wet mop, pulled it from its bucket, and began to clean the floor. "Watch your step," he said. The cops, too involved in their conversation to pay attention to him, walked through the doors at the end of the corridor.

Rigel left the hospital through the same doors he had entered less than an hour ago.

An LAPD patrol car blocked the exit from the rear parking lot to the road. Ten vehicles sat in cue waiting to leave the facility. The officers were inspecting each car and checking the identity of the occupants. The trunk of the lead vehicle was open, an officer rummaging through its contents.

A light rain fell. The night air smelled sweet and intoxicating, a blend of night-blooming jasmine and eucalyptus. Rigel took a deep breath, savored the invigorating floral aroma. He searched the parking lot for additional signs of police presence, saw none. No security teams roamed the grounds. The only attention being paid to the rear of the building was to the exiting vehicles.

Rigel removed his car keys from his pocket and sauntered across the parking lot. From the corner of his eye he saw he had caught the attention of one of the officers at the makeshift checkpoint. The cop turned on his flashlight and pointed it in his direction. Rigel waved, shook his car keys, and pointed to the back of the lot. The cop gestured to the last car in the cue, as if instructing him to take his place at the end of the line upon leaving. Rigel smiled and gave him a thumbs up.

A low wall separated the rear parking lot from the common roadway shared by a community of low-rise townhouses. The cop followed him with the flashlight as he walked across the lot. Reaching the driver's door of a nearby SUV, Rigel put the plastic case on the roof of the car along with his car keys and removed his service technician jacket. He took his time, deliberately drawing out the moment, until he achieved the desired result. Satisfied, the cop clicked off the flashlight and turned his attention back to the checkpoint. Rigel observed the officers. All were busy inspecting the vehicles. One employee, irate at having to wait so long to leave work, had stepped out of his car and begun shouting obscenities at the police. The entire inspection team turned their attention to him. The situation escalated to the point where they handcuffed the man and shoved into the backseat of a black-and-white.

The perfect diversion had presented itself.

Rigel collected his belongings from the roof of the car, turned the jacket inside out –now a solid black windbreaker– and hopped over the low back wall of the parking lot, away from the scrutiny of the authorities.

He had parked on a side street about a block from the hospital which he estimated to be a short walk from the townhouses. He planned to take his time, enjoy the stroll, and take in the sensorial gifts the night air offered.

He was passed by two late night joggers, both blonde, beautiful, typical of Los Angeles. Models or actresses, he thought. Strippers, maybe. One woman wore her hair in a ponytail while her running partner preferred to let hers bounce freely. They smiled at Rigel as they ran past. He wanted to stop them and ask if they could recommend a good Hollywood agent, someone whom he could trust to put his yet undiscovered talent as an actor to work. Or he could just knock them both out with two well-delivered blows, drag them into the alley they had just passed, enjoy them for a while, kill them, and take a souvenir or two from each for his collection.

No, not tonight. He needed to stay focused and make sure he didn't call any undue attention to himself.

Rigel watched them run around the corner. Pity. He could have shown them such a good time. But he had an assignment to complete. And he was a professional.

The women would wait. If the two runners were any example of what L.A. had to offer the city would prove to be an excellent hunting ground.

After receiving his final compensation for eliminating the Quest woman and fulfilling the terms of his contract he might even consider making the City of Angels his permanent home. He could be happy in this town, pursuing both his acting career and passion for killing.

So many women, so little time.

He would need a few more souvenir boxes.

And an agent.

25

CHRIS HANOVER WINCED as Jordan's nurse, Audrey Lane, dabbed a cotton ball against his neck wound, a visible reminder of his encounter with Jordan's attacker in the mechanical room. The antibacterial astringent stung as it bubbled on the surface of his skin and crept into the crevices of the laceration.

Nurse Lane looked surprised. "That hurts?" she asked.

"It's not that bad," Hanover replied.

Nurse Lane applied more of the solution into the deeper areas of the wound. Chris groaned.

The nurse smiled. "And I thought all FBI agents were tough guys."

Hanover looked at her. Nurse Lane was beautiful. Tall, blonde, with a slender build, high cheekbones and piercing blue eyes. Had she not chosen a career in nursing she could have been a fashion model in a heartbeat. She wore no wedding ring. Hanover wondered if she was married. "The guy tried to take my head off with a garotte and all I end up with is this scratch on my neck. That's not tough enough for you?"

"You couldn't just fight him off, huh?" Lane pursed her lips, tried to conceal a smile.

"The situation was a little more complicated than that."

"I'm sure it was. But you're trained in martial arts, right?"

"If you're referring to close quarter hand-to-hand combat, then yes, I am."

Nurse Lane smiled but said nothing.

"What does *that* mean?" Chris asked.

"What?"

"You're smirking."

"Am not."

"Yes, you are."

Nurse Lane tried not to laugh.

Hanover was getting perturbed. "Okay, *Bruce Lee*, suppose you tell me exactly what you would have done in my position."

"Well, I can think of one thing right out of the gate," Audrey replied.

"This ought to be good," Chris said. "Okay, I'll bite."

She smiled. "I'd have paid more attention in self-defence class."

"Funny."

"Especially the one when they cover how to survive an attack from a garrote-wielding psychopath hiding out in a hospital basement. I definitely wouldn't have missed that one."

"Oh, I get it. What you're telling me is that I *let* this happen."

"You went after the guy without waiting for backup. So yes, I suppose I am."

"Wow," Hanover said, "I'm impressed."

"With what?"

"How you've been able to amass such encyclopedic

knowledge about police procedure - how to handle a high-risk takedown, in particular - all the while maintaining your full-time gig as a nurse."

"Easy answer."

"Shoot."

"S.W.A.T."

Hanover rolled his eyes. "How could I have missed that? It's comforting to know your law enforcement expertise comes from watching television cop dramas."

"Oh, I don't watch S.W.A.T. to learn about law enforcement, or even police procedure for that matter," Audrey Lane replied.

"Really? Then why? I mean, let's face it. You could practically teach Psychopathy 101."

"You're so ill-informed."

"Enlighten me."

"Everyone knows there's only one reason to watch S.W.A.T."

"And that would be?"

"Shemar Moore. He can take me into custody anytime."

Hanover started to laugh, then winced. "I'll give you that. The man's one hell of an actor. Good looking guy, too."

"Dreamy."

"I wouldn't go quite that far."

"Dreamsville. Dreamalicious."

"You can stop now."

Audrey applied a liberal amount of Ozonol to the wound to prevent infection and wrapped the injured area with medical gauze. "There," she said. "That should do it. Now you can go back to chasing bad guys."

"Thanks," Chris said. "You know, you have a great touch."

Audrey smiled. "Thank you."

"Mind if I buy you a cup of coffee later?"

"As much as I'd like that, I can't. Hospital rules. No fraternizing with the patients."

"Then you leave me no choice."

"Is that so?"

Chris nodded. "Yep. I'm going to have to take you out to dinner. For purely professional reasons, of course."

Audrey laughed. "How is that?"

"You attend to Jordan, so there's a chance you might have seen something. Better yet, someone."

"And you think that by taking me out to dinner I can be of help to you in your investigation?"

"One-hundred percent."

Audrey smiled. "Then never let it be said I wasn't willing to cooperate with the FBI."

"Your government thanks you."

"So exactly where and when is this interrogation to take place?"

"Tomorrow night. 8:00 P.M. The Palm."

"Good choice."

Director Dunn approached and spoke to Nurse Lane. "How's Agent Hanover doing?"

Audrey winked at Chris. "On his way to making a full recovery."

"Good," Dunn replied. To Chris, he said, "I need to speak with you."

"Yes, sir."

"Please let me know if I can be of further assistance, Agent Hanover," Audrey said as she excused herself. "You can reach me here at the hospital."

Hanover smiled. "I'll be in touch."

Dunn waited for the nurse to leave. "Carmichael's here. He's got the blueprints you asked for. I've requested two additional agents, Carter and Lehman." Dunn motioned to the men conferring with Carmichael and Carnevale, reviewing the architectural layout of the hospital. "They'll be assisting in the search of the building. So will LAPD. Since you and Carmichael are the only ones who know what this bastard looks like, I'm splitting you up. You'll run point with Carter on Team One. Carmichael and Lehman will accompany Agent Carnevale on Team Two. I'll stay with Jordan. LAPD will keep the place locked down. If the sono-fabitch is in the building, we'll find him."

"Tell the men to watch their backs, sir. This guy's a pro. He won't hesitate to kill them if he gets the chance."

Nurse Lane approached the two men. "Sorry to disturb you," she said. She handed Chris a slip of paper. "For the pain, in case it gets worse."

"Thank you," Chris said, pocketing the note.

Nurse Lane continued. "Director Dunn, Mrs. Quest says she'd like to speak with you when you have a minute."

Dunn nodded. "Tell her I'll be right there."

"Of course."

Carnevale called out to Chris, held up the blueprint, and gestured for him to join the others in the waiting room. Chris waved back. He winced as he turned his neck.

"You sure you're okay?" Dunn said.

"Fine, sir. How's Jordan doing?"

Dunn shook his head. "She's tough as nails. The woman impresses the hell out of me."

"Me too," Chris agreed.

"I'm going to check in on her and see what she wants. Find this guy, Agent Hanover. He's coming after Jordan for a reason. We need to know what that is. If you've got to put a hole or two in him in the process so be it. Just bring him in alive."

"Yes, sir."

Dunn tapped his communications earbud. "Start the search. I'll be on comms if you need me."

"Copy that."

As Chris headed to the waiting room, he read the slip of paper Audrey Lane had handed him. He smiled. She had given him her phone number.

JORDAN WAS SITTING up when Andrew Dunn entered the room. Nurse Lane adjusted her pillow.

"Better?" she asked.

"Much," Jordan replied.

"Good. The CALL button is on the bed beside you. Press it if you need anything."

"Thank you," Jordan said.

Dunn waited until the door fell shut behind the nurse. "You asked to see me, Mrs. Quest?"

"I did," Jordan replied. In her hand she held the necklace which belonged to the Directors daughter, Shannon. She placed it in her lap. "I think I know where to find your daughters."

26

———

BEEP... BEEP... BEEP...

The GPS tracking dot suddenly reappeared on Tasker's phone. It had found Rigel. The contractor was less than two blocks away, moving in his direction. Tasker pressed the stereo MUTE button on the GT's steering wheel three times. With a *click*, the passenger seat cushion popped up. From a secret compartment, Tasker removed a loaded Tec-9 machine pistol which he'd converted from its default semi-automatic mode into a fully automatic weapon capable of firing multiple rounds with a single press of the trigger, along with a spare clip, customized sound suppressor, shoulder harness and two tear gas grenades. He pulled off the road, stepped out of the car, slipped into the rig, affixed the silencer to the end of the gun and drew back the bolt. After adjusting the harness for a comfortable fit, he grabbed his former Oakland A's team jacket and ball cap from the back seat, put them on, and sat back in the car. The blip on the screen pulsed. Rigel was close.

Although the assignments he fulfilled for New York

required substantial pre-planning, Tasker found his job as a contract killer remarkably easy. After receiving the electronic dossier from his handler, he would spend a day or two researching the target. He observed their daily routine, noted drive routes to and from work, pick up times if their children attended school, the restaurants or bars they frequented, times of day they walked their dog, and assessed their personal protection detail (if they had one) for areas of vulnerability or weakness. He believed most of his targets deserved their fate for being the self-important multimillionaire assholes or business executives they were. Men and women who had ruffled the feathers of the more powerful, only to learn just how unimportant they really were; the point being made by the delivery of a bullet to the back of the head.

Unless otherwise instructed by New York, Tasker was required to follow specific rules of engagement. Only the principal was to be eliminated, never members of their family. The death of a child was to be avoided at all cost (unless the child was the target). Only once in his professional career had this been the case. A fourteen-year-old microbiology and chemistry prodigy had made a game out of successfully circumventing the cash-cow patents of a major pharmaceutical company and selling the information on the Dark Web to the highest bidder. The firm, fearful of experiencing a catastrophic meltdown of its stock and a mass exodus of its shareholders, contacted New York and ordered the boy's termination. Although Tasker had been paid a staggering sum to fulfill the contract with no suspicion of foul play, it haunted him. Killing a man or woman and watching them die was one thing. But taking the life of a gifted kid was a whole different matter. Tasker had given the hit much consideration and refused to use bullets, poison, knives, electrocution or suffocation. When the boy was not in his home-based lab hacking drug formulations, he loved to skateboard. To his detriment, he had a habit of not wearing a helmet. Tasker's plan was simple but effective: slip into the family's garage in the dead of night, loosen the bolts securing the rear wheel assembly to the kid's board, remove and refasten the mounting platform using double-sided tape, then wait for the inevitable to occur. His plan succeeded. The following afternoon the local news reported on the boy's death following a catastrophic head injury which he had sustained in a freak accident at a local skateboard park. The back wheels had come flying off the kid's board as he raced down the half pipe on his first run of the day. He fell back, cracked his head open on the concrete form, and died at the scene. Tasker watched from a distance as the boy leaned forward and launched himself off the leading edge of the ramp, lost sight of him when he hit the ground, then observed the ensuing panic as fellow boarders ran to his aid. He was extradited from the scene fifteen minutes later by emergency medical personnel. New York congratulated him on the ingenuity he displayed in completing the assignment and extended the client's appreciation. Tasker stayed in town to attend a candlelight vigil held at the skatepark in memory of the dead boy. Weeks later, he was offered two more high-profile contracts involving tender age targets. He refused them both. Killing the boy had taken a greater psychological toll on him than he thought it would. One night, thousands of miles away from the skateboard park on the other side of the country, he was sitting in his hotel suite, lamenting on the loss of his pro-baseball career, the muzzle of the Tec-9 pressed against his temple, his finger on the trigger. Disgusted with himself for not having the nerve to end his own life as unemotionally as he had those of dozens of his targets, he threw the weapon across the room. After falling asleep in the early hours of the morning, he awakened to find the boys decaying corpse lying in the bed beside him, his skeletal arm draped over his shoulder. He could not move at the sight, much less scream. Summoning his courage, he jumped out of bed, retrieved the Tec-9 from the floor, swung around and targeted the bed. As he prepared to riddle the hellish corpse with bullets, he suddenly realized that the boy was not actually there. He had pulled the sheets off the bed while experiencing a horrific nightmare. A loosed thread from his pillowcase lay where he had envisioned the boy's remains to be. Filled with terror at the thought of returning to sleep, he instead packed his bags and checked out of the hotel. He hoped he'd left the boy behind.

The terms and conditions of his latest contract were crystal clear. The *entire* family was to be eliminated. There were to be no survivors. Michael Farrow, the principal target, and his wife, Mary, were already dead. The plane crash had seen to that. Only Farrow's daughter, Jordan Quest, and her two children remained. Killing the daughter would be easy, the children not so much.

Tasker dropped the Mustang GT into gear and pulled away from the curb.

The light mist that earlier had swept in and covered the moonlit ground in a pearlescent dew had now turned to rain. Fat droplets splattered on the windshield. Tasker checked Rigel's GPS signal once more, then glanced out the windshield at the low clouds. A bolt of lightning flashed across the sky, illuminating the car's interior.

A storm was coming to Los Angeles.

27

BEHIND SHANNON, ZOE, AND LILY the searchlights of the all-terrain vehicles swept through the forest, casting silver shadows over its dew-laden floor, startling its nocturnal inhabitants. A doe and its fawn raised their heads and sniffed the air, then bolted, the doe following closely behind its mother, their fight-or-flight instinct aroused by the snapping of twigs breaking under heavy footfalls.

Lily called back to her new friends. "Quit stomping," she said. "If your roll your foot from heel to toe the sound won't carry."

"Excuse me, Pocahontas," Zoe replied. "Next time I'll wear moccasins."

"Or Sketchers," Shannon added.

"A much better suggestion," Zoe agreed. "Note to self: Make Sketchers footwear of choice for late-night run through woods."

Lily disregarded the verbal jab. "We'll be getting off the trail soon. Stick close. Blend into the shadows. Listen to the forest. Be one with the night."

"One with the night?" Zoe said. "Please tell me you're not going to go all kung-fu Zen-master on us."

"Quiet!" Lily hushed. "There, up ahead."

"I don't see a damn thing," Zoe said.

"Me neither," Shannon added.

"That's the whole idea," Lily said. "Follow me and don't ask questions. We need to move fast."

Lily directed them off the path. The racing engines of the ATV's echoed through the forest. Uncle Emmett and his sons were closing in.

Lily pointed to a tree with a massive trunk. Its gnarly root structure snaked across the surface of the ground. "There," she said. "Behind that tree."

The girl ran ahead, slid to the ground, and began digging at the soft soil with her fingers. Shannon and Zoe stared down at her.

Lily looked up. "Well don't just stand there," she said. "*Dig!*"

The women dropped to their knees. "What are we looking for?" Shannon said.

"The edge."

"Of what?"

"A door."

"A *door?*"

"Just do it already!"

Shannon and Zoe followed the girl's instructions and explored the ground beneath their fingers until they felt the edges of the door.

"Well, I'll be damned," Zoe said.

"Clear the dirt," Lily demanded.

They dug a channel around the perimeter of the flat two-foot by three-foot metal door.

Lily located the recessed handle and pulled. The door

creaked but wouldn't budge. Time and exposure to the elements had rusted its hinge.

"I don't suppose anyone thought to bury a can of metal lubricant here too," Zoe said.

"Grab the handle and pull," Lily said.

"Move aside," Zoe said. She tugged hard on the handle. With a heavy creak the stubborn hinge gave way. Zoe raised the door. A surge of air wafted up from within the structure. A steel ladder anchored to a concrete wall led down into darkness.

"Get in!" Lily said.

Shannon and Zoe exchanged tentative glances.

"You're wasting time. Hurry!"

"You first," Zoe said.

"I can't," Lily said. "I have to go last."

"Why?" Shannon asked.

"I have to execute the countermeasures."

"Countermeasures?" Zoe repeated. "Who the hell was your dad, Lily? James Bond?"

The ATV's were fast approaching, the beams from their lighting system illuminating the forest canopy and surrounding trees. The smell of gasoline and burning motor oil carried on the fog. A light rain began to fall.

They could hear voices now above the roar of the machines, instructions being issued. The ATV's split off in different directions. The sound of one of the four-wheelers faded while the second machine, heading toward them, grew louder.

"*Go!*" Lily yelled.

Shannon and Zoe descended the ladder. Lily followed close behind. Once inside the structure the girl pulled down the lever-lock on the underside of the door and flicked on the lights, casting the underground chamber in a pale-yellow glow. A thin wire pull-cord ran down the side of the concrete wall. Lily pulled down on its metal handle. Shannon and Zoe heard a muffled *twang* sound from above the hatch door. The wire fell slack against the wall.

Zoe looked at Lily. "Countermeasures?"

Lily nodded. "There's a huge net of pinecones, needles and leaves suspended between the trees. Dad camouflaged it so that you could walk right under it and not see it. I released it. Everything fell to the ground. The hatch is covered now."

"Where are we?" Shannon asked.

"Dad's secret place." Lily looked up. "Don't worry. We're safe now. It's soundproof. They won't be able to hear us, much less find us."

Storage cupboards ran along the walls of the main corridor, each labeled according to its contents. Zoe opened the doors and peeked inside. In one she found a dozen cans of instant coffee and whitener, boxes of tea, a tall plastic container full of single-serve sugar packets, cartons of dehydrated ready-to-eat foods, canned beans and chili, powdered milk, dry pasta, shrink-wrapped cases of bottled water, soda, packaged nuts, dried fruit and more.

The shelving units on the other side of the hallway were stocked with a variety of items: porcelain mugs, dinner plates, plastic cups, paper towels, toilet paper, soap, shampoo, a medical supply kit, kitchen cutlery, knives in self-sharpening cases, books, board games, walkie-talkies, flashlights, batteries, topographical maps of the region, safety lighters, striking matches, boxes of beeswax candles, kerosene lamps, bottles of fuel, a portable stove, cans of Sterno camping fuel, two compasses, a hand-crank radio, and eight cans of bear spray. One section of the wall was outfitted with rock climbing gear. Miscellaneous camping items hung on hooks. Three large plastic storage containers sat on the floor. The first, labeled DAD, was full of clothes, a pair of hiking boots, several pairs of leather gloves and a rain poncho. The label on the second tub read JUNE. The third, LILY.

Shannon turned to Lily. "June was your mother?"

Lily looked at the floor. She nodded.

Shannon walked over to Lily and gave her a hug. "I'm sorry this had to happen to you. We're going to make it right."

"How?" Lily asked.

"I don't know yet. But we promised we would, and that's exactly what we'll do."

Zoe called out to her sister. "Shay, check this out." In her hands she held several booklets. Shannon thumbed through the publications and read their titles aloud: "Planning Guide for Response to a Nuclear Detonation... Radiological Attack: Dirty Bombs and Other Devices... Nuclear Attack Fact Sheet... EPA Emergency Preparedness and Response... Nuclear War Survival Skills Civil Defense Manual."

To Lily, Zoe said, "A soundproof concrete vault twenty feet or more underground... medical supplies... enough emergency food and water to last six months, maybe longer. Your mother and father were survivalists, weren't they?"

Lily nodded.

"This is an underground bunker," Shannon said.

"More than that," Zoe corrected. "It's a nuclear fallout shelter."

28

RIGEL'S MIND WANDERED as he strolled past the rows of townhouses that backed on to the parking lot behind Angel of Mercy Hospital. He enjoyed taking long walks in the rain and loved the smell of geosmin produced at these times. He learned that microbiological term, which referred to how oil compounds in plants combined with airborne bacteria during periods of rain to infuse the air with a musty smell from Sandra May Edwards, whose acquaintance he had made between assignments while attending a free acting workshop two years earlier in Burbank. Rigel found the effect of the geosmin and negative-ionized air to be refreshing and invigorating, the woman less so. Sandra May Edwards, who insisted on being addressed by her full name, had once been a Ranger in Death Valley National Park, which bordered California and Nevada. She left the U.S. National Park Service to pursue her call to acting after a chance meeting with Johnny Depp, the uber talented actor, in the Stovepipe Wells Village General Store while hiking through Mosaic Canyon. Mr. Depp (now *Johnny* to her) had complimented her on her perfect teeth, high cheekbones, symmetrical face, and positive energy, and asked if she'd ever thought about becoming an actress. She had not. But in time she came to believe Mr. Depp's sharply honed thespian senses had seen a potential for stardom in her that she had not seen in herself and concluded that by continuing to work for the State she was not living up to her full potential. Two months after their meeting, she submitted her resignation to the Parks Service and moved to Los Angeles to fulfill her destiny as a movie star. She made a point of telling Rigel it *had* to be the movies. "I was discovered by Johnny Depp, and Johnny Depp is a *movie* star," she said. "If I was intended to be on television, I would have been discovered by a *television* star. It's simple math, right?"

After a few minutes of trying conversation, Rigel concluded that Sandra May Edwards was as dumb as a brick and felt hard pressed not to tell her so. He wanted to point out that math had nothing to do with it, that Mr. Depp's generous compliment to her was him simply being the consummate gentleman which he was reputed to be, and that, in truth, she was about as attractive as corroded metal. But perhaps the greatest insult of all to Sandra May Edwards was that the woman couldn't act to save her life. Rather than say what was really on his mind, he opted to agree with her philosophy that 'nothing in life is as important as following one's true calling.' Sandra May Edwards had been so enamored with Rigel and his acting ability she immediately promised him a co-starring role in her first movie. Believing they had a chemistry 'so electric it transcended the screen,' she suggested they meet at her place later that week to work on their class assignment and enjoy a drink or two. Rigel quickly took her up on the offer. Shortly into the evening (and after handling as much of her pompous attitude and pathetic acting ability as he could take) he suggested they conduct an exercise of his own creation. Their homework assignment had been to better understand the intimacy of the craft by connecting with a past negative experience and exploring the range of emotions it incited. When he offered Sandra May Edwards the opportunity to go first, she drew a blank and could not recount a single such event in her life, not even the last time she had cried. She attributed this shortcoming to her eternally optimistic attitude towards life. She had buried her feelings of anger, fear, and panic so deep that any memory of them was foreign to her. Rigel's counsel was to impress upon her the three acting rules a coach had once taught him: first, that acting never *acting*; second, that real acting is *doing*; and third, that great actors never *fake it*. They practice and perfect every skill. He offered a suggestion. If she would put her trust in him, he would help her break through this mental barrier, and by the end of the evening have become a markedly better actor for going through the experience.

So overcome with gratitude that she was practically on the verge of tears, Sandra May Edwards emphatically accepted.

Rigel walked her into the kitchen, pulled out a chair, and instructed her to sit quietly for a few minutes with her eyes closed while he made a few necessary preparations. Sandra May Edwards teetered with excitement, eager for the session to begin. Rigel instructed her to take deep breaths while he massaged her shoulders, congratulated her for being willing to step outside her comfort zone, assured her that only good things would come from the exercise, and reminded her how proud Johnny would be of her were he there now.

He rummaged through her kitchen drawers and cabinets, found the items he was looking for, then returned to the woman, his hands wrapped in dish towels.

The first punch to Sandra May Edwards face knocked her out.

The second decimated her jaw.

When she had regained consciousness an hour later, Rigel was astonished at her emotional progress. Sandra May Edwards could emote feelings of sadness, rage, anger and hatred as convincingly as any Academy Award winning actor.

Honored to have made such a significant contribution to her development as an actor, Rigel was truly disappointed when Sandra May Edwards died in the chair. The training session had proved to be too much for her. Sad, he thought. The words of his former acting coach came to mind: 'In order for one to create art, one must be willing to make great sacrifices, even of oneself.'

He had once met a world-renowned acting coach in Miami who warned him against crossing the fine line between acting and *over*acting. Sandra May Edwards breakthrough had exceeded his expectations. Perhaps one day, after retiring from a successful acting career, he too would consider coaching. It didn't come as a surprise to him that he had a natural talent for it. But for now, life as a highly sought-after contract killer paid the bills. Still, it was nice to think about it. And planning for the future was always prudent.

He had taken the acting coach's advice to heart. If he was to pursue his dream of one day establishing himself as one of Hollywood's most celebrated actors, he would need to perfect his ability to *become* any role and take on the persona and idiosyncrasies of any character he would be asked to portray with uncanny accuracy. His current occupation permitted him the opportunity to do just that.

After tossing her apartment to make her death appear as if she had been the victim of a home invasion, Rigel slit her throat.

Though he continued to attend a few acting classes here and there to pass the time between assignments, Rigel soon began to feel he was no longer deriving any great benefit from them. After all, he was a natural. Finding work would be easy. He decided against attending 'cattle-calls.' He considered that indignant process of sitting in a room for the better part of a day with dozens of less-qualified actors just to read for a two-bit part to be a massive time suck attended only by hacks and wannabes. He would approach things differently. He would show up at the reading, walk into the room, introduce himself to the casting agent and director, and do his thing. If they didn't offer him the role on the spot (or worse, had the audacity to ask him about his past work such as commercials he'd been in or movie roles he'd played) he had only to present them with his treasured souvenir box and share his stories of how each valuable trinket had been acquired. After that, if they weren't impressed with his real-world skill to capture and captivate an audience, he wouldn't give them another minute of his time. Any disinterest shown on their part would serve as proof they didn't know what they were talking about and were not the supposed experts they presented themselves to be. The entertainment industry was full of scam artists. He believed his chances were extremely good that sooner or later his name would come up at a Hollywood 'insiders' party and that DiCaprio, Elba, DeNiro, Hopkins, Washington, Caine or Stallone would pick up the phone and call him. He would have to decline their initial offer, of course. If they really wanted him for the role, they would need to badger him until he accepted. In Hollywood, one should never appear too anxious. That would be unprofessional.

Rigel took a deep breath, invigorated once more by the fragrant smell of geosmin in the night air, and reflected on how lucky he was to be master of his own destiny.

He crossed the road from the townhouse complex, turned left at the end of the street, then headed north. His car was close by. The rain had begun to fall harder. Rigel pulled his collar tightly around his neck. He could feel the release of endorphins in his body. He felt on top of the world and had all but forgotten about killing the mechanical room engineer and his attempted murder of the FBI agent. His heart rate was normal, his breathing calm. Walking in the rain made him feel completely connected to the world and stimulated him on many levels. His concentration was markedly improved, as too his ability to react quickly. Beyond its restorative powers the rain entertained him by bringing music to the night. Fat water droplets drummed steadily on the roofs of parked cars. Overflowing water rushed along concrete gutters and fell through sewer grates with a low tympanic roll. Wind chimes tinkled in harmony above the front door of a well-kept bungalow.

Oil-dipped raindrops, strewn across the road like aqueous diamonds, sparkled in the headlights of a car that turned the corner behind him. Rigel looked over his shoulder. The vehicle slowed as it pulled over to the curb, killed its lights, idled. In a home across the street Rigel heard the *thump-thump-thump* of a heavy bass beat. Behind the doors a house party was in full swing. The car probably belonged to a pizza guy delivering a late-night order.

He turned the corner and saw his car parked at the end of the road. In a few minutes he would be out of the rain. He would log into the hospital computer using his cellphone, enter the passcode he had retrieved from the Laundry Services managers office, and look up Jordan Quest's patient information file. Taking her out at the hospital was no longer an option. She was now under the protection of the FBI. Alternate arrangements to terminate her would have to be made.

Rigel glanced back at the car parked across from the party house. It occurred to him he hadn't heard its door open or close. The driver had not left the vehicle.

The car pulled away from the curb, turned on its head-lights, then accelerated up the road toward him, gaining speed.

As the black Mustang GT approached, Rigel saw a short metal cylinder resting on its sill. He recognized it as the barrel of a silencer.

He darted across the lawn of the nearest house and shoulder-rolled to cover behind a Jeep Wagoneer parked in the driveway.

Thwup, thwup, thwup, thwup, thwup, thwup, thwup, thwup, thwup, thwup...

It was the sound of a suppressed machine pistol operating in fully automatic mode.

He was under fire. And unarmed.

The weapon spat out a steady stream of bullets, ripped holes in the vehicle, and blew chunks of brick and mortar off the wall of the house. A hall light came on inside the residence, followed by the porch light. The front door opened.

The Mustang screeched to a halt several houses down. A second volley of bullets blistered the house. The rounds missed Rigel completely.

Behind him, a wooden gate led into the back yard. Rigel

pulled the lid from a metal garbage can, scrambled to the other side of the Jeep and launched it into the air, sending it rolling across the neighboring lawn. The diversion worked. Gunfire followed. Rigel took advantage of the opportunity.

He ran around the car, raced up the walkway, tackled the teenager standing in the open doorway, knocked him back inside the house and held him down. A third spray of bullets serrated the front hallway, blew pictures off the wall, and shattered a glass vase filled with fresh flowers.

Rigel pressed the kids face against the floor. "Who's home?" he yelled.

The teens eyes were wide with panic. Rigel pressed down harder.

"J-just me," the kid said.

"You keep guns in this house?"

The kid nodded.

"Where?"

"Safe... downstairs."

Rigel closed the door. "Get up," he said. He forced the teen to his feet, shoved him down the hall. "You know the combination?"

"I think so."

"You have five seconds to open it or we're both dead. Understand?"

"Yes."

"Move!"

29

ANDREW DUNN SLID a guest chair across the room and took a seat beside Jordan. "You think you know where Shannon and Zoe are?" he asked.

Jordan nodded. "I got a flash off the necklace when the nurse handed it back to me. It was weak, but it might be something to go on."

"What did you see?"

"A ranch house, white clapboard with green trim and adjoining stables."

The anticipation in the FBI Director's voice quickly fell. "With all due respect Mrs. Quest, there are literally dozens of ranch homes, hobby farms and horse stables like that outside Los Angeles."

"I know."

"What makes you believe the one you saw is where we'll find my girls?"

"It's the only one with shackles hanging from the ceiling in the stables."

Dunn sat back in the chair. The thought of his daughters

bound in chains and imprisoned sent a chill down his spine. "Go on."

"I saw something else. But I don't know its relevance."

"Tell me."

"Is Shannon a fan of the circus?"

"The circus?" Dunn asked. "Not that I'm aware of."

Jordan held the necklace. "I keep seeing a circus... a hooded face... costumes. Somehow that's important. I just don't know how."

"There are a few professional circuses that still follow a circuit through small towns from here through to Arizona and into New Mexico," Dunn said. "Bands of grifters mostly. Do you think Shannon and Zoe could have been abducted by one of those groups?"

"I don't know," Jordan replied. "But it's worth investigating."

"I'll run a search," Dunn said.

"One more thing, Director."

"Yes?"

"The house. There's a darkness about it, a very negative energy. Something terrible happened there. I'm sorry, but that's all I'm getting for now."

Dunn stood. "Every little bit helps. You've no idea how much I appreciate your assistance in finding my girls, especially under the personal circumstances you're dealing with on today of all days. Thank you for trying."

"We *will* find them, Director."

Dunn nodded. "I just pray that when we do, we're not too late."

A knock came to the door. "Come in," Jordan said.

Chris Hanover entered the room.

"Anything?" Dunn asked.

"No, sir. We been through the facility from top to

bottom. There's no sign of Mrs. Quest's attacker. I don't know how he slipped out of here, but he did. Security is checking CCTV footage. If the closed-circuit surveillance cams caught a picture of him, we'll run a still through NCIC. If he's in the system, we'll soon know who we're dealing with."

Dunn was angry. "Tell them to look harder. If they can't find anything send the file to Quantico for analysis. The man's not invisible, for God's sake. It wasn't a ghost that did that to your neck. At least one camera in this damn place must have caught a picture of him."

"Yes, sir."

The Director turned to Jordan. "I'll have to insist we place your family in protective custody and move you to a Bureau safe house. This hospital isn't safe. It's clear someone wants to harm you and your family. I'm not about to let that happen." To Agent Hanover, he said, "You and Agent Carnevale make the arrangements. I want a full tactical team at the location. Mrs. Quest and her family are to be escorted out of here within the hour. Understood?"

"Copy that, sir."

Jordan sat up in her bed. "My family isn't going to any FBI safe house, Director," she said.

Dunn was taken aback by the objection. "We've followed this protocol hundreds of times before, Mrs. Quest. I assure you that you and your family will be safe."

"I'm quite willing to accept your offer of protection, Director," Jordan said. "But I'm not going to lock my family away in some hotel until the FBI figures out what's going on. We'll stay at my father's mansion, Farrow Estate. The place is a fortress. Its security system is state-of-the-art. Most importantly, my children are comfortable there. I don't want them to be any more upset than they already are. The same goes for my in-laws and Marissa. That is where we'll be the safest. And you're welcome to bring as many tactical teams as you like."

Dunn considered Jordan's proposal. "I don't know about this. We haven't vetted the location."

"You can send an advance team there right now," Jordan replied. "Agent Carnevale knows the address. But regardless, that *is* where we're going."

Dunn looked at Chris Hanover.

Hanover didn't wait to be asked for his opinion. "Sounds solid to me, sir."

Dunn agreed. "All right, Mrs. Quest. We'll take your family to the estate. But only on one condition."

"And that would be?" Jordan asked.

"That my men maintain overwatch," Dunn insisted. "I understand your father uses a private security team?"

"Yes. All ex-police or military. They've been part of my father's personal detail for years."

"Doesn't matter," Dunn said. "They're to stand down. Only FBI personnel are to be on the grounds."

"Agreed."

"And if there's even a hint of trouble you and your family are to follow our extraction protocol to the letter. Deal?"

Jordan nodded. "Thank you, Director."

Dunn nodded. "You can thank me when this thing is over."

The Director turned to Hanover. "Find Carnevale. Arrange tactical team transportation. Prepare to move the family to Farrow Estate."

"Copy that," Chris replied.

30

HARRISON TASKER YANKED open the secret passenger seat compartment, grabbed a second fully loaded magazine, stepped out of the car, shoved the clip into his waistband, and took a few seconds to observe the activity on the street. All quiet. No lights had come on in the neighboring houses. The street was empty. The Tec-9's sound suppressor had done its job. No one knew that the inhabitants of the charming two-story bungalow had come under siege.

It shouldn't have come to this, he thought. If he'd been able to catch up to Rigel a split-second earlier the man would be dead now or, at the very least, wounded. He could have walked up to him as he lay on the lawn, dying and bleeding out, and finished him off with a double tap; one bullet to the heart, the second to his brain. Standard operating procedure. Clean and simple. Problem solved. Easy as taking out the trash.

The irony of that analogy was not lost on him. In New York's opinion, that was precisely what he had been contracted to do.

But the kid had heard the rounds pierce the Wagoneer, ricochet off the front of the house and come to the front door to investigate. If Rigel had been hit, he would have seen him lying on the front lawn and tried to help him. He would have yelled for help and gotten the attention of his neighbors or ran back into the house and called 9-1-1. He wouldn't have made it more than a foot. Tasker would have been forced to cut him down with a dozen rounds from the Tec-9. Which would have presented him with a whole new set of circumstances to deal with. He wasn't fond of killing the teen. But the kid's death would be necessary if he was to avoid a police response. New York might be free of Rigel, but a family would be without its child. Instead of standing his ground like a man, Rigel had forced his way into the kid's home and taken refuge there. Tasker decided he would take every precaution to preserve the boy's life, so long as it didn't interfere with his primary objective of terminating the contractor.

Tasker approached the house with caution, staying low, using the bullet-riddled Jeep for cover. Back pressed against the wall, he crept forward and peered into the front window through a slight part in the drapes. No lights were on inside the house. Pieces of a bullet-shattered mirror hung on the wall but reflected no movement. One of the rounds had taken out the porch light and plunged the front of the house into darkness. Tasker considered returning to the Mustang to retrieve his night-vision monocular. The ability to see in the dark would have been advantageous. But at this moment, time and the element of surprise supplanted his requirement for the device. He knew Rigel would already have swept the house, bound, gagged or murdered its occupants, committed its layout to memory, and established a fortification point somewhere inside that would provide him with a clear line of sight to both the street and the front and rear entrances. To take Rigel down quickly he would need to breach the premises hard and fast, blister the place with gunfire, and force him into a position of retreat. It would be just like Rigel to use the kid for cover, thinking that might cause Tasker to hesitate or avoid taking the shot. He wouldn't. He had his orders. New York wanted Rigel dead and the Farrow contract was his now. That was all that mattered.

Tasker evaluated his options. Entering the premises through the front door would certainly put him directly in Rigel's line of fire. He would need to find another way into the home. He took a step back. Quietly, he lifted the gate latch and entered the back yard, stopping every few feet, listening for sounds of movement within the home that would give away Rigel's location. He heard nothing. He proceeded to the back of the house. From the ground floor basement window, a flash of light appeared, followed by the sound of muted voices, one urgent and demanding, the other fearful and pleading. The rain fell harder. Droplets splattering on the in-ground pool cover made loud *thwacking* sounds. Past the window well a set of sliding glass doors offered a possible point of ingress. Tasker tried the handle. Locked. He moved further along the back wall, checking each window as he went. Outside the kitchen entrance he found what he was looking for: a crank-style window, slightly ajar. Tasker eased the window open, removed a knife from his back pocket, cut the bug screen out of its frame, and slipped inside. He raised the Tec-9 to eye level and listened. No sounds came from beyond the kitchen or the second floor. A narrow shaft of light emanated from beneath a closed door in the hallway ahead, probably the entrance to the basement. Tasker walked along the kitchen floor to the edge of the hall. He could hear the voices clearly now. The boy was terrified, no doubt believing his life would end tonight and that he would die soon, alone and afraid, in the basement of the home that was his sanctuary from the outside world and the evil that dwelled in it. But that evil had introduced itself to him tonight, forced its way into his world, his life, his home. Tasker knew that after tonight the teen would never be the same again.

Anger welled in him.

He would not let the bastard get away with it. He would see to it that tonight James Rigel took his last breath.

Tasker advanced through the kitchen. He stopped suddenly when a floorboard squeaked under his weight.

The dim light beneath the doorway suddenly vanished. The voices in the basement fell silent.

He had made his presence known.

31

ZOE AND SHANNON explored the rest of the fully equipped, self-contained dwelling. The hexagon-shaped nuclear fallout shelter was unlike anything they ever had seen before. Six rooms branched off the main corridor. The first, the master bedroom, was fully furnished, with a king size bed and en suite bath. The second room was Lily's, clearly defined by the sign on the door which read, "Lily's Room. Keep Out!" The third room was an open-concept design that combined the living room with the kitchen and featured a wall-mounted television, shelves filled with technical manuals, dozens of books and magazines, a sofa, three easy chairs, a wet bar, wine rack, and a desk. The fourth room was the main bathroom with a tub, shower and toilet, the fifth the laundry room. The sixth, a maintenance room, housed two Honda generators which provided the place with light and power as well as equipment and devices to control heating, ventilation, and air conditioning.

"This place is incredible," Zoe said.

Lily smiled. "I know. My dad built it."

"For your Uncle Emmett?"

The girl shook her head. "For mom and me."

"I'm confused," Shannon said. "I thought this was your Uncle Emmett's property."

Lily shook her head. "This is our home. Uncle Emmett stole it from us."

"How is that possible?" Zoe asked.

The girl curled up in one of the chairs and told her story. "He showed up on our doorstep one day with my cousins, Ben and Basil. That was them on the ATV's. Uncle Emmett's nephew, Denny, was also with them. He's the one you killed."

"The clown."

Lily nodded. "Denny was mentally challenged. His mom was killed in a car crash a few years ago. Uncle Emmett adopted him. He liked to dress up and loved anything to do with the circus. My Aunt Chris, Uncle Emmett's sister, who died in the accident, had made half a dozen outfits for him. One day he'd dress up like a clown or a strongman, other days a lion tamer or big top announcer. The clown outfit was his favorite. But he was mean. I mean, real mean. He beat me up all the time just for fun. Dad said that when Aunt Chris died something broke in Uncle Emmett, my cousins too. We'd heard that the boys were always getting into trouble. Most of the time it had to do with drugs. When they showed up, I heard Uncle Emmett tell my Dad someone was after them. Ben and Basil had gotten in way over their heads with the wrong people and that they had no place to go. When Dad asked Uncle Emmett what the boys had done, he said they'd ripped off some drug-dealers. That's when Dad flat-out refused to let them stay with us. He told Uncle Emmett he didn't want that kind of trouble showing up on our doorstep. He started yelling at him and told him he had a lot of nerve putting our lives in danger because of Ben and Basil's stupidity. He closed the door in their faces. Uncle Emmett started banging on the door, saying they weren't leaving, that we had plenty of room and that as his brother Dad had a responsibility to him to let them stay. When Dad refused to open the door, Ben kicked it in. They walked into the house. He told Dad it was *theirs* now and that we'd better deal with it or he'd kill us. Dad lost it. He ran at him. That's when Ben pulled out a gun. He shot my father four times in the stomach, then shot my Mom. He wanted to shoot me too, but Uncle Emmett stopped him."

"Why didn't he kill you?" Shannon asked. "You're a witness."

"He said they needed someone to clean the house and take care of Denny."

"Motherf---," Zoe started to say. She held her tongue. "How long have these losers been living here?"

"A year, maybe longer."

"Jesus! You mean you've been their prisoner all that time?"

"Uh-huh."

"And they buried your parents in the horse stable?" Shannon asked.

Lily nodded. "Made me help."

Zoe looked at the girl. How could she have made it through such a horrifying ordeal and remained so psychologically intact? Perhaps, like her, Lily was damaged inside, beyond repair, but refused to let the world see her pain. She thought of how she too had once been forced to put up the fight of her life, and how killing her father was the price she had to pay to preserve her sanity. She'd been only a few years older than Lily at the time of her ordeal. But at least she had a choice, such as it was, and opted to accept the outcome of her actions no matter the cost. At least she hadn't been forced to watch her parents die at the hands of maniacs like Lily had, then cast into servitude. And she sure as hell had never been forced to bury her parents. What sort of animal could do that to a child?

Finally, Zoe asked, "Did you ever hear them talk about us?"

"Maybe," Lily said.

"What do you mean?" Shannon asked.

The girl turned in her chair. "A couple of weeks ago they were sitting at the kitchen table. I was making lunch. They always ate the same thing." She rolled her eyes. "Bologna sandwiches with mustard, ketchup, and mayo. Ben says he thinks he has a plan to get them out of trouble with the drug dealers. He tells Uncle Emmett and Basil about a conversation he'd overheard. A business associate of one of the drug dealers was asking if he knew anyone who could carry out a kidnapping. When the dealer asked who it was all he would say was that they were the daughters of someone important in the FBI. When the dealer said he didn't know anyone who could do it the guy threatened him. He told him that if he ever breathed a word of their conversation to anyone, he'd kill him and his family. Ben eventually found out who the guy was, contacted him, and told him that he and Basil could do the job. They were going to use the money the guy was offering to clear their debt with the dealers. Two days later I heard their car pull up and watched them pull you two out of the trunk and drag you into the barn."

"You didn't call the police?"

"Do you think I'd still be here if I could have called the police?" Lily exclaimed. "I couldn't. We have no phones anymore. The boys disconnected them. I looked everywhere but I couldn't find them. They either threw them away or hid them. Guess they figured that's exactly what I'd do the first time I had the chance. They have cell phones but they're never out of their reach. Then there's this..." Lily showed them her raw, chafed wrists. "They kept me chained up in the barn, just like they did to you. The only difference is they'd let me have a bath once a week. Uncle Emmett didn't want me playing with Denny if I was dirty."

Zoe shook her head. "This is insane."

Shannon removed a hardcover book from the bookcase entitled, "The Coldest October." It was one of several by the same author, a nuclear physicist by the name of Dr. Colton Maynard. She skimmed through its pages. "According to this guy we've continued to be on the brink of nuclear war since the Cuban missile crisis of 1962."

Lily took the book from Shannon and turned it over. The author and his family were pictured on the back cover.

Shannon recognized Lily from the photo. "That's you," she said.

Lily smiled. "And my mom and dad, Rose and Colton Maynard."

"Your dad was a nuclear physicist?" Shannon asked.

"He was *the* nuclear physicist," Lily replied. "Dad was the only civilian advisor to the Department of Defense in his field with top-secret clearance. Even had the ear of the President."

"What was his area of expertise?" Zoe asked.

"The long-term effects of nuclear retaliation by a foreign power on American soil," Lily answered.

"He built this place to protect you and your mom in the event of a nuclear war?" Zoe said.

"That's right."

"And no one else but you know it exists?"

"Nobody."

Shannon asked, "How long could we stay down here if we needed to?"

Lily shrugged. "That depends on how far we are from ground zero - the origin of the blast site. The place is stocked with enough provisions to last about four months. But we probably wouldn't have to stay in here any longer than one."

"Why is that?"

"Eighty percent of nuclear fallout occurs on the first day. It starts to dissipate after that. We'd have to stay inside for at least three weeks until the outside radioactive contamination had dropped to a low enough level that it would be safe enough for us to leave."

"Some fathers build their kid a treehouse," Zoe said. "Yours builds you a friggin' nuclear shelter."

"And some kids get to play with their dad in that treehouse," Lily replied. "I don't."

Zoe realized the inappropriateness of her remark. "You're right, Lily. I shouldn't have said that. I'm sorry."

Lily shrugged. "It's okay."

Shannon said, "You're quite a remarkable young lady for your age."

"Yeah, I know," Lily replied.

Zoe laughed. "And humble, too."

"I'm home-schooled," Lily said. "I tend to take after my dad. Solving complex problems comes easily to me, especially when they involve the application of logic, science or math." She pointed to the family's framed MENSA Supervised Test Certificates on the bookshelf. "My parents were both geniuses. Dad's IQ was 212, Mom's was 198. That level of intelligence is shared by less than one percent of the world's population. And as far as being humble goes, they raised me to be an independent thinker and say what's on my mind."

"So, you're a genius, too?" Shannon asked.

"Yes. But I'm not as smart as my parents. I only scored 185. Guess I screwed up a little."

"You got a few questions wrong on a test that confirms the intelligence level of some of the smartest people in the world," Zoe said as she sorted through the bottles in the wine rack. "Yeah, I can see how scoring a measly 185 could be utterly devastating. *Puleez*."

All but one of the bottles were sealed. Its foil capsule had been cut away, exposing the cork. Zoe tried to pull the bottle out of the rack, but it wouldn't budge. "Shay," she called. "Come check this out."

Shannon walked over to the rack. She tried to remove the bottle as well, couldn't. She examined it closely. "This stopper doesn't even look like a cork. You don't think..."

"I'm already one step ahead of you," Zoe said. "Yeah, that's *exactly* what I think." She pressed the faux cork with her finger.

With a *click* the wine rack popped opened. Zoe eased open the false door.

Clipped inside the cavity were two semi-automatic handguns. Three gas masks hung on hooks beside the weapons.

"Holy shit," Lily said.

Zoe smiled at her. "Potty-mouth," she teased.

32

RIGEL KILLED THE LIGHTS, clamped his hand over the teens mouth, dragged him across the basement floor and whispered in his ear. "One sound and I'll snap your neck like a toothpick. Got it?"

The kid nodded.

"Where are your parents?"

"Out," came the muffled reply.

"When will they be back?"

"Dunno."

Rigel took out his cellphone and swept the room with the glow of the screen. The gun safe stood in the corner of the room.

"You know the combo?"

"Maybe," the teen replied.

Rigel wrapped his hand around the kids throat and squeezed. "Now is not the time to get smart with me, son. I'll get out of this little predicament just fine. You, I'm not so sure about. Those rounds you heard tearing up the place? That's a machine pistol our friend is carrying. It'll cut you in half in a heartbeat. So, if you want to live long enough to get over acne, I suggest you tell me the code."

Rigel loosened his grip enough to let the kid catch his breath. "0-6-0-4-0-1."

"Let me guess. Your birthday? Mom's birthday? Parent's anniversary?" Rigel asked.

"My birthday."

"How original." Rigel entered the six-digit code, watched the LOCK status indicator light turn from red to green, then turned the handle. The door clicked open.

"Good job," he said.

Among the rifles standing in the safe were a Smith and Wesson M&P 15 .223 and Soviet SKS, both semi-automatic tactical weapons, a Remington 783 bolt-action rifle with scope and several target rifles. The collection of handguns mounted inside the safe door included a Taurus PTIII 9mm, Glock 19, Smith & Wesson Shield 45ACP, Ruger LC9S, Sig Sauer P238, and an Honor Guard 9mm. Boxes of ammunition were stored on the top shelf.

"Your dad knows his guns," Rigel said.

"He should," the kid said. "He's a cop. LAPD."

"We can't all be perfect," Rigel replied. He removed the Glock 19 from its mount, checked the clip, full, slammed it back into the weapon, then raised the back of his jacket and tucked it into his waistband. He lifted the Smith and Wesson M&P 15 out of the safe, repeated the inspection protocol, and laid the rifle on the workbench beside the safe. "I'll be needing these," he said.

The kid stared at the rifle.

"Don't even think about it," Rigel warned. He palmed the Glock. "By the time your hand has touched the stock I'll have put two in your head."

Now more angry than afraid, the teen asked, "Who the hell are you? And who's the guy upstairs?"

"Who I am is none of your business," Rigel said. "As for the guy upstairs, beats the hell out of me."

"You don't know him?"

"Never seen him before in my life. I'm thinking maybe road rage. Let this be a lesson to you. Drive safely. Watch your speed. And for God's sake, don't piss anybody off. You never know who's packing these days."

The floor creaked again, the sound nearer to the top of the stairs.

Rigel snatched the rifle off the workbench. His eyes had now adjusted to the near lightless basement. He noticed a door across the room. "What's in there?" he asked.

"Nothing."

"Answer the question."

"General crap. Christmas decorations, odds and ends, stuff like that."

"Does the door have a lock?"

"Why?"

"Does it lock?"

"Yeah."

"Good." Rigel grabbed the teen by his collar, pushed him across the floor to the room and opened the door. "Get in."

"Are you nuts?"

"Opinions differ." He shoved the teen inside and held up the tactical rifle. "Ever fired this before?"

"Yeah. Why?"

"Then you know how big a hole it'll punch through the door and *you* if you make a sound." He pointed his finger at the teenager. "By now I'm sure you've figured out I'm not the kind of guy who asks twice."

"I got that impression," the kid answered.

"Good boy."

"Screw you."

Rigel smiled at the teen as he closed and locked the storage room door.

Another creak. The gunman had reached the top of the stairs.

Rigel considered his options. He was well armed. If the situation came down to a gun fight, he was confident he'd be able to defend himself without difficulty. Besides, the gun safe behind him provided him with ready access to an arsenal of weapons and ammo should he need it. But the fact remained that he was at a tactical disadvantage. Despite having the armory at his disposal, he was still trapped in the basement. He needed to find a way out of the house that didn't include removal in a body bag.

He remembered seeing a cast-iron reloading press anchored to the work bench when he scanned the room with the light of the phone. Being a cop, the boy's father probably did a lot of field and range shooting to keep his reaction time quick and reflexes fast. The press meant the cop made his own ammo at home. Which also meant he kept the necessary shooting supplies on hand. Rigel had an idea. He returned to the open safe. On the top shelf he found what he was looking for. A large container of smoke-less gunpowder.

Rigel placed the container on the workbench. With a few more supplies he would have everything he needed to create the perfect diversion. On the shelf above the bench, he found several glass jars containing wood and metal screws, each labelled according to thread size and length. Additional jars were filled with nuts and bolts. A can of gunsmithing oil and two cleaning rags sat on the corner of the workbench beside the reloading press. On the opposite end of the bench lay a hammer and an open box of one-inch finishing nails.

Rigel thought about his acting classes and how they had emphasized the importance of improvisation. When the circumstances called for it, one must be able to think on their feet and adapt to any situation. The overlap of his acting lessons and their application to his professional life never ceased to amaze him.

He thought about the assassin upstairs. He too was a pro. Sloppier than Rigel, of course, but a professional, none-theless. He had been hired by someone to kill him. Only one answer made sense: New York. But why? He had the situation under control. The Farrow's were already dead. Just the daughter and her family remained, and very soon they too would be resting in peace for all eternity. There was more to the situation than he knew right now. He wanted answers badly, but even if he didn't get them that would be fine. He knew the players in the New York syndicate and how to find them. If necessary, Zippy could be kept busy for a very long time.

He grabbed the jars of wood and metal screws from the shelf, spilled their contents out over the workbench, removed and punched a hole in the metal lids with the claw end of the hammer, tore a cleaning rag into strips, soaked it in gunsmithing oil, fed each strip through the lid until it rested on the bottom of the jar, then packed the jars to the brim with screws and nails. Finally, he poured the gunpowder into each jar, shaking each one gently, watching the powder sift down and fill the gaps between the screws and nails. The jars now full, he screwed on the lids, leaving a six-inch strip of the wet cloth hanging from each container. He held the two makeshift bombs in his hands.

He was ready.

Across the room on a shelf stacked with camping supplies, Rigel found a spark lighter and a container of kerosene. He filled the remaining glass jars with the flammable liquid, fitted them with cloth wicks, and executed the final step in his plan.

The window well was much larger than he first thought it to be when he had taken refuge in the room. The latch was a standard bolt-action design and secured the window to its frame from the inside. Rigel released the mechanism and slid the window back. The damp night air rushed in, bringing with it the familiar fragrance of geosmin. Rigel breathed it in. Magnificent. What a perfect evening it had turned out to be.

Rigel returned to the workbench, picked up the Smith and Wesson tactical rifle, slid the work bench stool across the room, placed it under the window well to facilitate a fast exit, and slid the weapon out through the window onto the concrete walkway.

Ready to face his attacker, Rigel called out. "You have got to be the worse fucking shot on the planet, asshole."

The door to the top of the stairs flew open. Rigel lit the wicks on each of the kerosene filled jars, threw them as hard as he could and heard them shatter. Fire danced off the walls. An orange glow licked across the landing.

Rigel waited.

The assassin appeared in the doorway a second later. Rigel lit the wicks on the homemade bombs, threw them at the man and dove for cover. Round after round spat out of the machine pistol, splintering the wooden stairs and basement handrail.

Out of harm's way, Rigel heard the explosions. Wasting no time, he climbed onto the stool, crawled out the window, picked up the Smith & Wesson and ran.

Shards of glass, metal screws and nails flew at Tasker from all directions, embedding themselves in his face, hands, legs, and chest.

He fell to his knees on the fire-ravaged landing and dropped the Tec-9.

He couldn't stop screaming.

33

RIGEL HAD REACHED the backyard gate when he first heard the assassin's screams. The fire and nail bombs had created the perfect diversion, the attack crippling. The man could never have expected to find himself on the receiving end of such a well-calculated retaliation. His attempt to breach the landing behind a spray of bullets from the Tec-9 and take the basement by storm had proven to be a tactical error. Worse, it had put him in a position from which retreat was impossible. The damage inflicted upon him by the deadly combination of fire and shrapnel-filled bombs must have been severe. Which was exactly the point.

Rigel opened the gate, unzipped his jacket, hid the rifle against his body, and walked past the bullet-riddled Jeep to the sidewalk.

The sound of the explosions had been louder than anticipated. Neighbors had come out of their homes to investigate the noise. They stood huddled together in the rain, staring in horror as the fire began to spread throughout the house. The main floor hallway was now fully involved.

Behind the rain-pelted windows flames climbed the walls, illuminating the interior of the home. Fire licked across the living room floor and rolled across the ceiling, hungrily consuming everything in its path. Thick black smoke billowed out from beneath the front door.

Across the street, an old man and his wife shared an umbrella in the pouring rain. He watched Rigel walk past the house and called out. "What happened?"

Rigel kept the barrel of the Smith & Wesson hidden behind his leg as he turned to reply. "No idea," he lied. He pointed to the assassin's Mustang GT parked a few doors down. "I was driving past the house and heard the explosion. Shook the damn car. Thought I'd have a look to see if I could help."

"And?"

Rigel gestured at the house. "The place is cooked. I called 9-1-1." Another lie. "Fire department is on the way."

Distracted by the arrival of another neighbor, the old man turned his attention away from Rigel. Rigel walked to the assassin's car. The driver's side window on which the machine pistols silencer rested when he had come under fire was down. Rain blew into the car, soaking the interior. Rigel checked the ignition. No key fob. He circled around to the passenger side of the vehicle, opened the door, rummaged through the glove box, found the vehicle registration, and read the name on the document: HARRISON TASKER, New York, NY.

Who the hell was this guy? Why had he been sent to kill him? And the most important question of all: How had he been able to find him?

Only two answers made sense. New York was behind this. But why? He had worked for the syndicate for most of his professional career. As to how he had been found only one answer made sense. He was being tracked. His car had been tampered with. A device of some kind had been placed inside or beneath the vehicle and broadcasted his location to Tasker. But the more he thought about it that didn't make sense. His car was still half a block away. If the vehicle itself was being tracked Tasker would have found the car, waited for him to return to it, then tried to kill him. But that wasn't what had happened. Tasker had rolled up and opened fire on him when he was still on foot. They had to be tracking him by some other means. Of course, he thought. His smartphone. Whoever hired Tasker had hacked the phones operating system and was tracking his location in real time. Even if he was wrong, if some other technology was being used to locate him, he'd still need to lose the phone. If Tasker's screams were any indication, the pursuit was already over and the man dead, consumed in the fire. Nevertheless, he wasn't prepared to take any unnecessary chances. New York knew his reputation. After all, they had profited from it on numerous occasions. They would have assumed he would be hard to kill. If Tasker had been sent to kill him and failed, New York would soon know about it. Others would follow. The pursuit would continue until he was dead. The rules of the game were clear.

Rigel removed the slip of paper from his pocket on which he had written the Laundry Services managers computer password for Angel of Mercy Hospital. He powered up the phone, entered the URL, logged into the hospital computer network and followed the prompts.

PATIENT LAST NAME: Q-U-E-S-T
   PATIENT FIRST NAME: J-O-R-D-A-N
   PROCESSING...

STATUS: OBSERVATION UNIT, SUITE 604, BED 2
ATTENDING: PAUL TREMAINE, M.D.
NOTES: FBI/MEDICAL PERSONNEL ONLY. NO VISITORS PERMITTED

THE TARGET WAS STILL at the hospital. Despite the heavy FBI and police presence he would need to find a way to get to her. He had slipped into her room undetected once before. He could do it again. This time he wouldn't leave until she was dead.

Rigel knew how the Feds operated. If he didn't get to the hospital soon, he would lose his window of opportunity to kill her. They were probably preparing to move her, likely to an FBI safe house, which would complicate matters somewhat but not prove to be an insurmountable problem.

Sirens in the distance. Getting closer.

The authorities were en-route to the burning house.

Someone had called 9-1-1. Very thoughtful.

Having acquired the information he needed, Rigel removed the cover on the back of his phone, pulled out the SIM card, tossed it on the ground, and crushed it under foot. If his phone was being used to track him it wouldn't be any more. Without a functioning chip-card the device was useless. Assuming his car was free of similar tracking devices he would now be invisible, a ghost.

Rigel noticed the Mustang's passenger seat cushion rested on an odd angle. He lifted the seat and found Taskers secret weapons compartment. Empty foam cut outs outlined the shape of the Tec-9 machine pistol, its sound suppressor, and secondary clip. Two OC foggers, more commonly known as tear gas canisters, sat in their respective holders. Rigel pocketed the devices.

The horn of an approaching fire truck sounded three long blasts. It would be on-scene any second.

Rigel slammed the door of the Mustang and walked down the street. He would be back to his own car in a matter of minutes, then on to the hospital.

He hoped the pungent smell of tear gas wouldn't over-power the intoxicating aroma of the woman's perfume.

34

EYES WATERING FROM the acrid smoke, Harrison Tasker swept his hand across the fire-ravaged floor until his fingertips found the Tec-9's shoulder-sling. He drew the weapon to him, used the wall for support, forced himself to his feet, and shuffled back into the kitchen, away from the rising fire.

Tasker had warned New York the man would be difficult to take down.

Blisters had formed on his face and hands, the result of direct contact with the flames. Shards of glass, metal screws and finishing nails were embedded in his arms and legs. He attempted to remove a piece of the shrapnel, couldn't. The pain was unbearable. He knew he desperately needed medical attention. If the shrapnel remained in his body for too long the wounds would become infected. Sepsis would follow, then death. But his injuries would have to wait. He summoned his strength and focused his attention on reacquiring his target. James Rigel had a reputation for being an expert evasion strategist and had just proven it by using the tools at his disposal to ingeniously defend his position in the basement. Tasker needed to find a way to successfully breach the room, get downstairs, and eliminate the bastard.

The fire in the hall was growing fiercer by the second and had now encroached upon the kitchen. He had a minute, two at the most, before it would spread out of control and cut off his access to the basement entirely. He had to act quickly.

Tasker searched the kitchen. In the cabinet beneath the sink he found an assortment of aerosol cleaning products: canisters of furniture polish, stainless steel and antibacterial counter surface sprays, oven cleaner, barbeque grill degreaser, and foaming tub and tile cleaners. All were neatly organized in a portable plastic caddy. Tasker hauled the caddy out of the cabinet and stumbled back along the hallway. At the end of the narrow corridor crackling and hissing accompanied the smell of burning wood. The fire had found the front of the house, started to consume the dining and living room furniture. A mirror shattered from the scorching heat. Chandelier bulbs popped in their light sockets.

Tasker knew he had only one shot at this. For his plan to work he would have to walk back into the fire, breach the basement landing, and move down the stairs despite the intolerable pain electrifying every nerve in his body. Rigel had probably prepared a secondary defense, and if it proved to be as effective as his first Tasker knew his chances of survival would be slim.

He forced the Tec-9 into his blistered hand, fingered the trigger, tried to steady himself, couldn't. Screw it, he thought. You only live once.

Tasker shuffled through the open doorway, stumbled down the first few stairs to the open landing, tossed the caddy of aerosol canisters into the darkness below and fired a barrage of rounds into the room. *Boom!-boom!-boom!-boom!-boom!-boom!-boom!-boom!* The bullets ripped through the pressurized canisters. A succession of fireballs lit up the room. Tasker stood on the staircase and braced himself for Rigel's retaliation.

The room remained dark and still. The smell of incinerated chemicals drifted up from the basement.

Tasker leaned against the handrail and slumped down the stairs. He swung the machine pistol high to low, left to right, his brain conducting an instantaneous threat assessment of every shape and shadow in the room as fast as his eyes could adjust to the darkness.

Nothing moved.

Across the room, a stool lay on the floor beneath the ground level window well he had walked past outside. The window stood open. Gusts of wind blew skeins of rain into the basement.

Tasker froze. Was the fallen stool a diversion? Had Rigel staged the scene and hidden himself away in the shadows, waiting for him to take the bait... the proverbial mouse to the cheese?

It was then he noticed the small room.

Tasker trained the Tec-9 on the door but stopped short of pulling the trigger.

The teenager.

He remembered Rigel shoving the kid through the doorway when he invaded the house. What if the kid was in there, bound and gagged, unable to call out, or being used as a human shield? Were other members of the family in the room as well?

This was a war between professionals. Tasker saw no good reason for civilians to be caught in the crossfire. He yelled at the door. "Let the boy go. He doesn't need to die today."

No response.

"Now, Rigel."

Movement within the room. The sounds of shuffling, coughing. The chemical cloud produced by the exploding canisters had seeped under the door, found its way into the small room.

As he suspected, the room was occupied. A voice called out. "It's me."

"Me who?"

"Tim... Crawford."

Tasker leveled the Tec-9 at the door. "Come out... slowly."

"I can't," the teen replied. "I'm locked in here."

Tasker noticed the deadbolt on the doorframe. It had been engaged from the outside. Which meant it would have been impossible for the teen to have locked himself in the room in this manner. Still, maybe this was another ploy to distract him. Perhaps Rigel was still in the room, hiding where Tasker could not see him, ready to surprise him at the opportune moment, shoot him in the back, then murder the boy and his family, lock them all in the cellar, and leave it to the fire to consume them and reduce their bodies to ash.

Tasker investigated the open basement. Except for the furnace, there were no major obstacles behind which Rigel could hide and not be seen.

The teen coughed again. "I smell smoke," he yelled.

"That's because your house is on fire."

"*On fire*?" the kid replied. "Jesus Christ! Open the door!"

Tasker shuffled to the door and released the latch. The teen was on his knees, choking on the smoke and chemical fumes. He looked up at Tasker. "Who the hell are you?"

"LAPD," Tasker lied.

The kid wiped his face. "My Dad's LAPD," he said, coughing into his sleeve. "You don't look like LAPD to me."

"Undercover narcotics."

"Right," the kid said. He rose to his feet and pointed at the Tec-9. "I suppose you're gonna tell me that's standard issue?"

"I was driving past your house, saw the fire, broke down the door, and found you here."

"Bull."

Tasker ignored the remark. "You're welcome. Now stop talking and get out of here."

"Who's Rigel?"

Tasker didn't reply.

The teen pressed. "Before you opened the door, you called me 'Rigel.' Is that who locked me in here? This *Rigel* guy?"

Tasker pointed to the stairs. "Just leave, kid."

In the faint light of the room the embedded glass shards glittered on Taskers black face and hands. Tim noticed the screws and nails sticking out of his jacket and pants. "Jesus! What the hell happened to you?"

"It's nothing," Tasker said. "Go."

The kid began to walk toward the stairs. "All right," he said. "Come on."

Tasker leaned against the wall. "No," he said. "I'm done. Leave me here."

"The hell I will."

Tasker shook his head. "I won't make it halfway up the stairs."

"Yeah, you will," Tim said. "Lean on me."

"Look, kid..."

"You tellin' me you'd prefer to die down here?" Tim said.

"What do cops say... 'Not on my watch?' No way, mister. Not gonna happen. You saved my life. Now I'm gonna save yours."

Tim helped Tasker to the foot of the stairs. "Wait here," he said. Tasker leaned against the wall. The kid ran to his father's workbench, pulled a fire extinguisher from its wall bracket, then ran back and cradled Taskers arm over his shoulder. "We'll be out of here in a minute," he said. "You ready?"

"Just get me to my car," Tasker said. "Black Mustang, parked across the street."

At the top of the stairs they heard the sound of sirens. Emergency vehicles were closing in on the burning house. Tim blasted the hallway with a heavy blanket of foam and extinguished the flames blocking their path. He referred to the sirens. "They'll be here any second."

"I can't be here when they arrive," Tasker said. "No cops, Tim."

"No kidding," Tim replied as he helped Tasker out the front door. "I never would have guessed."

35

THE FBI ESCORT TEAM pulled into the main entrance of Angel of Mercy Hospital and exited the three Chevy Suburban's. Hanover and Carnevale met with S.W.A.T. Commander Alexander Callum and mapped out their route to the Farrow Estate. Callum spoke to his team. Within minutes, Marissa, Emma, Aiden, David, and Paula Quest had been safely transferred to the armored vehicles.

Dunn heard Callum's status report in his earbud and acknowledged the Commander. "Copy that," he said. He turned to Jordan. "Your family's secure, Mrs. Quest. Time to go."

Dr. Paul Tremaine was conferring with Audrey Lane at the nurse's station. Jordan walked to the desk.

"Thank you for trying to save Keith's life," Jordan said.

"You have my deepest condolences," Tremaine said, shaking her hand. Jordan hugged her nurse. "Good luck, Mrs. Quest," Audrey said.

As Jordan and Director Dunn waited for the elevator the events of the day flashed through her mind. In less than twenty-four hours she had lost her husband, Keith, her parents, and Rock Dionne, whom she witnessed sacrifice his life to save hers. She had lived through the experience of the plane crash and narrowly missed being killed by the tractor trailer as it slid over her on the highway and slammed into the jet, killing its driver, her family, and the flight crew. She recalled the onset of the vision prior to the occurrence of the tragic events; a warning provided by her mysterious gift. Not being able to stop the doomed flight would haunt her for the rest of her life.

Suddenly, Jordan was again struck by the Gift. She closed her eyes, connected with the vision, and saw the man; tall, black, athletic build, standing in the aircraft hangar beside her father's jet, a tool of some kind in his hand, wearing a fire department uniform. The man had *two* faces, which meant to Jordan that another soul was connected to him in death. The faces morphed, first the black man's face, then the face of the second man. He had been responsible for taking this man's life. This feeling was strong, and she learned long ago that when she felt this way she was never wrong. The dead man's spirit was trying to come through, to connect to her, speak to her... possibly even warn her. Jordan tried to understand the message, but the symbolism confused her: the man, dead, in the trunk of his car; a horse in full gallop; the three-star tattoo on the hand of the man who had attacked her in her room, a fierce battle between the tattooed man and the killer of the man in the trunk. But perhaps the most prominent aspect of the vision was the feeling it gave her that the men were *near*. Despite assurances from the FBI that she was safe, Jordan intuitively knew the danger to her and her family was far from over.

Andrew Dunn spoke. "Are you okay, Mrs. Quest?"

Jordan hesitated. "I'm fine."

Dunn could see she was worried. "Your apprehension is understandable, but you can relax. Your family is under our protection now. We won't let anything happen to them. The agents waiting downstairs are highly trained. They'll have you and your family home before you know it, safe and sound."

"Thank you, Director."

The elevator doors opened. Jordan and Dunn stepped inside.

As the car descended Jordan was struck by a sensation of impending danger.

Lights cutting through the night...

Engines racing...

A subterranean room...

Gas masks...

Three figures in motion... two adults, one child.

Jordan waited for the vision to end. "I connected with Shannon and Zoe," she told the Director.

"Where are they?" Dunn asked.

"In hiding," Jordan replied. "Somewhere below ground. Wherever it is, they're safe. At least for now."

"You said earlier you saw a ranch house with stables and shackles hanging from the ceiling. Should we still be looking for that?"

"Yes. I don't sense that's changed. I'd know if it had. That building is still important."

"Could one be connected to the other? Are they being held in the basement of the ranch house?"

"It's possible."

The Director heard the desperation in his own voice. He was too close to the case and he knew it. He should never have allowed himself to become involved in the investigation. Had the circumstances been different, had this happened to any one of his agents, he would never even have permitted them access to the file, much less participate in the resolution of the case. Personal involvement led to poor judgement, poor judgement led to unnecessary mistakes, and mistakes to lost lives. It was much easier on the other side of the desk. He had been in situations like this before with undercover agents who had been pulled out of deep cover, their operation blown, but not before their families had been kidnapped, tortured, or killed. He'd watched them fall apart, no longer useful to themselves or the Bureau. Some had been unable to live with the guilt and taken their lives, while others threw their loyalty to the Bureau and the justice system out the window, taken matters into their own hands, sought out the killers, and exacted their revenge. He was standing in their shoes now. He understood how they felt. How could he not get involved? *His* daughters were missing. All he wanted was for them to be alive and safe, and if that wasn't to be the case then he too would tender his resignation and perpetrate righteous justice on the person or persons responsible for invading his world and harming his children, because no human need is greater than that of a parent to protect their child.

The elevator door opened. Chris Hanover stood in the lobby. Grant Carnevale waited at the front entrance. Both agents held their weapon at their side.

"All clear, Director," Chris said. "We're in the lead car. Jordan's family will follow in the second unit. The assault team will ride in three."

"Intersections?" Dunn asked.

"LAPD's got us covered all the way to the estate. We're good to go."

"And the advance team?"

"Carter and Lehman are on their way. Ms. DeSola gave them the entry codes for the gate and the residence."

Jordan said, "Before we leave, I want to speak to my children."

"Of course," Dunn replied. "Agent Hanover will walk you out."

HANOVER OPENED the back door to the Suburban. Emma and Aiden leaned forward and gave their mother a hug.

"How are you guys doing?" Jordan said.

"Scared," Emma said.

"Me too," Aiden replied.

"I know, babies," Jordan replied. "But we're going to go to Grandma and Grandpa's house now. We'll be safe there." The day had been as hard on them as it had been on her. She was proud of her children for the strength they had shown under such difficult circumstances.

"Want to know a secret?"

"What?" they asked in unison.

"Grandma and Grandpa wanted to tell you themselves, but I guess I'll have to do it for them. You guys both have your own rooms now."

"Really?" Emma asked. "Cool!"

"I know!" Jordan shared in her jubilation. "Because we both know how loud your brother is when he snores!"

"Hey," Aiden said. "I don't snore!"

Jordan teased him. She winked at her daughter. "Like a freight train, right?"

"More like two freight trains... full of honking geese."

"Three freight trains, full of honking geese... playing the bagpipes."

Aiden crossed his arms. "Very funny."

Jordan gave him a friendly poke. "Just kidding, buddy."

"Was not!" Emma said.

Jordan smiled. "You two be good. Uncle Grant's going to ride with you. Listen to him and do exactly what he says."

"Yes, Mom," the children replied.

"All right. I'll see you soon." Jordan closed the car door.

She turned to Director Dunn. "I want to ride with my kids. They'll be more comfortable if I'm with them."

Dunn shook his head. "Not happening. It's clear that whoever is trying to harm your family has made you their primary target. We need to separate you from them as much for their safety as yours."

"And if we're attacked en route?" Jordan asked. "What happens then?"

"We break off. LAPD will provide cover until we get to safety. But don't worry. It won't come to that."

"Forgive me for saying, Director, but I don't share your level of confidence. Whoever is coming after my family was able to take down the jet and get close enough to me to try to kill me in my room. I wouldn't underestimate them."

"Agreed."

"One more thing."

"Yes?"

"If we come under fire, you'll give me a gun. No questions asked."

The Director shook his head. "That's not a very good idea, Mrs. Quest."

"You carry a Glock 9-millimeter, correct?"

Dunn nodded. "It's standard issue."

"A G17M to be exact," Jordan continued. "Safe action trigger, 17 rounds per clip, twelve- to eighteen-inch wound penetration effectiveness depending on the size of your target and whether your round hits center mass, the chance of which will probably be no more than twenty percent after factoring in heightened awareness, adrenaline, and the fact that your target will most likely be moving, not stationary."

Dunn smiled. "You've had small arms defense training."

"Honest answer?"

"Please."

"I'm probably a hell of a lot more proficient with that weapon than you are."

Dunn smiled. "Considering how effectively you were able to defend yourself earlier tonight that wouldn't surprise me one bit."

Commander Callum opened the door to the lead vehicle. "Advance teams are on their way, Director," he said. "Time to roll."

Jordan and Dunn stepped into the vehicle. Callum closed the door behind them.

Next stop, Farrow Estate.

36

ZOE REMOVED ONE of the handguns from its hook in the hidden compartment, racked the weapon, caught the bullet in <u>mid-air</u> as it jumped out of the breech, and checked the clip. "Full," she said. She fed the ejected round back into the magazine, readied the weapon, and slipped the gun into her waistband.

Shannon inspected the second gun. "Same here," she replied. "Walther PPK's," she said. ".32 caliber, eight-round capacity. Nice. How are we for ammo?"

Zoe held up a single box of bullets.

"That's it?" Shannon said.

Zoe nodded. "Afraid so. How much do you want to bet Uncle Emmett and his boys are gun freaks? Which means they'll be heavily armed." She poured half the box of bullets into Shannon's hand and pocketed the remaining rounds. "If you have to take the shot..."

"... make it count," Shannon finished.

"Exactly."

Shannon turned to Lily. "You told us you needed to be

last through the hatch because you had to engage counter-measures, right?"

Lily nodded and pointed towards the ladderway. "I released the leaf net."

"Are you sure it worked?" Zoe asked.

"My father and I tested it a dozen times. It's foolproof."

"Not that I don't trust you," Zoe said, "But I'd prefer to see that for myself."

"You can," Lily replied.

"How?"

"By using the periscopes and night vision cameras."

Zoe looked at Shannon and threw her hands in the air. "Sure, why not. Because who would think of building a nuclear fallout shelter and *not* install periscopes and night vision cameras."

"Not me," Shannon said.

"Me neither." Zoe continued. "While I was at it, I'd prob-ably throw in a few more goodies, like maybe a Jacuzzi."

Shannon shrugged. "I'm more of a lap pool girl, myself."

"Why not both?"

"I could work with that."

"And a bowling alley."

"Five or ten-pin?"

"I'm not fussy."

"Mini-putt?"

"Absolutely. And a batting cage."

"Most definitely."

"Home gym?"

"There's room for a Bowflex."

"Basketball court?"

"Now you're talking."

"Hilarious," Lily said. The girl rose from her chair and walked across the room. "*This*," she said, tapping the side of a six-inch wide metal tube which extended two feet down into the room from the ceiling, "is a periscope. The second one is in my parent's room. This one rises twelve feet above ground, the second twenty. Dad painted them to look just like tree trunks. They even have branches attached to special collars so that when the periscope turns the branches don't. It's ingenious."

"Your father was one smart dude," Zoe said. She lowered the periscope handgrips and looked through the eyepiece. "Hmm," she muttered.

"What?" Lily asked.

"Good thing you've got a second one. This one's broken. I can't see a thing. Just darkness."

"That's because it's nighttime," Lily said. "This is a basic periscope. Which means light needs to reflect off its mirrors for it to work." She glanced at Shannon and rolled her eyes. "I thought everybody knew that. *Duh.*"

"Hey!" Zoe said. "Nobody likes a smartass. Especially when she's a *genius* smartass. But point taken just the same."

Lily smiled.

"And the cameras?" Shannon asked.

"There are four of them," Lily replied. "Installed in the treetops. All infrared, so we can see in the dark. If you didn't know where they were, you'd never see them from the ground. They're camouflaged, too. Together they cover a thousand-foot perimeter so that outside conditions can be monitored."

Lily turned on the camera's display monitor. The screen was divided into four sections. Each gray image captured a different section of the forest. The bottom right corner of the screen glowed bright white.

Zoe pointed to the picture. "How come this one's not working?"

"It's working just fine," Lily said. "Give it a second."

The bright glow disappeared. The picture flickered into view as the ATV drove under the camera. "The lights from the ATV hit the camera lens head on," Lily explained. "That's why it whited out." She tapped the screen with her finger. "That's Ben," she said. "He's the one who killed my parents."

"Which direction is this camera pointing?" Zoe asked.

"This is camera number four," Lily replied. "It covers the west perimeter of the forest. It points toward us."

"Which means he's driving *toward* the camera and away from us."

Lily nodded. "That would be correct."

"And the others?" Shannon asked. "Where's Basil and your Uncle Emmett?"

Camera's one, two and three captured no movement. The forest was quiet.

"I don't see them," Lily said.

"But if they were still in the forest you would, right?"

"As long as they're within camera view, yes," Lily said. "It would display their image as clear as day."

"Looks like they've given up trying to find us," Shannon said. "We should get out of here while we can."

"And go where, Shay?" Zoe said. "We don't have wheels. And I'm pretty sure those three psychos wouldn't be stupid enough to leave their car keys in the ignition."

"We need to examine our options," Shannon said. "As I see it, we have two choices. One, we stay here for as long as we need to and wait them out, or two, we figure out a way to steal their car and hightail it to the nearest police station."

Zoe walked across the room and sat on the sofa. "There is a third option," she said.

Shannon stared at her sister. "I've heard that tone before," she said. "I already know I'm not going to like this."

"We play their game," Zoe finished. "But that'll mean getting a little dirty."

"What are you thinking?"

"About the promise we made to Lily." She patted the sofa. "Come here, genius girl. Take a seat."

Lily sat beside her.

Zoe put her arm around her. "We promised we'd keep you safe, that we'd never let them touch you again, and that we'd come back for your mom and dad. That's exactly what we're going to do."

"How?" Lily asked.

Zoe directed her response to Shannon. She removed the gun from her waistband. "We're going to take back your house."

37

SHUFFLING OUT OF the front door of his burning home, Tim Crawford dropped the spent fire extinguisher on the veranda and helped Harrison Tasker down the front steps. Tim's neighbor, Ron White, ran to their aid.

"You okay, Tim?" White asked.

"I'm fine, Mr. White," Tim answered.

White helped Tim carry Tasker down the stairs. "You're going to be okay, mister," he said. "Fire departments on the way." The old man saw the particles of glass, screws and nails embedded in Tasker's face and body. "Sweet Mother of God!" he said. "We have to get you to a hospital."

Tasker whispered in Tim's ear. "That can't happen. You need to get rid of this guy."

"I know," Tim replied quietly.

Tasker nodded at his Mustang GT parked down the street. "That's my car."

Ron White asked, "Is anyone else in the house?"

"No," Tim said. "Just me."

"Thank God. Where are your parents?"

"Police awards ceremony."

"Have you called them yet?"

"No, sir."

"Okay," White said. "I have your dad's cell number. I'll take care of it. You two going to be okay if I leave you for a minute?"

"We're good," Tim said. "Thanks, Mr. White."

"All right. I'll be back."

Tim watched his neighbor return to the crowd and place the call to his father.

He turned to Tasker. "Soon as my dad finds out what's happening here, he'll make a few calls of his own. When that happens, you'll never get out of here. The street will be crawling with LAPD before you know it."

"Just get me to my car."

"You're in no shape to drive?"

"I'll be fine."

"No, you're not. In case you hadn't noticed, you're pretty messed up. No offense."

"None taken. It's all right. I've been hurt worse than this."

The two shuffled across the street to Taskers car. "So, what are you *really*?" Tim asked. "Military or something?"

"Or something."

"Delta Force?"

"The keys are in my pocket," Tasker replied. "Open the door."

"CIA?" Tim asked. He fished out the keys and opened the driver's door.

Tasker moaned as the teen helped him into the driver's seat. A wave of pain shot through his body. He gripped the steering wheel, steadied himself. "There's a medical kit in the trunk. White box, red cross. Get it."

Tim found the kit and handed it to Tasker. "You're not Delta or Central Intelligence Agency," Tim said. "That leaves NSA. You're National Security Agency, right?"

"You forgot Homeland," Tasker said.

"You're Homeland Security?"

Tasker removed a blister pack containing six capsules from the box, pushed two of them through their foil backing, swallowed them. He leaned back, closed his eyes, and waited for the heavy-duty pain killer to take effect. A few seconds later he answered the question. "No. None of the above."

"Then who are you?"

Tasker looked at the teen. "I'm Death."

It took a second for the answer to register with Tim before he understood what Tasker meant. "You're a hitman?"

Tasker didn't reply. The drug had started to work, the pain to abate.

"The guy that tried to kill me, the one you called Rigel. Is he a pro, too?"

"You shouldn't be asking these questions," Tasker said.

"You were after him, weren't you?"

"Yeah."

"Why?"

"I can't tell you that. Let it go."

"Let it go?" Tim said, pointing to his home which was now fully involved. "Have you seen my house?"

"It's just brick and wood," Tasker said. "I'm sure your parents are insured."

"Oh, of course," Tim scoffed. "Because every insurance company on the planet covers home invasions by machine-gun-toting-bomb-throwing-mad-ass-hitmen. I'm pretty sure that's a separate policy. Probably costs my dad an extra ten bucks a month."

"You'll get a new house," Tasker said. "Put it all into perspective. You're still breathing, right?"

Tim paused. "Thanks to you." He closed the car door.

"You're going to be all right, kid. You'll see."

Tasker started the car. He looked in his rearview mirror. A fire engine raced around the corner on its way to the Crawford home followed by an ambulance and four LAPD squad cars.

"I'd call that one hell of an over-response," Tasker said.

"Yeah. Looks like dad called in the cavalry."

"You better get back there. Your parents will be showing up any second." Tasker dropped the car into gear. "Thanks for your help, kid. You saved my life tonight."

"Don't mention it," Tim said.

Tim stepped away from the car. The rain, which had begun to fall harder since they had escaped the home, pinged off the roof of the Mustang. Orange rivers ran down the back window, reflecting the blaze. Tim watched his parent's bedroom windows blow out with a *boom!* The crowd stepped back as emergency vehicles arrived on the scene and took up positions in front of the Crawford home. The quiet residential street was now the epicenter of an urban disaster.

"I'll take that as my cue to leave," Tasker said. "I'd say see ya around but... you know."

Tim nodded. "Where are you going?" he asked.

"To work."

"After Rigel?"

Tasker nodded.

"Good," Tim said. "Do me a favor when you find him?"

"What's that?"

"Set fire to the bastard."

"I'll add it to the list."

Tim watched Tasker pull away from the curb, then joined the crowd in front of his house. Mr. White ushered him over to the paramedics even though he wasn't in need of their assistance.

The Tec-9 hung inside Tasker's jacket. He winced as the Mustang rounded the corner and the weight of the weapon pressed against the screws, nails, and glass shards embedded in his body. He should have removed the gun before getting into the car. But the sight of a stranger standing on the street beside Tim, strapped with a machine pistol, might not go over very well with the neighbors.

Light from an overhead streetlamp washed over the passenger seat and briefly illuminated the interior of the car. Tasker noticed the compartment cover under which hid the Tec-9 and military grade ordinance was ajar. He pulled the car to a stop at the curb and lifted the cover.

The foam inserts that held the OC foggers were empty. The tear gas canisters were gone.

Rigel!

Tasker turned on his phone and opened the tracking app.

Rigel's signal had disappeared. No locator blip appeared on the screen.

He had lost the target.

"Dammit!" Tasker yelled. He threw the phone on the passenger seat. He needed to think through the situation, to rely on his experience and intuition in the absence of technology. How could he find Rigel now? Where would he go?

Tasker slammed his foot on the gas pedal and raced down the street. He would return to Angel of Mercy Hospital, take out the protection detail, and assassinate Jordan Quest and her family quickly and professionally.

For now, Rigel would have to wait. He would eventually resurface. When he did, he would make sure his death was slow. And exquisitely painful.

38

J AMES RIGEL REACHED his car, slid the <u>Smith</u> <u>and Wesson</u> tactical rifle he had stolen from the teen's father into the footwell of the front passenger seat, then dropped to his knees and examined the underside of the vehicle for the presence of a tracking device. He checked inside the engine compartment, under the wheel wells, inspected the trunk, looked under the seats, opened the glove box, and discarded its contents onto the floor.

Nothing. As far as he could tell the car was clean. He could find no unusual devices of any kind.

He considered leaving the car on the street and stealing a new set of wheels, thereby being assured his new ride would be free of tracking devices. But that might bring with it a new problem. It was now ten o'clock in the evening. Although most individuals had retired for the night and no longer had an immediate use for their vehicles until morning, it was possible that the car he chose to steal could belong to a shift worker who, upon heading out the door for work and finding their car missing, would call the police right away. Rigel couldn't take the chance of calling unwanted attention to himself. It was best to stay with the vehicle he was driving and hope it was bug free. He started the car and drove down the street. One block over, Angel of Mercy Hospital rose above the <u>rooflines</u> of the houses. Red and blue lights danced off the medical facility's concrete walls and mirrored glass windows. The police were still on site. Rigel removed the Glock from his waistband and placed it between the seats for quick access.

He was careful to avoid parking in the same lot he had used on his previous trip to the hospital. Instead, he turned into the parking lot of a nearby apartment complex and viewed the activity taking place at the front entrance from an inconspicuous distance.

Two black Chevy <u>Suburban's</u>, unmarked FBI S.W.A.T. vehicles, were pulling out. Rigel watched the men assigned to the third and last vehicle converse with an FBI agent dressed in full tactical gear. The neck of one of the men was wrapped in white medical gauze. Rigel recognized him as the agent who had pursued him into the mechanical room earlier in the evening after his attempt to kill Jordan Quest had failed and with whom he had struggled until the ill-timed intervention of the maintenance engineer. Zippy must have done an effective job after all. Too bad he hadn't had another few minutes. He could have saved the hospital the cost of a few feet of sterilized dressing. The fed would be in the morgue. One less cop in the world to worry about.

The agent stepped into the vehicle. The Suburban's brake lights glared. This must be the detail assigned to protect his target. They were moving her.

Change of plan. There would be no need to try to kill her in the hospital. He would follow the motorcade from a safe distance, watch where they took her, plan his next attack carefully, then strike when they least expected it, hard and fast, and take out the woman and her family.

As the third SUV rolled down the ramp, an unmarked LAPD sedan took its place at the rear of the motorcade. Rigel waited until the vehicles had traveled a dozen car lengths past him before pulling out of the apartment complex and merging into the traffic flow.

He fell back and followed the motorcade.

39

HARRISON TASKER SLOWED as he approached Angel of Mercy Hospital. The black and white LAPD units which had earlier been inspecting vehicles at the staff parking exit in search of the assailant had since left the hospital and returned to patrol. A convoy of three black SUV's, escorted front and back by two unmarked LAPD sedans, pulled out of the main entrance. He had seen these same vehicles earlier in the evening when he had come to the hospital in search of Rigel and Jordan Quest and been informed by security about the attack on the FBI agent. He suspected Rigel had been the attacker. The guard told him Jordan was upstairs being treated for her injuries. Miraculously, she had survived the horrific jet crash of which he'd been the architect. But any opportunity for him to kill the woman and her surviving family members had been rendered impossible by the sheer police presence. It was in his best interest to leave the hospital before being detained and questioned by authorities.

Once again, Tasker opened the GPS tracking software

and waited for Rigel's location to appear on the screen. Perhaps a simple technical glitch had been responsible for the previous loss of signal. No luck. The bastard had figured out he was being tracked and either disposed of his phone or found a way to jam the signal.

Sitting behind the wheel of the Mustang, every part of Tasker's body felt as though it was on fire. The glass shards and metal debris embedded in his hands and body from the shrapnel bombs were a part of him now. They poked out at jagged angles beneath the surface of his fire-ravaged skin, the result of his direct exposure to the inferno in the hallway and were now impossible to remove by any means other than surgery. Pain ravaged him. Tasker desperately wanted to pull the car over, rip open the medical kit, down another dose of pain killers and rest. But his priority now was not to lose visual on the motorcade. Jordan Quest was in one of the cars. He had a contract to fulfill, which he now figured would likely be his last. The damage to his body from the makeshift bombs and the fire was irreparable and severely restricted his mobility. He was having difficulty maintaining a grip on the steering wheel. It slipped in his hands as he changed lanes. The damage to the nerves in his body was severe. His left hand felt heavy, cold, and numb. He tried to lift the Tec-9 with his right hand but instead fumbled with the weapon. His melted skin had congealed around the shrapnel, and with even the slightest amount of exertion, pulled against the bits and pieces of embedded foreign matter. The accompanying grating action felt as though a thousand razor blades were slicing away at his body from beneath his skin. He would not be able to lift the weapon while driving, much less fire it. The pain from the kickback alone would result in a loss of control over the gun and trying to aim it with any degree of precision would be damn near impossible. Bullets would spray everywhere but in the direction of their intended target and leave him vulnerable to taking return fire. Tasker remembered Tim's last words when he'd left him standing in front of his burning home: *When you find him, set fire to the bastard.* He looked at his hands. He wanted to scream in anger. His career as a professional assassin was over and he knew it. He would see to it that Rigel suffered a long-lasting death when at last he located him, partly to satisfy New York's wishes, but also because he simply despised the man. But now in his depleted state, granting young Tim Crawford his wish seemed as satisfying a battle plan as any.

The motorcade sped up, opening the gap between them. Tasker maintained his speed and distance behind the vehicles so as not to arouse suspicion or give the police a reason to believe they were being followed. Only a few vehicles shared the road. Perhaps the city's residents had been dissuaded from venturing outside by weather reports that warned of the severity of the storm that threatened to sweep across Los Angeles, bringing with it heavy rain, thunder and lightning. The rain had begun. Flashes of lightning serrated the night, followed by the low rumble of thunder. Rigel groaned as he raised his hand and engaged the windshield wipers. The rubber blades swept back and forth intermittently.

Ahead, a car pulled out of an apartment complex and merged into traffic. Tasker watched it fall in behind the unmarked LAPD sedan.

40

ZOE TOOK CHARGE. "Stay on those monitors, Lily. Let us know if you see anything we need to be concerned about. Shay, you and I will go through the cupboards. There are a couple of backpacks hanging on the wall beside the ladder. Grab anything you think we'll need, especially if it can be used as a weapon. After that, we're out of here."

"Got it," Shannon said. Lily nodded.

Together the women divided the items and filled the packs. Shannon's contained knives and forks, a safety lighter, two packs of matches, candles, three canisters of bear spray, two small cans of Sterno camping fuel, a flashlight, spare batteries, several packets of dehydrated food, and two bottles of water. Zoe's pack contained the same items plus a kerosene lamp, a bottle of fuel, and the hand crank radio. Lily's contained food, water, a flashlight, the medical kit, and a map of the region.

"That should do it," Zoe said. She unhooked the climbing ropes from the wall, gave one to Shannon. "Here's the plan: If we run into trouble outside, we separate. It'll be harder for them to catch us if we split off in separate directions. Lily will stay with you. If those assholes should catch up to you, don't think twice. You pull out that Walther, point it, and unload every last round into them. Getting Lily out of this hellhole is priority one. Deal?"

"Deal," Shannon replied.

Zoe hugged her sister. "Shay, I know you're way out of your comfort zone here. But we've got to do what we've got to do." She pointed to the infrared camera monitors. "Those guys are drug dealers and murderers. We know for a fact they've killed Lily's parents. God knows how many more lives they've taken. We're not going to give them the chance to take ours. Okay?"

Shannon's voice was unsteady. Her body trembled. "Okay," she said.

Zoe held her firmly by the shoulders "*Promise me, Shannon.*"

Shannon took a deep breath. "I do. I promise."

"Good," Zoe said. She pointed to the top of the ladderway. "You'll need to keep it together up there. Once we leave here, we're not coming back. Like Lily said, releasing the leaf-net camouflage over the hatch cover was a one-shot deal. We can't re-enter the shelter *and* cover up the hatch. Which means if they search the forest a second time, they'll find it. It won't matter that we've locked ourselves in. They'll trap us inside, and with no secondary exit this place won't be a shelter anymore. It'll be a crypt."

"How do you figure that?" Lily asked.

"For starters," Zoe said, "the hatch cover is made of steel. They could weld it shut and trap us down here with absolutely no way of getting out. Sure, we might have fresh air. But eventually our food and water supplies would run out and we'd starve to death. Or the generators will die. That means no heat, ventilation, or air conditioning. Or maybe they drill a hole in the hatch cover, hook a hose up to the ATV's exhaust, feed it through, fill the place with carbon monoxide until they figure we're dead, then blow it up. Or they skip the gas because they realize an explosion could probably be seen or heard and instead pump the place full of water and drown us like trapped rats."

"You're giving this way too much thought," Shannon said.

"I'm just keeping it real," Zoe said. "This is a *one-way* trip. We leave and don't come back. Agreed?"

Shannon looked at Lily. The girl nodded.

"All right," Zoe said. "It's settled. Grab your packs. I'll leave first. Shannon, you follow. Lily, you'll stay three rungs below Shannon. We'll wave you up when it's clear."

"Why can't I come up right behind you?" Lily protested.

"Because if for some reason the cameras have malfunctioned, and Emmett and his sons are still out there in the forest looking for us, we'll have enough time to drop the hatch, brush enough leaves over it so it can't be seen, and make a run for it. Which means they won't find *you*. If they catch us, we'll just tell them you're long gone. You'll still be safe down here, at least for the time being."

"But..."

"No buts, Lily!" Zoe warned. "The topic isn't open for discussion. You may be the kid genius here, but I've been in a situation like this before and lived to tell about it. You'll do what I say *to the letter*. Because all our lives depend on it, not just yours. Am I clear?"

Lily stared at the floor. "Clear."

"Good," Zoe said. She placed her foot on the bottom rung of the ladder and looked up at the hatch.

Fight or flight.

Life or death.

Live.

She turned to Shannon. "Ready?"

Shannon nodded. "Ready."

Zoe let out a long breath. "Okay," she said. "Here we go."

At the top of the ladder, Zoe removed the Walther PPK from her waistband, raised the handgun to eye level, released the lock, pushed open the hatch, and scrambled up and out of the shelter. She knelt on the wet ground and swung the weapon left to right.

The light drizzle that had fallen when they had first escaped the stables had since transitioned to a hard rain. It felt cold and quickly soaked her to the skin.

The forest air carried with it the sounds of the night.

Horses whinnied in the distant stables. In the house that had been Lily's prison for the last year, men argued.

"Clear," Zoe said.

Shannon and Lily scrambled out of the shelter and joined her at the surface.

"Now what?" Shannon asked.

"I have a plan," Zoe said. "Follow me. Stay close."

"What are you going to do?" Lily asked.

"What should have been done a year ago," Zoe replied as she walked in the direction of the house. "I'm going to chop the head off the snake."

41

THE FIVE VEHICLES merged into the right lane, rounded the corner, and headed for the Interstate. Two turns later they entered the highway. Rigel slipped in behind them, changing lanes frequently to avoid detection, and followed them for several miles until they reached their exit and stopped at the light. Each of the Suburban's had taken a separate lane. The first prepared to turn left, the second maintained the center lane, intending to continue straight through the intersection, while the third signaled a right turn. Both LAPD sedans sat behind the center lane vehicle. When the light turned green, the cars sped up and changed lanes, the center car switching with the left, the left with the right; a tactical evasive maneuver, like a Las Vegas street hustle of *find-the-pea-under-the-shell* but with cars traveling at high speed.

As a professional, Rigel was trained to pay attention to minute details. The SUV the injured agent had gotten into bore one subtle difference to the other vehicles: its running lights were marginally brighter than the other two Suburban's. A problem with its electrical system perhaps, but nonetheless evident. To Rigel's trained eye it wouldn't have mattered if ten cars were assigned to the motorcade. The brighter lights of the vehicle gave it away. Rigel watched it race across the road from the right lane to the left and execute a hard-right turn at the next intersection.

He followed the car and pulled into the driveway of a home with an unobstructed view of the long road down which the vehicle had traveled. The car slowed, turned left, then proceeded up a steep hill to a stately stone mansion. Two men in business suits, accompanied by uniformed members of the LAPD, met the vehicle at the gates. Rigel observed the driver as he exited the car. It was the same FBI agent he had seen at the hospital dressed in full tactical gear. The passenger exited the vehicle and shook hands with the other police officers. In the harsh security perimeter lights of the mansion Rigel could make out the bandage around his neck.

Bingo.

He watched the Suburban proceed beyond the main gate and drive to the front entrance of the immense home.

Rigel put his car into gear and drove across the street. An estate home, similar in size and design to the one at which the agents had arrived, was under construction. He parked out of sight, pulled a protective plastic tarp off a bundle of clay roofing tiles, and went to work. He pulled the trunk release lever, stepped to the back of the car, removed a long narrow suitcase, released the thumb latches, clicked open the case and withdrew a sniper rifle. He attached its scope and inserted the clip. He removed his phony service techni- cians' jacket, folded it neatly and placed it in the trunk. From a travel bag, Rigel removed a pair of bulletproof Kevlar pants and tactical jacket and put on the clothing. He placed the OC foggers, spare rifle clip and the Glock he had stolen from the teens home into the pockets of the vest, along with Zippy. Now well-armed and protected against assault from small-arms fire, Rigel walked through the wet, dark grounds of the construction site. The home shouldered into a large parcel of undeveloped hillside on the road opposite the mansion. Rigel ascended the hillside, found cover, and rested the rifle barrel on a tree branch. He turned on the scope, adjusted the eyepiece and brought the mansion into sharp focus. A four-foot concrete wall surrounded the property. Built into the front gate was a bronze plaque bearing the name of the property: Farrow Estate.

Jackpot.

Rigel retracted the rifle and continued through the trees, keeping a close eye on the two agents patrolling the grounds.

Cloaked in the darkness, weapon in hand, enveloped in the powerful smell of geosmin rising from the ground beneath his feet, footfalls dampened by the falling rain, Rigel maneuvered cautiously through the hillside. Lightning flashed across the sky and lit up the night, followed seconds later by a giant *boom*. Rigel counted the seconds before the next bolt of electricity cut across the clouds and a second thunderclap shook the ground: one... two... three... *boom!*

The storm was rolling in, gaining momentum, intensity, and ferocity. It would be upon him any second. He would use it to his advantage.

Rigel identified his ideal vantage point. He settled himself into position at the foot of the tree, readjusted the scope, and sighted the two sentries.

42

SPECIAL AGENTS CARTER and Lehman met the motorcade at the front entrance of the Farrow Estate and conferred with Director Dunn as Chris Hanover and Jordan exited the lead vehicle.

"Mr. Farrow's on-site security walked us through the estate, sir," Carter said, raising his voice over the hammering rain. "The place is a fortress. Top of the line Crestor security system, cameras everywhere except for the bathrooms and bedrooms, external cams with thermal imaging heat sensors, you name it. The Bureau should be lucky enough to have a safe house as secure as this."

Jordan smiled.

"Speaking of Farrow's detail," Dunn said. "Have they been relieved?"

"Yes, sir," Lehman answered. They asked if they could maintain a communications link with us from another location."

Dunn shook his head. "Not a chance. Until this is resolved, its Bureau-personnel only on comms."

"Yes, sir," Lehman answered. He looked over his shoulder. "Words out about what went down at the hospital. How's Chris?"

The men watched Hanover open the doors to the second and third SUVs. He stepped aside as Emma and Aiden jumped out of the second escort vehicle, hugged their mother, then followed Marissa into the house. Paula Quest exited the third car, followed by her husband, David. Jordan joined her in-laws. Chris accompanied them into her parents' home.

"Hanover's Hanover," Dunn replied. "No need to worry about him. The man's as tough as they come."

"Do we know who attacked him and Mrs. Quest?"

"Not yet," Dunn replied. "Hospital CCTV's pics weren't clear. Quantico's working on it."

Carter surveyed over the property. "This place is enormous. There's a ton of ground to cover. You want us inside or out, sir?"

"Out," Dunn said. "You'll take the rear and east side of the estate. Lehman, you've got the front and west. Hanover, Carnevale and I will be inside with the family. We'll be checking comms frequently. Stay sharp."

"Yes, sir." The agents took up their assigned positions.

Andrew Dunn walked up the steps to the landing and watched the two LAPD escort vehicles exit the main gate. Carter and Lehman were right. The property was massive. He considered calling the Bureau to request additional personnel but changed his mind.

They had taken every precaution. Multiple units had been used to transport the family. Evasive driving procedures ensured they hadn't been followed. The grounds had been vetted by a trusted advance team. He was worrying over nothing. The Quests were safe now and would remain so. He had called in favors and put all available resources into finding whoever was responsible for the death of the Farrows and the attempt on Jordan's life. He wondered if he would have exerted the same degree of effort had the target been anyone other than Jordan Quest. Had he allowed himself to become compromised? Was he trying to keep the woman alive simply because she was a target in danger and that was his job, or was there more to it than that? Was it because she was Jordan Quest, the acclaimed psychic... and the only person he knew with the ability to shorten the window to help him locate his missing daughters? That was the truth, and it made him feel ashamed. But he was a father first, and nothing was more important to him than the safe return of his beautiful girls. If he had to compromise himself professionally to make that happen, so be it.

He stood under the portico and watched Carter round the west corner of the estate and disappear out of sight.

For reasons he couldn't explain he drew his weapon and held it at his side. Thirty ounces of cold comfort.

Once again, he reminded himself that all precautions had been taken.

Trust your team.

God dammit Shannon, Zoe... where are you?

"Director Dunn?" Marissa DeSola stood in the doorway, a cup of hot coffee in her hand. The aroma was enticing. "Please, come inside," she said. "I've put out some food. You and your men need to eat."

"That's very kind of you, ma'am," Dunn replied. "Thank you. I'll be right there."

Marissa smiled. "De nada," she said. "No problem."

Despite the rain and the coming thunderstorm, the night seemed preternaturally still.

Dunn holstered his weapon and followed her into the house.

He couldn't shake the feeling he was being watched.

THWUP. Thwup.

Two rounds left the silencer of Rigel's sniper rifle seconds apart and found their targets on the east and west grounds of the estate.

In an instant, FBI Special Agents Carter and Lehman fell dead.

43

THE TRIO KEPT LOW, moving cautiously through the forest until they reached the edge of the clearing. Emmett's car, a late model Chevy Impala, was parked in the dirt driveway facing the road. The ATV's sat in the backyard.

"I'm going for the car," Zoe whispered to Shannon. "With any luck, the old man *was* dumb enough to leave the keys in the ignition."

"And if he didn't?" Shannon asked.

"I'll hot wire it."

"Do you even *know* how to hot wire a car?"

Zoe nodded. "My birth dad's car was a piece of junk. It had no keys. No biggie. If you know which wires to cross, you're good to go."

Ahead in the damp grass, Shannon spied the stun stick she had dropped when she'd run back to help Zoe. She crept out of the clearing, retrieved the weapon, gave it to Lily.

"You know how to use this?" Shannon asked the girl.

"Yes," Lily replied.

"Good. If we get separated and someone catches you, ram it straight down their throat."

"Or *up* somewhere else," Lily replied.

Zoe smiled at Lily. "Now who's the badass?"

The girl smiled back. "I am."

"Damn straight."

"Now what?" Shannon asked.

Zoe opened her backpack, removed the emergency radio, set the volume level to zero, then rapidly cranked its charging handle, powering up its internal generator. The display glowed. "You two run to the back of the stables. Wait for me there."

"What are you going to do?" Shannon asked.

"Create a diversion," Zoe said. "When I do, all hell's gonna break loose. They're going to come after us. When you hear me call out don't hesitate for a second. You haul ass to the car, and we get out of here. Got it?"

"Got it."

"Good. All set?"

Shannon and Lily nodded.

"Go!"

Zoe ran straight ahead through the open field towards the back of the house. Shannon and Lily ran to the stables. Zoe slid to a stop under the kitchen window. She could hear the voices of the men inside, muted by the teeming rain. They were arguing, each blaming the other for losing their hostages in the dark woods. Lightning raked the low clouds. A tremendous boom sounded above her, so powerful that Zoe felt the concussive pressure of the thunderclap in her chest. The electrified air made her skin tingle. When she saw Shannon and Lily had made it safely to the stables, she executed her plan. She crawled on her hands and knees to the opposite end of the house. She'd already calculated approximately how much time she would need to run from where she sat crouched under the back porch to the car: eight seconds. If she tripped and fell or lost her footing and slipped on the wet grass, it would be game over for all of them. The success of her plan relied one hundred percent on her making it to the car in time. Zoe peered over the edge of the porch. All clear. She placed the radio on the wooden deck, pointed it toward the kitchen window, cranked the volume control knob all the way up and turned it on.

Bon Jovi's, 'Livin on a Prayer' blasted out of the speaker.

Zoe ran as fast as she could. She circled the house and made it to the old Chevy.

The car was unlocked, the driver's side window left down. No keys were in the ignition. Zoe jumped into the rain-soaked front seat, closed the door behind her, tucked her head down and reached under the steering wheel.

The music stopped playing.

Someone had found the radio, turned it off.

She fumbled in the dark. *Where were the damn wires?*

Zoe froze upon hearing the voice outside the vehicle. "I figured it was you."

She raised her head.

A man stood at the door; his shotgun aimed directly at her. "Out of the car," he said.

Zoe slowly sat up in the seat. The man was in his early twenties, tall, well built, with a hard, angular face and cold, deep-set eyes. Zoe stared at him. "Just curious," she said. "Are you Ben or the other dipshit brother... Basil?"

"Does it matter?"

"Does to me."

The man set the shotgun muzzle on the window frame. "Why?"

"I want to know who's left," Zoe said. In one smooth

motion she yanked up on the seat adjustment lever, collapsed the seatback of driver's chair, pulled the Walther PPK out of her waistband, and fired several bullets through the door panel, then threw open the door, rushed out of the car, jammed the gun into the man's stomach as he fell and emptied the remaining rounds into him. Dead, Zoe searched his pockets and found what she was looking for.

Shannon heard the gunshots and looked around the corner of the stable. Zoe was on the ground, straddling the man's body.

Zoe saw her and called out: "Catch!" She threw the dead man's cell phone to her sister. "Take Lily. Get as far away from here as you can, then call the police."

Shannon caught the phone. "What about you?"

Zoe heard footsteps running across the back porch, coming her way. "Don't worry about me," she yelled. "I'll find you. Go!"

44

H ARRISON TASKER CONSIDERED making a move on the motorcade, cutting off the lead car, shooting it out with the agents assigned to protect the family, opening the doors to each vehicle and riddling its passengers with bullets, photographing the dead bodies of Jordan Quest and her family and emailing them to New York as proof he had completed of the first half of his contract, then pursuing Rigel, finding and killing him too, and finishing the job.

This was what he *wanted* to do. But in his state of waning vitality, he instead chose to follow the detail at a distance.

The same car that had pulled out of the apartment complex when he drove past Angel of Mercy Hospital was still ahead of him as they exited the interstate. Now four car lengths ahead, it followed the black SUV's around the corner and down a long winding road flanked on either side by multimillion-dollar mansions. Most of the homes were occupied. Others were still under construction.

Tasker stopped the Mustang at the corner and watched the vehicle drive down the road. Was this nondescript car part of the motorcade? He hadn't thought so. Perhaps it was an unmarked follow vehicle, its officers assigned to trail the detail, report on any suspicious traffic activity, and warn them if they thought the motorcade had picked up a tail.

Taskers suspicions were quashed when the car turned on its signal light and pulled into the driveway of an estate home under construction. Perhaps the vehicle belonged to a contractor checking on the progress of his workers. Coincidence. He watched the motorcade continue to the end of the street, drive through a pair of open gates, climb a hill, and park under the portico at the main entrance to the grand home. He realized he would need a better vantage point if he was to observe the activity taking place at the mansion. Tasker drove ahead and turned down an adjoining street which ran parallel to the road on which the brightly lit mansion was located. This street too was lined with luxury homes in similar phases of development. He chose a home for which construction was near completion, pulled into the driveway, and turned off the car. Rain battered the roof and windshield of the Mustang. Painfully he reached over, opened the glove box, and removed the night vision monocular. Summoning his strength, he forced open the car door and pulled himself out of the vehicle.

The unfinished mansion stood like a monolith against the backdrop of the bleak rain-battered night. A concrete balcony surrounded the building. Tasker struggled up the front steps, followed the landing around to the back of the house and peered through the monocular at the massive property.

Three men stood on the front steps of the estate. One of them appeared to be in charge, giving instructions, pointing to either side of the mansion. Tasker watched two of the men walk off in opposite directions; one to the west side of the estate, the other the east. The man on the front steps watched the motorcade leave, then removed his weapon and held it at his side. But why? Had something spooked him? Tasker scanned the estate for signs of movement but saw only the two men patrolling their assigned sectors. The grounds were quiet. A woman appeared in the doorway and spoke to the man in charge. He acknowledged her, then holstered his weapon and followed her into the house, but not before taking a long last look around.

Tasker surveyed the grounds once more, saw nothing.

A wooded hillside flanked the estate. Tasker slowly scanned the forested area with the monocular. A fiery heat signature blazed into view. The figure stood against a tree, arms elevated, head forward, body locked. Tasker recognized the shooting stance. The man who had been standing on the steps had reason to be concerned. He *was* in danger.

Tasker couldn't hear the shots being fired. The silencer flared twice. The monocular caught the orange trail of the first bullet as it ejected from the weapon, followed by the second. The figure lowered the weapon, relaxed his stance, and began to walk through the woods toward the estate.

Tasker swept the monocular back toward the mansion, following the flight path of the rounds.

Two men lay on the ground, shot by the sniper, presumably dead.

"Rigel," he said.

He returned the monocular to his jacket pocket, shuffled back along the landing, and struggled down the steps back to the Mustang.

He needed to get to the estate as quickly as his wounded body would allow, find Rigel, and kill him.

Somehow.

45

E MMETT AND BASIL ran from the back porch to the front of the house upon hearing the gunfire and stopped dead in their tracks at the sight of Ben laying crumpled on the ground beside the old Chevy. Zoe stared at the men, pointed her gun at them, fired.

Click.

Zoe felt her stomach drop. Seconds ago, in the moment of composed panic when she'd come face-to-face with Ben's shotgun and fired through the car door panel to save her life, she had forgotten to *count* her shots. Every last round had been expended into Ben. The gun was empty.

Emmett yelled: "You fucking bitch!"

Zoe dove on top of Ben's blood-soaked body for cover as the old man fired. The round whizzed past her ear. She fumbled in her pocket for the spare bullets. She could hear the old man and his son walking down the steps towards the car.

Emmett yelled above the teeming rain. "I'm gonna take my time with you, missy."

Zoe ejected the clip from the gun, fished several of the

bullets out of her pocket, tried to reload the clip, couldn't. Fingers slick with mud, blood, and rain, she dropped both the magazine and the rounds. The men were less than twenty feet away. They would be on her at any second. No time to search for the bullets.

"Y'all didn't just kill my boy and my nephew," Emmett continued, spitting away the rivers of rain trickling down his face and seeping into the corners of his mouth. "Ya'll fucked up my payday."

Fifteen feet away...

"You know what you and your sister were worth?" Emmett yelled.

A bolt of lightning flashed across the sky. Zoe felt the ground shake beneath her as a peal of thunder shattered the night.

Ten feet away...

"Twenty-five grand," Emmett yelled. "That was our cut. *Twenty-five-thousand dollars.* For a simple snatch-and-grab."

Nine feet away...

"Your daddy made himself some downright nasty enemies during his time in the *F-B-I*. We didn't give a shit about you. You two were just... what they call it? Payback."

Eight feet away now. Basil had separated from his father. He was approaching Zoe from the other side of the vehicle.

Then she saw it.

Under the Chevy.

Ben's shotgun.

Six feet away...

Zoe stretched out her arm, clawed at the gun, raked her fingers across the stock, caught the trigger guard, pulled it towards her, and grabbed hold of the weapon with both hands.

Three feet away...

Zoe heard the sucking sound of the men's shoes as they sunk into the wet muddy ground.

"I'm gonna find out what you taste like, girl," Emmett said. "Gonna peel you back, layer by layer..."

Zoe pulled herself out from under the car and rolled onto her back. She clutched the shotgun against her chest.

Emmett again. "... take you right down to the bone."

Zoe leveled the shotgun and waited.

Fight or flight.

Life or death.

Live.

As the old man rounded the corner, Zoe pulled the trigger. The blast lifted him off his feet and sent him traveling through the air. Emmett landed flat on his back six feet away, very dead.

Without hesitation, Zoe scampered to her knees and threw herself against the side of the car for balance. She turned the weapon on Basil but could not react fast enough. The man fired. The bullet ripped through her right shoulder. As the shotgun fell from her grasp, she managed to catch the trigger and squeeze off one last shot. The upward trajectory of the round caught Basil in the neck, decapitating him instantly. His body stood in front of Zoe momentarily, hands and fingers twitching, then fell. Zoe turned away from the ghastly sight.

She recalled hearing a *ping* after Basil's bullet tore through her shoulder. She struggled to her feet and inspected the section of the door against which she had been sitting and found the bullet hole.

Basil's round had passed through her shoulder and into the door, a through-and-through. No bullet was lodged in her shoulder. Thank God for small mercies.

Zoe surveyed the corpses around her. "You two got off lucky," she said.

Live.

She yelled, her words drowned out by the fierce rain. "Shannon... Lily... where are you?"

No response.

She had last seen them last running south, away from the stables, toward the county road.

Zoe picked Basil's semiautomatic pistol up off the ground, wiped away the mud, checked the clip. Full. She grabbed her waterlogged backpack, slung it over her shoulder, shoved the weapon into her waistband, and started down the road in search of Shannon and Lily.

46

T HE AGENTS WERE DEAD. Headshots. Delivered seconds apart to opposite sides of the estate. No time to react, no opportunity to warn the targets inside the mansion of the imminent threat to their lives.

The grounds now unprotected, Rigel snaked his way through the trees and down the hillside to the concrete wall which surrounded the Farrow estate. He dropped to one knee, leveled the weapon on the wall, and surveyed the interior of the home through the rifle scope.

No activity. No shadows played on the walls of the illuminated rooms. Nothing moved. The family and their protection detail were somewhere inside the massive home. Which meant Rigel could not gain a visual confirmation on any of his targets. This was a purely tactical play, a secondary line of defense should the perimeter be compromised, which it had.

Rigel eased himself over the stone perimeter, ran across the floodlit grounds and reached the wall of the estate undetected. One of the dead sentries lay several feet away. Rigel knelt, inventoried the body, and found the man's identifica-tion inside his jacket pocket: *Francis Carter, Special Agent, Federal Bureau of Investigation*. Rigel shoved the ID into the front pocket of his tactical vest. Though not as meaningful a souvenir as the trinkets he had collected from his victims, it was a valuable acquisition just the same. The official FBI credentials would come in handy in the future. In his line of work every small advantage helped.

Rigel pulled the two-way communications earbud out of Carter's ear, fitted it into his, and listened.

A voice said, "Carnevale, report."

"North sector clear," came the reply.

The voice again. "East sector, status report."

No reply.

The voice repeated the request. "East sector. Carter. You there?"

Francis *Carter*, Special Agent.

Rigel replied on the dead man's behalf. "East sector clear."

"Copy," the voice said. "West sector, report."

No response.

The west sector of the estate was being covered by the second agent he had shot and killed. The man's communica-tion device operated independently. Rigel was unable to fake the second response.

"West sector... *report*."

Silence followed.

"*Lehman?*"

Nothing.

The voice assumed the worst: "Be advised Lehman is down. Callum, cover the west sector. Carnevale and Hanover, move the family."

The time had come to make his move. He would take

out the rest of the detail, one by one, until he found the family and killed them all.

He remembered the sweet smell of the woman as she lay in her hospital bed. He wouldn't underestimate her this time, much less give her an opportunity to defend herself. The second he located her he would kill her. Then he would *take* her. Jordan Quest, daughter of deceased tech billionaire Michael Farrow, and one of the world's most gifted psychics, would herself become the ultimate prize in his collection. His body shuddered at the thought of such a conquest. He was lucky. Life was good.

Rigel dragged Carter's corpse behind a row of shrubs in front of the mansion wall and dropped it on the ground, out of sight, then circled the estate and found the body of the second sentry laying on the ground at the foot of a floor-to-ceiling picture window. Inside the mansion, the S.W.A.T. team commander came running down the stairs. Rigel raised his rifle and fired. The bullet disintegrated the glass and found its mark in Callum thirty feet away. Rigel wasted no time. As Callum tumbled down the staircase, he advanced into the room and fired a second round into the agent. Callum's lifeless body rolled down the last few steps. Rigel stopped it with his foot.

Rigel called out. "Honey, I'm home!"

Upstairs, the children screamed.

47

"I'VE GOT THIS!" Hanover yelled. He ran past Carnevale and Dunn toward the sound of the crashing glass and the voice of the intruder announcing his presence from the Great Room below.

To Carnevale, he said, "You know the layout of the house?"

"Every inch," the agent replied.

Below, a massive wall mirror reflected the shooter's image as he stepped over shards of broken glass and entered the home. Hanover immediately recognized him as the orderly he had chased into the bowels of the hospital just hours ago, and who would surely have killed him had it not been for the unexpected intervention of the mechanical engineer, Abe Carmichael. "I'll deal with this sonofabitch," he said. "Get the family out of here!"

Andrew Dunn's cellphone rang. The unfamiliar name on the display read BEN MAYNARD. He took the call. "This is Dunn."

"Dad?"

Dunn's heart slammed in his chest. "Shannon?" he cried. "Is that you?"

Grant Carnevale overheard the call, saw the Director's reaction, and immediately called the Bureau. "This is Special Agent Grant Carnevale," he said. "I need an emergency track and trace on the cell phone of Director Andrew Dunn. Ping the caller's coordinates and dispatch a Hostage Rescue Team to the location ASAP." He called out to Dunn. "Bureau's on it. Keep her on the line."

Dunn nodded. "Where are you, honey?" he asked his daughter.

"I don't know."

"Is Zoe with you?"

"She told us to run."

"Us?"

"Lily and I. They killed her parents."

Lily?

"Are you safe?"

"I'm not sure. I hear gunshots. Lots of them. Close by."

Dunn was terrified at the thought of his daughter being hunted by armed killers. "Listen to me very carefully, Shannon. HRT has been scrambled. They're on their way to you right now. You need to find somewhere to hide. Can you do that?"

"I don't know... maybe... yes."

"Good. And keep this line open. Do not hang up on me. Got it?"

Shannon voice suddenly changed, became subdued, introspective. She no longer sounded frightened. "Dad?"

"Yes, honey?"

"I love you."

"I love you too, baby girl."

The pressure of the ordeal was taking its toll on her. She broke down, began to sob.

"I know how scared you are," Dunn told his daughter. "I promise it will be over soon. You'll be back home before you know it. But you need to hold it together just a little while longer. Can you do that for me?"

"Yes."

"Good. Take a deep breath."

Shannon stopped crying. She inhaled deeply, let it out. "I'm okay."

Lily screamed. *"Zoe!"*

Shannon turned. Her sister was walking toward her, gun in hand, soaked to the skin, covered in blood and mud. Shannon threw her arms around her. "You're alive!"

Zoe returned the hug. "I'm fine. Bad guys... not so much. You two okay?"

"We're fine," Lily answered.

Zoe pointed to the phone. "Dad?"

Shannon nodded.

Zoe held out her hand. "Gimme." Shannon handed her the cell phone. "Hey, Dad," she said. "What's up?"

"Zoe, honey," Dunn asked. "Are you okay?"

"To be honest, I'm wet, cold, tired, pissed off and could use a stiff drink or three. Other than that, I'm good."

Carmichael broke in. "Sir, we have a lock on the phone. HRT is in the air. They're en route to the location."

"Help is on the way, Zoe."

"I heard."

"Stay where you are. Do you think you can signal the chopper when you see it?"

"Don't worry. They won't have any trouble finding us."

"That's my girl."

237

In the background of the call, Zoe heard gunfire. "Dad?" she said.

No reply.

"Dad... are you okay?"

Nothing.

"*What's happening?*"

The line went dead.

THREE ROUNDS RICOCHETED off the corner of the wall behind which Chris had taken cover. The gunman was proceeding up the stairs, his shots calculated, timed to keep the agent pinned down and unable to return fire.

Hanover turned to Dunn and Carnevale. "Get them out of here! Now!"

The agents fled down the corridor with the family. A metal canister bounced off the wall and rolled to a stop at Chris' feet. It started to spin.

A cloud of tear gas hissed out of the OC fogger. Chris covered his mouth. The noxious vapor stung his eyes, seared his lungs.

Hanover fought his body's desire to surrender to the incapacitating cloud. He swung his arm around the corner and fired blindly at the intruder.

Then he ran.

T ASKER LEFT THE site of the unfinished home, drove the Mustang GT to the end of the street where he had a clear view of the mansion, and parked the car. He fumbled through the contents of his medical kit, removed the emergency vial of Morphine, ripped the syringe out of its plastic wrapper, filled it with the drug, forced out the air bubble, jammed the needle into his leg, pressed down on the plunger and injected the contents into his thigh. Within seconds the drug produced the desired effect. The firestorm of pain coursing through his body began to subside.

Three muzzle flashes, followed by concussive gun blasts, drew his attention to the upstairs balcony inside the mansion. A floor-to-ceiling windowpane at the back of the mansion had been blown out. Smoke swirled at the top of the stairs. Tasker watched as the man who taken cover at the top of the stairs turned and ran as his pursuer closed in on his position.

Rigel.

Tasker tested himself, moved his fingers, hands, arms,

and legs. The drug was working. His body was by no means as functional as it had been before the attack in the teenager's home, but at least he was mobile. He had no idea how long the pain-suppressing effect of the drug would last in his grossly debilitated state. Based on the extensiveness of his injuries, logic dictated he had only minutes before the pain returned with a vengeance. Fueled by adrenaline, pain suppressed by the morphine, motivated by revenge, Tasker climbed out of the car, forced himself over the low border wall of the estate and shuffled up the hill to the back of the mansion. He stood in the shattered window frame on the shards of broken glass, pulled the Tec-9 out from under his jacket, and listened.

The great house had become as still and silent as death itself.

HANOVER, Dunn and Carnevale moved the family into the upstairs study. Chris locked the ornate solid brass doors behind them.

The room was twenty feet tall, circular, and filled with books from floor to ceiling. Polished mahogany bookshelves wrapped around the upper and lower floors. Ten feet above, a brass walkway divided the room into two levels. Access to the walkway was made possible by a wheeled ladder attached to the second level railing. The ladder moved freely and could be rolled across the floor to any point in the room to access the bookshelves above.

Hanover turned to Carnevale. "A library?" he said. "How the hell are we supposed to defend ourselves in here?

"We don't," Jordan said.

Frustrated, Hanover looked at Jordan. "I'll need a better answer than that."

Jordan turned to her children. "Kids, you know where to go," she said. "Don't be scared. We'll be right behind you. Paula and David, you're next."

The agents watched the children scamper up the ladder and run along the brass walkway.

"Jules Verne!" Emma yelled at her brother.

"20,000 Leagues Under the Sea!" Aiden replied. "I know, I know." He found the novel and pulled it towards him. The bookcase panel labelled "Classics," popped open. The children pushed it back, stepped inside, and disappeared behind the shelves.

Hanover turned to Jordan and smiled. "That is just too cool."

"Everybody up," Carnevale said. "Follow the kids. Hurry!"

RIGEL WAITED for the tear gas cloud to clear, then rounded the corner, fast and wide, finger on the trigger. He expected to be met by retaliatory fire but instead found the corridor empty. The agents and the family were gone. Rigel listened to the acoustics of the hallway. His footsteps made a hollow sound on the marble floor, a slight reverberation. The sound in the corridor carried. Which meant the *lack* of any sound right now indicated they were close by. If they were still on the run, he would have heard their footfalls in an adjoining corridor. He walked down the hall and assessed the floor for possible escape routes or hiding places.

The door to the guest bathroom was open. Rigel looked inside. It was big, but not big enough to accommodate six adults and two children.

Clear.

He entered the media room next. Stocked bar. Four rows

of seats; eight in the back row, then six, then four, finally two. A two hundred sixty-two-inch C Seed flat screen television, one of the biggest in the world, was mounted on the wall. Who the hell needs a home theatre with a seating capacity for twenty and a TV that big, Rigel thought. Ostentatious asshole.

Clear.

One room remained at the end of the hall. Twin brass doors, both closed. Shadows danced in a slit of light at the bottom of the doors, then darkness fell upon the room.

Rigel opened fire as he advanced on the door. *Pling... pling... pling... pling... pling... pling... pling*. The bullets failed to penetrate the solid brass, merely deflected off the metal. The ejected rounds tinkled on the marble floor.

Rigel had one tear gas canister left. *Gas them out*, he thought, *then make entry*.

He positioned the OC fogger at the foot of the door, jammed the nozzle into the narrow gap, then pulled the pin and waited for the gas to take effect.

Five seconds elapsed, then fifteen, twenty. No choking, coughing, screaming or pleas for help came from inside the room. Only silence.

Somehow the family had escaped.

Rigel knew they were still somewhere within the mansion. They *had* to be.

A noise downstairs. Footsteps on broken glass.

Rigel turned and ran back along the hallway.

Had the targets somehow evaded him, made their way downstairs and were now escaping through the blown-out kitchen window?

Rigel became enraged. If this was the case, he would find them and shoot them down faster than they could run.

Every last one of them.

49

Z OE HANDED THE cellphone back to Shannon.

"What's wrong?" Shannon asked.

"Nothing," Zoe lied. "Bad connection. We're good." After all they had been through, she wasn't about to tell her sister about the gunfire she had just heard in the background of the call and its abrupt termination.

"Dad's sending a chopper," Zoe said. "C'mon. We need to go back."

"To the house?" Lily asked. "What about Uncle Emmett and the boys?"

"They're no longer a concern."

Shannon and Lily stared at Zoe. They understood what she meant.

Zoe put her hand on the girl's shoulder. "I told you we'd make sure they never hurt you again, Lily," she said. "You're safe now. The FBI are on their way. They'll need a place to set down. It's almost pitch-black out here. If the phone dies, they'll lose our signal and might fly right over us. We'll wait in the clearing between the house and the woods and wave them down with our flashlights."

The girl's clothes stuck to skin. Her teeth chattered. "You have clean clothes in the house?" Shannon asked.

Lily nodded quickly.

"Good," Shannon said. She rubbed Lily's arms, tried to warm her. "Let's get you into something dry. Sound good?"

"Uh-huh," Lily said.

"COVER HER EYES," Zoe told Shannon as they approached the driveway. "Lily doesn't need to see this."

They walked around the old Chevy past Basil's headless corpse, Ben's bullet riddled body and Uncle Emmett, who was missing the middle of his chest. Shannon forced down the rising gorge in her throat.

"Better them than us," Zoe said.

"I know," Shannon replied.

They reached the back of the house. "Take genius girl inside to change," Zoe said. "I'll wait out here and listen for the chopper."

Shannon turned to her sister. "You okay, Z?"

Zoe forced a smile. "Never better."

Shannon hugged her. "I love you. You know that, right?"

"Yeah, yeah, yeah..." Zoe replied. There was a catch in her voice. Even in the driving rain Shannon saw a glisten in her eyes. Her smartass attitude returned. "Stop wasting time. You're gonna make us late for our own damn rescue."

LILY CHANGED QUICKLY. She didn't want to spend a minute longer in the house than she had to. Shannon waited in the doorway. Although the immediate threat to their safety had been resolved, she couldn't help but feel they were still in danger. Rain hammered the roof. A flash of lightning lit up the room, followed by a peal of thunder. The ceiling fixture above her shook. To Shannon, it felt as if the storm was feeding on the dark energy of the house. She could tell Lily felt it too.

"Hurry," Shannon said.

"I'm ready," Lily replied. She had changed into jeans, a T-shirt, white sneakers, and a bright yellow jacket. She held her wet backpack in her hand.

"All right," Shannon said. "Let's get out of here."

Lily followed. "Wait!" she yelled. She turned and ran back into the room.

"What is it?"

Lily dropped to her knees in front of her dresser, rummaged through the bottom drawer, and removed a framed picture of her parents. She looked up at Shannon. "It's all I have left."

Shannon nodded and held out her hand. "Come on, sweetheart."

The lights in the house flickered. The power went out. The house fell into darkness.

Shannon removed the flashlight from her backpack. Lily did the same.

"Follow me," Shannon said.

ZOE JUMPED when the door opened behind her. Residual tension. Shannon and Lily joined her on the porch.

"Everything okay?" Shannon asked.

"Yeah," Zoe replied. "The place just creeps me out."

"Six dead bodies on the property will do that to you. Any sign of the chopper?"

"Not yet."

"We should move into the clearing. They'll see us if we flash our beams."

"I have a better idea," Zoe said. She opened her backpack and removed the kerosene lamp, spare bottle of fuel, and the lighter she had taken from the fallout shelter. "We're gonna make damn sure they see us."

Zoe ran down the stairs to the stable and opened the main doors. The horses whinnied at the intrusion. She opened their stalls and yelled. Shannon and Lily watched as the animals trotted out of the building and ran into the open field.

Zoe walked to the porch and poured a jagged line of kerosene over the deck and back wall of the ranch house. A dirty sweatshirt lay on the seat of a wicker deck chair. Zoe used it to wipe her fingerprints off the lamp.

She asked Lily, "Was Uncle Emmett left or right-handed?"

"Right."

"Wait here." Zoe ran back down the stairs to Emmett's corpse, wrapped his right hand around the lamp, then ran back.

"We watched the bastard set fire to the house," Zoe said. "Right?"

"That's what I saw," Shannon replied.

"Me too," Lily said.

"Good," Zoe said. She lit the wick. "It's best if you two go to the clearing. I don't exactly have a ton of experience in the arson department."

Shannon took Lily by the hand and walked with her into the open field.

Zoe wrapped her damp sleeve around the metal handle and stepped off the porch. When she was a safe distance away, she looked over her shoulder at Lily.

The girl nodded, as if giving Zoe permission to burn her family's home to the ground. It didn't matter. It wasn't her home anymore. It had stopped being her home the day Emmett and his boys had walked into her life, murdered her parents, and made her their slave.

Zoe tossed the burning lamp. Its glass globe shattered against the wall of the house. Its flame found the trail of combustible fluid. *Whoosh!* A line of fire erupted across the porch.

Zoe turned, walked into the clearing, held Lily's hand. Shannon took hers.

Above the noise of the torrential downpour the house crackled and popped. Fiery embers cast off from the structure and drifted upward like fireflies dancing in the rain. The wooden porch was the first to go. They watched the fire climb the walls, claim the roof, and seep into the home. Before long, the ranch house was fully involved. The crackling had become a roar. The flames grew stronger and reached high into the night sky. The brightness of the fire illuminated the property. From where they stood, they could feel the heat of the fire.

Shannon turned to Zoe. "You hear that?" she said.

Zoe recognized the blade-churning thrum of an approaching helicopter. She nodded. "Our ride's here."

50

R IGEL QUIETLY SET down the sniper rifle on the marble floor, removed the Glock 19 from his tactical vest, and peered around the corner.

Clear.

He brought the weapon to his eye, trained the front sight over the balcony railing, and looked down. Shards of glass from the blown-out window had been tracked inside the home. The twinkling path crossed a fine Persian rug, led into the Great Room, past the fireplace and out of sight. He had not been in that room. When he breached the house, he immediately followed the screams upstairs. If the family and their protective detail had made it unheard downstairs to the first floor, why wouldn't they have just continued out the door? Something was wrong. Perhaps a third sentry had been patrolling the grounds. Had he missed him? Had he heard the shot and followed him into the house? Impossible. His surveillance had been thorough.

He needed to know.

The mansion was immense. Finding the family and their guardians was proving to be more of a challenge than he thought. But first he needed to investigate the glass trail, find out where it led and *who* had made it.

Rigel kept his back to the wall, descended the staircase, stopped on each step, listened.

Silence.

He entered the Great Room, swept it with the Glock, and took cover behind a six-foot marble reproduction of the famed statue, Venus de Milo. No gunfire. Fragments of glass in the doorway led to an adjoining room. Rigel stepped out from behind the statue and moved towards the room, keeping the entranceway in his gunsight. A tray of candies sat on a side table beside a reading chair; Werther's Creamy Toffee, his favorite. Rigel unwrapped one of the treats and popped it in his mouth. He pocketed the rest, reached the wall, and glanced around the corner.

The Music room was decorated with guitars and signed photographs of the artists who had played them. Some instruments stood inside locked display cases. Others hung from neck rests anchored to the walls. Rigel recalled reading an article on the Huffington Post website a few months ago in which Michael Farrow had mentioned his appreciation for the instrument. He had reached out to some of the greatest guitar players in the world and gained their endorsement for the establishment of the Farrow Center for the Performing Arts. The artists had signed their instruments, and Sotheby's had facilitated the auction. In just one evening, he and the world's musical elite had raised fifty million dollars. The project now funded, Farrow matched the donation dollar-for-dollar. Five hundred musically gifted but financially underprivileged children were admitted into the exclusive music education program. The guitars in this room were not for sale. This was his private collection. Which is why, had he still been alive, Farrow would have been devastated to watch the first five of the priceless instruments splinter into pieces by the rounds fired from the Tec-9.

Rigel dove for cover as the bullets shattered the display cases, felled instruments from their mounts, and cut through the wall above him. He scrambled behind a wooden display case in the middle of the floor. The sound was a machine pistol. He remembered the Mustang outside the kid's house, the tear gas and Tec-9 foam cut-outs in the false compartment under the seat and the identification in the glove box: *Harrison Tasker*.

The assassin had followed him here. But how? He had destroyed the SIM card in his phone and thoroughly inspected his car for GPS tracking hardware, found none. Yet here he was, in the Farrow home, trying once again to kill him.

Rigel shook his head. Some guys just don't know when to quit.

He called out. "That you, Harrison?"

No reply.

A shiny metal pick guard from a splintered guitar lay on the floor beside him. Rigel picked it up and angled it around the corner of the case. Its mirrored surface reflected the room. He searched for Tasker.

No luck.

"Is this because I broke into your car?" Rigel taunted. "Don't blame me. You left it unlocked." He slid to the other side of the case, angled the pick guard once more. "I've got to give you credit, though. The compartment under the seat? Smart. Wish I'd thought of that."

Nothing.

"I'm guessing you're here 'cause I pissed somebody off. Mind telling me who?"

Silence.

He's injured... force him to shoot... make him waste his rounds... listen for the click... take him out before he can reload...

"You must be feeling pretty messed up right now, Harrison," Rigel continued. "Sorry about that. But you've got to admit the whole fire-and-nail-bomb thing was a brilliant move on my part. Then again, it worked out a hell of a lot better for me than it did for you. Can you even fire straight? Probably not."

There. Movement. Reflected in the pick guard. Around the corner at the entrance to the room.

A spray of bullets cut into the floor beside Rigel. One round caught the pick guard. The plate flew out of his fingers. He drew his hand back quickly.

Rigel laughed. "Whoa! Nice shot! Or was that just luck?"

A second display case stood several few feet away. If he could make it there without being cut down by the Tec-9 he'd be out of the assassin's direct line of fire. Tasker would be forced to relinquish his position in the room. Rigel removed the candies from his pocket.

"I'm working a theory over here, Harrison," Rigel yelled. "Want to know what it is? I think New York's got you on their payroll and they sent you to kill me. Why, I don't know. Frankly, I don't care. But here's the thing. You and I both know that's not going to happen. You're done, Harrison. Finished. But being the fellow pro that I am, not to mention an incredibly generous guy, I'm going to make you an offer. Screw New York. You don't have to die today. I'll let you walk out of here in one piece while you still can. I'll even throw in an early retirement bonus. How does two million bucks sound? Go buy yourself a nice place in the Caribbean. Sip Pina Colada's by the pool and live out the rest of your days in style. Sound good?"

"Not in a million years," Tasker replied.

"You sure about that?" Rigel said.

"Positive."

"That's a shame." Rigel replied. He threw a handful of candies across the room.

Tasker reacted. He fired in the direction of the sound.

Rigel dashed to the safety of the second display case. He watched the foil-wrapped sweets skip across the floor. Tasker's rounds caught one of the candies and blew it apart; a terrible death for a Werther's if ever there was one.

Rigel kept moving. He slid along the floor to the wall, then rose to his feet. Tasker was twenty feet away. He trained the Glock straight ahead and waited. The assassin had inconvenienced him enough for one lifetime. The second the man entered the room he would kill him, then get back to the business of eliminating his targets and their protective detail.

He waited.

Ahead, glass crunched underfoot.

S HOOP-SHOOP-SHOOP-*shoop-shoop-shoop...*

Zoe, Shannon, and Lily heard the heavy rotor churn of the FBI's Tactical Helicopter Unit as it approached, its blades slicing through the driving rain. The Black Hawk circled the burning ranch house, hovered above them, then scanned the grounds with its powerful search-light. The pilot engaged the air-to-ground communications system, his voice booming through the loudspeaker over the sound of the storm and the raging fire.

"This is the FBI. Get on the ground! Place your hands behind your head. *Do not move!*"

The two women and the girl complied. Zoe and Shannon tossed their weapons aside.

Ropes fell from the open doors of the chopper. Agents from the Hostage Rescue Team fast-roped from the bird and zipped down to the ground, one hand on the wind-tossed rope, the other on their weapon. The first two agents were followed by two more. They approached the trio with caution, keeping them squarely in their gun sights.

"Identify yourselves," the lead agent demanded as he secured their handguns.

"Zoe Dunn," Zoe said. The wicked rain pelted her face as she looked up at the agent. "This is my sister, Shannon. The girl is Lily Maynard."

The agent spoke into his microphone. "This is Reed. We have the package." To Zoe, he asked, "Everyone all right?"

Zoe nodded. "Tell your men there are four dead. One in the barn, three by the car."

Reed motioned to the two agents. "Check it out," he said. "Anything else we need to know?"

Zoe shook her head. "No," she replied.

A second HRT agent, a woman, spoke to her. "Who killed them?" she asked.

Zoe looked up. "I did."

"Hands behind your back," the agent said.

"She didn't do anything wrong," Shannon protested. "It was self-defence. She saved our lives!"

"If that's the case she's got nothing to worry about," the agent replied.

"It's all right, Shay," Zoe said. The agent zip cuffed her hands and brought her to her feet. "They're just doing their job."

"We want to speak to our father, *right now*," Shannon insisted.

The Black Hawk touched town. Four more agents deployed from the chopper. The team headed toward the burning building.

Reed listened to a status report in his earbud from his agents: "Confirmed. Four down. Vital signs absent."

"Copy that," Reed replied. The two women and the girl were soaked to the skin. Lily shivered. Shannon wrapped her arms around her, pulled her close, rubbed her arms.

"Come on," Reed said. "Let's get you out of the rain."

Seated in the helicopter, shivering under a warm blanket, Lily spoke. "Agent Reed, my parents are buried in the barn. The first stall on the right."

"Your parents?" Reed asked.

Zoe interjected. "They were murdered by the guys I killed."

"Just what the hell happened here?" Reed asked.

Zoe stared at the agent. "Payback," she said.

"I don't know why, but for some reason I believe you," Reed replied. He handed Shannon a headset. "What do you say we call your father?"

"Thank you," Shannon said. She slipped on the earphones and adjusted the microphone.

Reed tapped the pilot on the shoulder. "Open a channel. Put her through to Director Dunn."

52

THE AGENTS FOLLOWED the children and the family through the secret labyrinth hidden between the walls of the estate. Hanover heard the muted sound of gunshots and breaking glass.

He stopped, drew his weapon, turned, tried to determine the specific location of the gunfire, couldn't. The sound seemed to be coming at him from all angles.

"It's the acoustics," Jordan said. "The passageways inter-connect, so they form one giant echo chamber. I used to play in these corridors all the time when I was a kid, just like my kids do now. I could hear my father playing his guitar or listening to music on the opposite site of the estate. My guess is its coming from the Music room."

"How far away?" Hanover asked. He kept his weapon trained down the corridor as if expecting the gunman to come around the corner at any second and open fire.

"Ten thousand feet, maybe fifteen," Jordan replied.

"Did you say ten *thousand* feet?"

"Give or take."

"Just how big is this place?"

"The main house is forty thousand square feet. That doesn't include the indoor pool, underground garage, wine cellar, or the Collectibles vault."

"You have no idea how small my condo feels right now," Hanover said. He holstered his weapon. "The garage... can we get to it from here?"

"Of course."

"What side of the estate is it on?"

"The east."

"And the Music room?"

"The west."

"Good. Then that's where we're going. We'll drive out of here. S.W.A.T. can deal with the intruders."

The family reached the end of the corridor. Carnevale waited for Chris and Jordan to catch up. He was holding his weapon at his side. He too had heard the shots.

Hanover informed him of the plan. "Sounds good," Carnevale said. "We'll take the Rolls Silver Shadow. Thing's built like a tank. The more metal around us the better."

"In case the gunmen open fire on us?" Jordan asked.

"Exactly."

"I won't do that, Uncle Grant."

"Won't do what?"

Jordan stopped. "I won't put my children in the line of fire. Not for a second. You need to call in S.W.A.T. Have them find whoever is in the house and put an end to this."

"S.W.A.T. can't possibly get here in time, Jordan," Carnevale replied. "We need to get you and your family out of here right away."

Chris added, "That sound you heard? That's not just any gun. It's a machine pistol. Whoever these guys are they came to play. And they brought the heavy artillery with them. We're talking multiple rounds per second. We're simply not equipped to go up against that kind of firepower."

"All the more reason to call S.W.A.T.," Jordan insisted.

Carnevale sighed. "Okay, Jordan. Here's what we'll do. We'll go to the Collectibles vault instead. It's impenetrable. Everyone will be safe in there. Once we're inside, we'll call S.W.A.T. Deal?"

"Deal," Jordan agreed.

"Does that work for you, Chris?" Carnevale asked.

"You bet."

"Good. Let's go."

OUTSIDE THE ENTRANCE to the Collectibles vault, Andrew Dunn's phone vibrated. He took the call. "Shannon?" he said. "Are you all right? Thank God." The Director leaned against the wall. Hanover and Jordan stood beside him, anxiously awaiting a status update on the safety of his daughters. Carnevale escorted the Quests, Marissa, and the children into the cavernous room. Hanover had expected the call would come soon. He hoped the outcome would be a favorable one. After speaking to his daughter, Dunn received a briefing on the situation at the ranch from Agent Reed. "Thank you," Dunn said. "Extend my appreciation to your team. Tell them I'll speak to them personally upon their return... Zoe said *what?* My God! Show her every courtesy. If she says it was self-defence, then I can assure you that's exactly what it was. I'll be in touch shortly." Dunn ended the call.

"All good, sir?" Hanover asked.

The Director was quiet. He looked at his phone for a moment, then returned it to its case. He stared at Jordan. "Agent Reed just filled me in. The reading you took from

Shannon's necklace in the hospital room... the ranch house, the stables, the shackles hanging from the ceiling... all of it was accurate. You said you saw some kind of connection to the circus. They found a teenager in the stable dressed in a clown suit, dead. His neck had been broken. There was a young girl with Shannon and Zoe. Her name is Lily. You saw her, too. They *had* taken shelter underground. Lily took the team to the place they'd been hiding. Some sort of bunker. You were right about it all, Jordan. I don't know how you saw what you did. I sure as hell can't explain it and frankly, I don't care. All I care is that my daughters are safe now, so too is the girl with them. I'll never be able to repay you for that. All I can say is thank you." The stress of the last week was evident in Dunn's voice. He was close to losing his composure in front of his agents. He swallowed hard, reeled in his emotions.

Jordan hugged him. "You're welcome, Director. I'm glad I could help."

Dunn exhaled sharply. "It's about damn time we turned this thing around. Agreed?"

He took out his phone and punched in a number. The call was answered a second later. "Agent Reed," he said, "Dunn again. We have a situation here. I need your help."

More gunfire. It sounded closer.

"Everyone inside," Hanover said. He turned to Carnevale and Dunn. "Lock down the room." He started to close the door behind them. Jordan stopped him.

"What are you going to do?" Jordan asked.

"Go after them."

"The hell you are," she replied. "You don't know the layout of the house. I do. There are a million places to hide. They'll gun you down the second they hear you coming. I'm guessing that S.W.A.T. is at least twenty minutes out, maybe longer. And you already told me you're not equipped to deal with automatic weapons, remember?"

"All true," Chris said. "But if you think you're coming with me you're out of your mind. You need to stay here with your family, Jordan." The Collectibles vault featured a heavy bank-style door with keycode access. Valuable antiques sat on the shelves. "This room's impenetrable. You'll be safe in here until help arrives."

Jordan stepped out of the room and into the hallway. "And if we're not?" she said.

"Meaning?"

"Whoever is trying to kill my family almost killed us both at the hospital and probably took out the agents Dunn assigned to patrol the grounds. Now they're somewhere in the house, looking for us. For all we know they have the override code to the security system. Which would give them access to the vault, in which case they could just open the door, open fire, and kill us all."

"Director Dunn and your godfather would never let that happen."

"They wouldn't stand a chance against a machine pistol. *Dozens of rounds per second* you said." Jordan stepped back into the room and spoke to her family. "Under no circumstances is anyone to leave this room. We'll be back soon." She closed the door, entered the pass code, locked it, and began to walk down the hall.

Hanover raised his hands. "Just where do you think you're going?"

"To find whoever is in my house."

"That's not happening."

"Wanna bet?"

"Get back in the room, Jordan."

Jordan stared down the agent. "There's a lot about me you don't know, Chris. I have certain... *skills*."

"I'm aware of that, Jordan. But psychic abilities won't help you in a gun fight."

Jordan ignored the comment and continued down the hall. "I'm ending this now," she said, "with or without your help."

Hanover watched her walk away. "You realize you're unarmed, right?"

Jordan stopped and looked back. "That's a matter of opinion," she replied. "You coming?"

Hanover shook his head. "Something tells me I don't have much choice in the matter."

"No, you don't."

Chris followed her down the corridor. "Where are we going?"

"North wing. Training room."

"As in *gym*?" Chris asked. "You might want to put off your workout for a day or two."

"I need to pick up a few things."

"Like what?"

"You'll see."

53

FOLLOWING THE BARRAGE of gunfire, flecks of gold-foil danced in the air, then fluttered to the floor.

Candy wrappers.

Fucking candy wrappers!

Tasker stepped forward to better his view of the room but stayed clear of the threshold. To cross it would be suicide. Once again, he had been taken in by Rigel's diversion. *Stupid!* He was trying to fight the man while raging a battle within his own body. The morphine that had pinned down the pain long enough for him to navigate the barrier wall, enter the house, and get back into the fight was wearing off. The pain receptors in his nerve cells retaliated. The Tec-9 shook in his grasp. He dropped the gun to his side and leaned against the wall for support. Darkness rose and fell in front of his eyes. He was on the verge of losing consciousness. He willed himself to stay on his feet and hang on, if even for a few more minutes, long enough to find Rigel and finish him off. He raised the machine pistol and pushed himself off the wall.

Shawn Mendes came to his aid. The famed pop singer stood beside Michael Farrow behind a glass-framed auto-graphed poster which reflected Rigel's position in the room. Rigel's back was pressed against the wall, his weapon trained on the doorway, waiting for Tasker to enter the room.

No more surprises, Tasker thought. Not again.

He wrapped his arm around the corner, slammed the Tec-9 against the wall, and fired blindly into the room.

The awkward, shaky motion of the gun coming at him from around the corner telegraphed Tasker's feeble attempt to mount an attack. Rigel retraced his steps and darted back across the floor, passing the display case behind which he had earlier taken cover. He kept running, building up as much speed as he could, then cut hard around the second display case, shoulder-rolled into the middle of the room, rose to one knee, Glock in hand, targeted Tasker, and fired. The single round caught the man in his leg and dropped him to the ground. The Tec-9 fell from his hand and clat-tered on the hardwood floor. Tasker slid down the wall and sat. The weapon lay beyond his grasp. The pain from the gunshot wound rode a wave throughout his entire body from one nerve synapse to the next. The darkness rose again. He watched Rigel walk toward him.

Rigel kicked away the Tec-9 and stood over the man. "Harrison Tasker, I presume," he said. "Nice to meet you."

Tasker looked up. "Wish I could say the same."

Rigel sat on the floor, crossed his legs, and placed the Glock between them.

Tasker's breathing had become labored. He was having difficulty maintaining his balance. He stared at the gun. "What's this?" he asked.

"Call it a last chance at redemption," Rigel said.

"What the hell is that supposed to mean?"

Rigel made himself more comfortable. He stretched out on the floor, leaned on his elbow. "It means for every correct answer you give me I'll give you an inch." He nudged the Glock toward Tasker. "Wanna play?"

Tasker groaned. His body swayed. "Fuck you."

Rigel pulled the gun back. "Seriously, Harrison? You came here to kill me. I'm giving you that opportunity. You want it or not?" He inched the Glock forward again.

Tasker looked at the weapon. The gun was only four inches from his hand.

"Question one," Rigel said. "Who sent you?"

Tasker's eyelids fluttered. He could feel eternal darkness settling in.

"Answer the question, Harrison," Rigel said. He pushed the Glock forward another inch. Added incentive.

Tasker wondered what lay in store for him beyond this world.

"Was it New York?"

He had always wanted a family, should have had a family.

"They rescinded my contract, didn't they?"

The gun was now just two inches from his hand. *Two damned inches.*

"Are you working alone?"

Cold overtook him. His body shuddered. He dropped his head and closed his eyes. So this was death.

Rigel saw that the man was slipping away. "No way you get to die that easily," he said. The killer rose to his feet, pulled Zippy out of his pocket, yanked out the metal lanyard, and wrapped it around the man's neck.

As Tasker slumped forward, his hand fell on the Glock. Though his body was failing him faster than his mind, his sense of touch recognized the textured surface of the weapon's handgrip and communicated the message to his brain. As the steel cable tightened around his neck, he clamped his fingers around the gun, raised it as high as he could, and squeezed the trigger.

The lanyard fell slack as the round lifted Rigel off his feet, sent him staggering backwards into the <u>Great Room</u> and the Venus de Milo. The heavy marble statue tilted with the impact of his body but held its ground. Rigel had taken the hit to his shoulder. He checked his vest. The slug was lodged in the material. He plucked it out and threw it across the room.

The Glock! he thought. How could he have been so careless?

Tasker dropped his arm but maintained a loose hold on the gun. He looked down at the weapon, urged his fingers to cradle the handgrip, find the trigger, and lift the gun. Impossible. His strength was gone.

Rigel shuffled back to Tasker. The weapon lay in his hand, his fingers slack.

"Sonofabitch," Rigel said, favoring the pain in his shoulder from the gunshot. Zippy hung around Tasker's neck. Rigel yanked on the steel lanyard. The metal cord cut deep, serrated the flesh, severed the carotid artery. Tasker gurgled. Blood flowed freely from his neck. His hands flailed helplessly at the wire. He kicked at the ground, his body convulsing and twitching until at last he sat still. It was over. Harrison Tasker was dead.

"It's about time," Rigel said. He pulled Zippy out of the man's neck, ran the serrated steel cord across the dead man's jacket, removed fine particles of flesh and blood from the weapon, then retracted the garrote.

He picked up the Tec-9, draped the sling around his

neck, shoved the Glock into the front pocket of his bullet-proof vest, and walked out of the Great Room.

In the main lobby he stopped, listened, pulled the last Werther's out of his pocket, unwrapped the candy, and popped it in his mouth.

The estate remained cemetery silent.

His targets were still here, hiding somewhere within the massive house. He could feel it.

He set out to find them.

54

MORE GUNFIRE.

"It's coming from the Great Room," Jordan said.

"How can you be sure?" Chris asked.

"Like I said, I know this place. I can tell you the location of every sound in the house from within these walls. That definitely came from the main floor."

They made their way through the secret passageway until they had arrived at the Training Room.

"We're here," Jordan said. She pushed a button on the labyrinth wall.

The hidden entrance, disguised as one of many mirrored panels that ran the length of the wall of the Training Room, clicked open. They stepped inside.

"Holy crap," Chris said. He looked around the room. "What the hell are you training for?"

The room featured a lap pool, Jacuzzi, urethane dumb-bells of varying weights on chrome stands, barbells, training racks and benches, two treadmills, an elliptical Cross-Trainer and rowing machines, a Rockwerx indoor rock-climbing wall, state-of-the-art Pilates equipment, heavy bags, speed bags, grappling dummies, Ensolite training mats, head, hand and foot gear for martial arts training and sparring, and elastic hand wraps. Opposite the fitness area were two specially designed ranges: a soundproof indoor shooting range for handgun practice and a knife-throwing target range.

"I'm the daughter of a billionaire," Jordan replied as she walked across the training mat toward the ranges. "My family has received more than our fair share of death threats over the years. Unfortunately, that comes with the territory. I can't always rely on bodyguards. Rock designed this place for me. He trained me so that I'd know how to protect myself."

"Rock Dionne... your father's head of security. The man who died in the crash."

"That's right." Jordan replied. "He taught me how to shoot, throw, and fight. I'm going to show him he didn't waste a second of his time."

A safe was built into the wall beside the shooting range. Jordan punched in the combination, opened the door, removed a Heckler and Koch VP9 9mm tactical handgun from the shelf, racked the weapon, fitted it into her waistband, then walked to the knife throwing range. Three perfectly balanced, stainless steel Gil Hibben throwing knives in a black nylon shoulder harness hung on a wall hook. Jordan slipped into the rig.

"Need anything else while we're here?" Chris said. "Blowgun, maybe? Poison darts?"

"You're joking, right?"

"Hardly. You train like a friggin' ninja."

"I wouldn't go quite that far."

"Says the woman strapped with the semi-automatic handgun and wearing the three-pack of knives."

"I like to be prepared."

"No," Chris said. "Packing an overnight bag with fresh underwear and a toothbrush is being prepared. Keeping a flashlight in your glove box is being prepared. Hell, taking a pee before a long drive is being prepared."

"Would you rather we just ask them nicely to leave?"

"You know, if Dunn were here, he wouldn't let you leave this room."

"Well, he's not. You are."

"I shouldn't let you, either. It's too dangerous."

"But you will."

"Because I have no choice in the matter?"

"Precisely."

"And because if I tried to stop you, you'd probably kick my ass?"

"I would never assault a federal agent."

"Good to know."

"Subdue... possibly. Incapacitate... maybe. But assault? Never."

"Every man and woman in law enforcement thanks you."

"Come on," Jordan said. She walked back toward the hidden mirror-door. "There's one more thing I need to do."

"And that would be?"

"Level the playing field."

55

R IGEL EXPLORED THE first floor of the grand home. He held the Tec-9 high, close to his body, eyes locked on the front sight, the weapon trained directly ahead, searching each room for his targets.

He recalled the specific condition of the Quest contract: *no survivors*. The entire family was to be wiped out. The payout was huge. His mind drifted back to his battle with Harrison Tasker. The man had been discourteous enough to die before telling him whether or not New York had, in fact, rescinded his contract to kill the Quests. Regardless, he would be paid. He would factor any financial loss into the creation of a new contract. The competition would pay him any amount of money he demanded in exchange for the carefully planned execution of the New York syndicate bosses, especially if the murders were carried out in ways that would not draw attention to his benefactors. He would make the killings look like a series of accidents: a fatal heart attack from a failed pacemaker; a family dinner at a fine restaurant ending in death from anaphylactic shock. Each assassination would be made to order, no clues left behind.

His most profitable contract had earned him thirty million dollars for three months of work in Columbia. Reconnaissance and planning accounted for eighty-five of those ninety days; the terminations completed in the remaining five. The deaths, undoubtedly his best work to date, had been front page news for a week in *El Tiempo*, the country's largest newspaper. Framed reprints of the articles hung on the living room wall of his Florida home. The posters served as excellent conversation starters. When once a dinner guest asked why he chose to display such grisly art, he told her the truth; that *he* had carried out the contracts and been responsible for the deaths. He shared with her the story-behind-the-story, elaborating on the exciting details of each hit, only to realize, too late, that in his enthusiasm to impress her he'd crossed the line. The look on her face and sudden change in demeanor gave her away. People had a strange tendency to become uneasy upon hearing a confession of murder, especially when they found themselves in the presence of the murderer himself. He was then forced to rectify the situation, and nothing puts a damper faster on an otherwise enjoyable evening than killing your guest in order to guarantee her silence. Living in the Sunshine State had its benefits, among which included the Everglades and its plenitude of hungry alligators. He took pride in keeping them well fed.

Rigel moved through the house, clearing the solarium, twin kitchens, dining room, ballroom, cigar room and reading room. The lower levels of the estate were next. He was about to descend the marble staircase when the home suddenly plunged into darkness.

Rigel froze, heard a whirring sound above him, looked up. It came from a camera mounted high in the ceiling.

Inside the labyrinth, Jordan used her cell phone to log

into the mansion's security system. She zoomed in on the intruder standing at the top of the stairs and opened the speaker. Her voice boomed over the house-wide intercom: "Who are you?" she asked. "What do you want from me?"

Rigel lowered his weapon and smiled at the camera. "Good evening, Mrs. Quest," he replied. "Nice place you have here. A little much for my taste. But hey, each to his own."

"Answer the question."

Rigel displayed the Tec-9. "That's rather obvious, isn't it?"

"Who sent you?"

"Someone who has unfinished business with your father."

Hanover turned to Jordan. She muted the phone. "What is he talking about?" Chris asked.

"I don't know," Jordan replied. "Follow me."

Together they traversed the labyrinth. Jordan captured the electronic image of the intruder on her phone and instructed the system to FOLLOW. The security system locked in on Rigel and tracked his movements as he searched the house.

Jordan and Chris exited the labyrinth by way of the Great Room. Tasker's body lay in the adjoining entrance to the Music room. Despite the obvious fatal laceration to the man's neck, Chris checked his pulse. He looked at Jordan and shook his dead. "He's dead."

"Good guy or bad guy?" Jordan asked.

"He's not one of ours," Chris replied. He saw the glass shards in his face and hands, the steel nails sticking out of his body. "Jesus," Chris said. "What the hell happened to this guy?"

"Look at his neck," Jordan said. "Same injury as yours.

How much do you want to bet the guy who did this is the same one who attacked you in the hospital?"

"And you."

Jordan looked at her phone, located the man. "He's on the move," she said. "Games Room, East wing. Straight ahead."

They removed their weapons. Chris stepped ahead. "Stay behind me. I want him taken alive. We need to know who he is and who sent him."

"That's what fingerprints and DNA are for," Jordan said.

Chris took her by the arm, stopped her. "Listen up, Jordan. No heroics. Got me?"

Jordan nodded. "Whatever you say." She stepped past him, raised the Heckler and Koch, and proceeded down the hall. "Games Room," she repeated.

56

R IGEL ENTERED THE games room.

The bespoke twelve-foot ash pool table, a work of art recognizable even in the dark room, sported purple speed cloth. Matching chalks sat on its rails. Aramith balls, precisely positioned, sat ready to break in their wooden triangle. An exquisite bank of Tiffany lamps hung above the table they served. A rack on the wall held eight pool cues.

Rigel removed one of the cues, placed its tip on the playing surface, pressed down on the shaft, and scored a tear down the cloth as he walked the length of the table. In the corner of the room a security camera whirred and panned, following his every step.

Rigel looked up at the camera. "I'm guessing you can see and hear me, Mrs. Quest."

"I can," the speakers replied.

"Kind of gives you an unfair advantage, doesn't it? You able to see me, but me unable to see you."

"Works for me," Jordan said. They reached the main

foyer. She muted the microphone and whispered to Chris. "Down the hall. Last room on the right."

"Got it," Chris replied.

Rigel laughed. "Smart lady." He removed the triangle, tossed it across the room, placed the white ball behind the break line, readied the cue and sighted the shot, but stopped short of taking it. He removed a hundred-dollar bill from his pocket, showed it to the camera, then placed it under the ball.

"Care to make a little wager? A hundred bucks says I find you before the cops arrive."

Rigel waited.

No reply.

He continued. "Not rich enough for you, huh?" He took out a second hundred and slid it under the first. "Better?" He waved the cue at the camera. "How many of those have you got in this place? Forty? Fifty? I'm guessing fifty, minimum." Rigel leveled the Tec-9 at the camera and pulled the trigger. *Brrrrrrrrrrrrr*. The camera blew to pieces. Hot brass casings bounced off the pool table and fell on the floor.

"Make that forty-nine," Rigel called out. He sprayed the room again, fatally injuring the opposing players on a neighboring foosball table and decimating two vintage pinball machines: a Bally *Eight Ball* and R. Gottlieb *Arabian Knights*, then blew out the LCD displays of five classic video games: Pong, Frogger, Space Invaders, Pac-Man, and Star Wars. A final blitz of gun fire annihilated a classic Skeeball Alley Bowler.

Jordan and Chris advanced down the hallway towards the Games Room as the ejected casings tinkled on the hardwood floor. Jordan looked at Chris and pointed to her phone. She shook her head. One of the rounds had struck and severed the camera cable hidden behind the wall. The screen was black, the live visual feed from the room to her phone lost. They were proceeding blind now. Fifty feet of open hallway separated them from the shooter.

The next room, a guest bathroom, lay ten feet ahead. Twenty feet beyond it was the entrance to the art gallery. The doors to both rooms, normally kept closed, stood open. The intruder must have cleared them in his search for the family prior to investigating the Games Room.

Chris motioned to Jordan and pointed to the bathroom. The two moved quickly down the hall, slipped into the room and hid behind the door.

Footsteps in the hallway, outside the Games Room.

Rigel called out. "You never took me up on my wager."

Closer, in front of the art gallery now.

Hanover placed the barrel of the Glock in the crack of the doorframe. He would wait for the man to pass, sight the back of his head, the 'light switch' as sharpshooters called it, take the shot, kill him instantly, and end the terror.

"Maybe I should have made it a thousand?" the man called out. His voice was loud, just a few feet from the doorway. It echoed off the walls of the long hallway. "Just how fast is the police response time in this neighborhood, anyway?"

Hanover steadied his breathing, waited.

Rigel stopped within inches of the door. Strange... the camera at the end of the hallway failed to whir or pan. Was the security system no longer tracking him? Had the woman escaped?

No, she was here. He could sense her presence. But more than that, he could *smell* it. Jordan's perfume. The same exhilarating blend he remembered from his visit with her in her hospital wafted in the hallway: Indian jasmine... Rosa centifolia... cardamom... carnation... benzoin... fruity citrus...

Rigel dropped low and shoulder-rolled past the entrance to the bathroom.

Hanover heard the man, saw him roll past the door, tried to reacquire the target, lost him. He pushed Jordan aside as a hail of bullets ripped through the bathroom door. All but one round hit high. The last bullet found its mark and caught him squarely in his shoulder.

Chris groaned and dropped to the ground. His Glock clattered across the polished marble floor.

Through the bullet holes in the splintered door he watched the assassin rise to his feet.

Jordan moved to the center of the bathroom, crouched down, closed her eyes, and listened. She knew how far the shooter was from the door: Six feet.

The hundreds of hours she had spent training with Rock Dionne came to her all at once: stay low... move fast... hit hard... never retreat.

Stay low, move fast, hit hard...

Jordan ran toward the doorway as fast as she could, threw herself on the floor and slid into the hallway, opening up on the intruder with the Heckler and Koch, squeezing off round after round. Each of the ten bullets found their target.

Rigel was unprepared for the counterattack. He was sure it was the woman who had been hit with multiple rounds from the Tec-9. The rest should have been easy, pure clean up. He wasn't naïve enough to believe that she would willingly give up the location of her family within the great house. No matter. At the least his principal target would be dead. He would find the rest of the family before the police arrived, kill them and the FBI agents, and make good his escape. But now he found himself in uncharted territory, staggering backward as round after round from the woman's weapon struck his body armor with brutal force. The last bullet blew his index finger off his shooting hand. Rigel screamed. He clutched his hand and dropped the Tec-9.

Never retreat...

Jordan jumped to her feet, drew a knife from its sheath, and threw it at the gunman. The weapon sailed through the air, caught Rigel in his throat and brought him to his knees.

Fingers wet with blood, Rigel clawed at his throat. Jordan walked toward him, pulled a second knife from its sheath, looked down on the gunman, drove her foot into his chest, pinned him down.

Hanover staggered out of the bathroom and into the hallway, weapon drawn, expecting a gunfight. Instead, he saw Jordan straddled atop the intruder, a knife lodged in the man's throat, a second blade pressed against his neck.

"Put it down, Jordan," Chris said.

"He tried to kill us," Jordan replied coldly, her voice shaking. "He came into this house. He wanted to kill my family, my *children*."

"But he didn't," Chris reminded her. "You stopped him."

"Not good enough."

Chris stood beside her. He placed his hand on her shoulder. "We have him, Jordan. It's over."

Jordan stared into Rigel's eyes. "It'll never be over. I have to live with this for the rest of my life."

"I promise you you'll get the answers you need."

With her free hand, Jordan grabbed the handle of the knife embedded in the man's throat. Rigel gurgled.

Chris warned her. "Right now, it's one-hundred percent self-defence, Jordan. I'll swear to that in court. But the second you turn that blade everything changes."

Jordan's hand trembled on the handle. She wanted to drive the blade in deep, twist it, finish him.

"Think about Emma and Aiden," Chris said.

The faces of her children flashed through her mind.

She had already endured enough tragedy.

No more.

She let go of the knives, threw her hands aside.

Chris helped her to her feet. Rigel stared up at her from the floor. His eyes were vacant, his breathing labored, unsteady. He coughed up blood.

"No matter," Jordan said. "The blade nicked his carotid. He's done." She picked up the Tec-9, slung it over her shoulder and turned to Chris. "We need to get to the vault and let the others know we're safe."

The artwork on the hallway wall trembled, the floor vibrated. They heard the drone of a helicopter rotor. The craft was hovering above the house.

"Hostage Rescue Team," Chris said. "They'll be inside any second."

Jordan looked down at Rigel. His good hand, fingers intact, lay across his chest. "What about him?"

"He's not going anywhere," Chris said. "Let HRT take out the trash. Let's go."

Jordan and Chris walked down the hallway. "How's the shoulder," she asked.

"Hurts like a sonofabitch."

"You pushed me out of the way back there," Jordan said.

"I know."

"You saved my life."

"I was just doing my --"

Bang! Bang! Bang!

The gunshots came from behind. Two of the bullets glanced off the wall. The third narrowly missed Chris' head.

Jordan spun around. The attacker lay on his side, a pistol in his outstretched hand. He was firing wildly. Jordan leveled the Tec-9 at the man she mistakenly thought she'd mortally wounded and pulled the trigger. She held it down as she walked towards him, watching his body dance on the floor as round after round tore through his head, torso, arms, and legs. Jordan didn't stop firing until every last round in the machine pistol had been spent. Gray smoke poured out of the silencer.

Chris pried the Glock out of the dead man's hand. "He must have had it hidden in his vest," he said. "My focus was on the Tec. I never thought to clear him. Jesus, Jordan. I'm sorry."

Jordan pulled the knife out of Rigel's throat, wiped clean the blade on his slug-riddled body armor, then returned the weapon to its sheath.

"I'm not," she replied. "Not one damn bit."

57

"F OLLOW MY LEAD," Chris told Jordan. They stood in the front entrance of the grand home, watching the agents deploy from the FBI Black Hawk helicopter as it set down on the front lawn of Farrow Estate. "Let's go inside. HRT will secure the scene. Which means they're going to treat you as a hostile until they know what's going on. Drop your weapons on the floor and stand beside me."

The Hostage Rescue Team stormed the home. Chris displayed his Bureau credentials, identified himself first. "This is Jordan Quest," he told the tactical force commander. "This is her family's home. We have two hostiles down, one in the east wing, the other the west. Director Dunn and Special Agent Grant Carnevale are guarding the family in a locked room on the premises. There are two agents outside. Both may be down. Tell your men to sweep the grounds."

"Copy that," the Commander said. He motioned to his men. The agents dispersed. "You two okay?"

"Never better," Jordan replied.

. . .

JORDAN CALLED to her godfather from outside the vault. "Uncle Grant, it's me. I'm unlocking the door. Agent Hanover is with me."

Jordan entered the code. The heavy metal door to the Collectables vault clicked open. The two agents stood in the middle of the room, their weapons trained on the door as it swung open.

"Step inside, slowly," Director Dunn said.

"What's going on?" Jordan asked.

"It's all right, Jordan," Chris said. "Just do as he says."

The two entered the room.

"Walk past us," Carnevale said.

Chris and Jordan complied.

Dunn and Carnevale advanced past them, cleared the hallway, re-entered the room and holstered their weapons. "Sorry," the Director said. "We needed to be sure you weren't being forced to open the door at gunpoint."

"I understand," Jordan said.

The family emerged from behind a large wooden shipping crate in the corner of the room. Emma and Aiden heard their mothers voice and ran to her. "Mom!"

Jordan dropped to her knees, capturing the children in her arms. "Hi, babies," she said. "Are you guys all right?"

"Yeah," Aiden replied. He pointed to the remains of a shattered ceramic bowl on the floor. "Emma broke one of Grandpa's antiques."

"Me?" Emma exclaimed. "You're the one who took it out of the box."

"You're the one who dropped it!"

"Which wouldn't have happened if you'd left it on the shelf where it belonged!"

Aiden raised his hand, dismissed his sister. "Whatever,"

he replied. "No big deal. There's a whole pile of them in the box. No one's going to miss one stupid bowl."

Chris leaned over and whispered in Jordan's ear. "That wasn't just any old bowl, was it?"

Jordan shook her head. "It was an Asian Ding bowl from the Chinese Northern Song Dynasty."

"Expensive?"

"It was valued at four hundred thousand dollars."

Chris gasped. "Four hundred grand? For a *bowl*?"

"It wasn't just any bowl. It was a piece of history."

Blown away by the value of the insignificant looking piece, Chris shook his head. "No problem," he said. "I'll replace it for you."

Jordan chuckled. "You will, huh?"

"Piece of cake."

"And exactly how do you plan to do that?"

Chris smiled. "Give me a lump of modeling clay and a little water. I'll whip you up a new one in no time. Shouldn't cost more than five bucks."

Jordan laughed. "Remind me to never let you near this room again."

HEARING VOICES IN THE VAULT, the Hostage Rescue Team rounded the corner and entered the room. Dunn and Carnevale identified themselves. Dunn instructed the team to lower their weapons and stand down.

"Are the premises secure?" Dunn asked.

"Yes, sir," the Commander replied.

"Fatalities?"

"Four. Two of ours, two of theirs."

Dunn nodded. "Have your men escort the family out of

here. Take a route around the deceased. I don't want the children seeing the bodies."

"Copy that."

ON THE GROUNDS of the estate the night was alive with the flashing lights of emergency medical service units and FBI sedans. The EMS attendants provided blankets to the family and assessed them individually. Other than the emotional trauma of the ordeal, all were reported to be in good health.

Hanover sat in the back of an ambulance. A paramedic gingerly removed his jacket, opened his shirt, and inspected the bullet wound. After checking on her family, Jordan stepped into the back of the ambulance and sat beside him. She looked at the wound. "Ouch," she said. "That looks nasty."

"It's not so bad." He turned, showed Jordan his back. "Bullet came out the other side. Give me a week and I'll be as good as new."

"A week?"

"Okay, maybe a month. Give me a break. I've never been shot before. Can't say I'm liking it very much, either."

"How's the neck?"

"It only hurts when I talk."

"Too bad. Audrey will be disappointed when she finds out you'll be out of commission for a while."

"Audrey?"

"Nurse Lane?" Jordan reminded him. "Angel of Mercy Hospital? My nurse? The one with the hots for you?"

Chris smiled. "Oh, *that* Audrey. It's my shoulder that needs rest. The rest of me works just fine."

Jordan laughed. "I'm sure it does." She watched as law enforcement personnel came and went from the mansion. A coroner's van pulled up to the front entrance. Two atten-dants exited the vehicle. Taking their instructions from the HRT Commander, the men opened the rear doors of the van and removed two steel gurneys. The bodies of Carter and Lehman, the agents tasked with protecting the grounds, were placed in the van. Moments later, a second van pulled in behind the first. The black-bagged bodies of James Rigel and Harrison Tasker were removed from the home. Jordan stepped out of the ambulance and watched the vehicles drive down the winding driveway and leave the property.

Chris eased into his shirt and jacket and stood beside her. "Don't focus on them, Jordan," he said. "Focus on your family."

"That's easier said than done."

"I know."

"I need answers, Chris. I need to know why this happened."

"You'll get them."

"This was a professional assassination attempt. Someone *ordered* this."

"We'll find them, Jordan. Count on it."

"What if you don't? What if this isn't over?"

"Your family will be under FBI protection for as long as it takes, until we make an arrest."

Jordan's voice broke. "I'm scared, Chris. Not for me, but for my kids."

Hanover couldn't think of an appropriate response. Instead, he put his good arm around her and provided her with what she needed the most that moment: compassion.

Jordan leaned into him. For the first time since being told by Dr. Tremaine that Keith had died, she cried.

.   .   .

Andrew Dunn and Grant Carnevale walked to the ambulance.

"You okay, honey?" Carnevale asked.

Jordan wiped away her tears. "I'll be fine, Uncle Grant."

"Yes, you will," her godfather replied. "And we'll be here with you all the way. But right now, we need a favor."

"Of course," Jordan replied. "Anything."

"Director Dunn's daughters have been taken to a hospital in Ridgecrest, north of Los Angeles. HRT needs to return to base. Any chance we can borrow a Farrow Industries chopper?"

Jordan opened her phone and called the heliport. "Consider it on the way."

58

ITHIN THIRTY MINUTES of receiving Jordan's call the Farrow Industries Eurocopter EC155 touched down on the front lawn of the estate. Andrew Dunn ran to the chopper and took his place in the passenger seat.

"One hell of a night, huh?" Sam Cooper said, referring to the inclement weather. The pilot waited for the director to buckle up before handing him an in-flight communications headset.

"You have no idea," Dunn replied over the rising whine of the twin Turbomeca engines. The helicopter lifted off, banked hard to the left, then sped up, following a north-by-northeast heading to Ridgecrest. "What's our ETA?"

The pilot referred to the route information displayed on the digital flight control. "Forty-five minutes," he replied. "Fair warning, though. Final approach could get a little rough. Ridgecrest's got the Sierra Nevada's to the west, Cosos on the north, Argus Range on the east and El Pasos on the south. When you factor in updrafts, downdrafts, and cross-winds from those surrounding mountain ranges, plus rain, thunder, and lightning, well... let's say this promises to be an interesting flight."

"Fine by me," Dunn replied. "Just as long as you get us there in one piece."

Cooper smiled. "Haven't lost a passenger yet."

Dunn smiled. "Try not to break that record tonight."

"I heard about the crash," Cooper said. "Still can't believe it. How's Jordan holding up?"

Rain lashed across the cockpit window. Thousands of feet below, the city of Los Angeles stood its ground against the raging storm.

"She's keeping it together," Dunn replied. "Which is the most anyone could expect from her right now."

"Any idea how it happened?"

"We'll know soon enough."

"You want my two cents?"

"Sure."

Cooper was emphatic. "There's no way in hell that jet just fell out of the air," he said. "All Farrow Industries aircraft, including this one, are serviced by corporately employed aircraft mechanics. If it crashed it's because someone outside the company tampered with it, end of story."

"Anyone come to mind who might be motivated to do that?" Dunn asked.

"Nobody I can think of. Michael and Mary were good people, you know? Considerate and generous to a fault. The kind who wouldn't hurt a soul."

"Someone out there doesn't share that sentiment."

Cooper shrugged. "Maybe not. But I'll tell you this. None of our guys were responsible for the crash. Not a chance."

"Let's hope you're right," Dunn replied.

Forty-six minutes after leaving the Farrow estate, the

extra minute lost to rough weather, the corporate chopper set down on the helipad at China Lake Regional Hospital in Ridgecrest.

"Bird's at your disposal for as long as you need it," Cooper called out as Dunn opened the cockpit door. "I have to clear the helipad. Hospital rules. Call for pick up when you're ready to leave."

"Thanks, Coop," Dunn said.

"You've got it."

Dunn ran across the tarmac, entered the facility, presented his credentials at Patient Registration, and was directed to the second floor. His daughter's room wasn't hard to find. A member of the FBI's HRT tactical team stood guard outside the door. He recognized the FBI Director and stepped forward to greet him.

The agent introduced himself. "Special Agent Thomas Ford, sir. HRT Los Angeles. Your daughters are inside."

"Thank you, Agent Ford," Dunn replied.

Safe and sound. Thank God.

Dunn entered the room. Zoe was sitting up, her bandaged shoulder in a sling. Shannon sat in a guest chair beside her. Lily sat on the end of the bed, legs curled under her.

"Director Dad!" Zoe exclaimed as her stepfather entered the room. "It's about damn time you got here."

Shannon stood and gave her father a big hug. Dunn kissed his daughters.

"I leave you two alone for a week and this happens," Dunn teased. "You guys okay?"

Zoe raised her wounded shoulder. "Other than receiving this little souvenir and being detained on suspicion of murder, I'd say we're good."

"About that," Dunn said. "I was briefed on the situation.

You're both lawyers, so you tell me. Were you defending yourself?"

"This was non-criminal homicide to the letter," Zoe said. "I was facing an imminent threat to my life under existing and extenuating circumstances, the result of which would have resulted in the commission of a murder; mine, to be exact. Had I not taken the action I did we wouldn't be having this conversation right now."

"Good enough," Dunn said. "Consider the matter closed."

"Happy to," Zoe said. Lily was holding her hand. "Dad, Shannon and I have someone special we'd like you to meet. This is Lily. She saved our lives. Lily, meet our father, Andrew Dunn."

Lily stood. "Pleased to meet you, sir."

"Not half as much as I am to meet you, Lily," Dunn said.

Shannon said, "Without Lily's help we would never have made it out of there alive."

"I don't know what to say, Lily, other than thank you," Dunn said. He gave the girl a hug.

"By the way," Zoe told her father, "Lily's a genius."

"Smart, huh?" Dunn replied.

"No, really," Shannon added. "Lily's a *real* genius. A one-hundred percent certified smarty-pants. Even has the creds to prove it."

Lily blushed. "*Had* the creds, you mean."

Shannon replied, "We'll go back to the fallout shelter and get them."

"Fallout shelter?" Dunn said.

"Yeah," Zoe added. "They're on the wall. Beside the periscope."

"*Periscope...*"

"It's a long story, sir," Lily said.

Dunn laughed. "It certainly sounds like one."

Lily lowered her head and stared at the floor. Dunn sensed the girl's sadness. "How did you come to find yourself in the company of my daughters, Lily? Where are your parents?"

Shannon put her arm around her. "They're gone, Dad. We'll fill you in on the details later. Now's not the time."

The severity of the matter was obvious. Dunn asked, "Who's taking care of you, Lily?"

Lily shook her head. "Just me."

"You don't have a family member you can stay with?"

Lily didn't answer. Dunn saw the girl was on the verge of tears. "Then it's settled," he said. "Until this whole matter is rectified, you'll stay with us." He winked at Lily. "That is unless you've already had as much of these two troublemakers as you can handle."

Lily smiled. "They *can* be a little difficult."

Dunn laughed. "Tell me about it! So, what do you say? You want to hang out with us for a while?"

"Thank you, sir," Lily replied. "I think I'd like that."

"So would I," Shannon said.

"Ditto," Zoe added.

"Good," Dunn said. "Then consider yourself one of the family."

Shannon held out her pinky finger to Lily. Zoe did the same. "Told you we'd take care of you," Shannon said. "Remember?"

"Yes, you did," Lily said. "Thank you."

"Sister pinky swear?" Zoe said.

The girls locked fingers. "Sister pinky swear," Lily replied.

Dunn opened his phone and placed a call to Cooper. To

the girls he said, "There's a helicopter on its way to pick us up. It'll be here shortly."

"Are we heading back to New York?" Shannon asked.

"No," her father replied. "We'll be staying in L.A. for a few days. I have funerals to attend. Plus, there's someone I want you to meet."

59

A TEAM OF FBI agents, assigned by Andrew Dunn before his departure for China Lake Regional Hospital, maintained a vigil over Farrow Estate throughout the night, wary that yet another attack against the family might follow the failed assassination attempts of the last few hours.

Chris slept in a reading chair in Michael Farrow's study. Twice in the early hours of the morning he bolted out of the chair, drew his weapon, and raced up the stairs with members of the protection detail to investigate the origin of the screams. In both instances their response led them to Emma's room where they found her sitting up in bed, clutching her sheets, and calling out for her father. Now Jordan was sitting beside her on the bed, holding her in her arms, rocking her, consoling her frightened daughter.

No immediate threat.

Stand down.

Chris stayed with Jordan as the accompanying agents returned to their posts.

"Everything okay?" he asked.

"Fine," Jordan said, smoothing her daughter's hair. "Just a nightmare."

"Second one tonight."

Jordan nodded. "With probably a few more yet to come."

"Poor kid. How's Aiden?"

"Still asleep. He's always handled stressful situations much better than his sister."

"Sounds like he takes after his mom."

Jordan smiled. "Don't be fooled," she replied. "Inside, I haven't stopped screaming."

With her mother's encouragement, Emma settled back into bed. Jordan tucked her blanket around her and stroked her head until she fell asleep.

"I won't be sleeping anytime soon," Jordan said. She lifted herself slowly off the bed, careful not to disturb the child. "The kids will need me again soon enough. I could use a coffee. Care to join me?"

"Sure," Chris said.

Jordan and Chris sat in the kitchen sipping French Roast and talking. On the opposite side of the room, the window that Rigel had earlier shot out and through which he had entered the home had been sealed off with thick plastic sheets. The forensics team carefully inspected sections of the damaged window frame, dusting it for fingerprints. Outside, spotlights mounted on portable light stands washed the manicured backyard in harsh white light. Lost in thought, surprised by an unexpected camera flash beyond the opaque plastic barrier, Jordan jumped in her chair and spilled her coffee on the table. An FBI photographer stepped out from behind the sealed window and snapped another picture of the scene. The second flash was followed by a third, then a fourth, a fifth.

Chris retrieved a dish towel from the counter and wiped the table.

"You okay?" he asked.

"A little jumpy, I guess."

"That's understandable," Chris said. "Try not to worry. There are ten agents stationed on the grounds and around the perimeter of the estate, plus another eight in the house. No one will get to your family again, Jordan. We won't let that happen."

"I know."

"Then what's wrong?"

Jordan rubbed her temples. "I know what's coming. A full-on assault by the media... paparazzi... relentless requests for interviews. Even the funeral service will be a circus."

"Can't your father's company handle the PR?"

"Yes, Farrow Industries public relations will do the best they can. But there's nothing the press likes more than to cover a tragedy. And I'm not sure if I'll be able to hold it together at the funeral."

"Jordan, you're the strongest woman I've ever met," Chris said. "Don't let them take that strength from you. Show them you've got this. And if you need me to be there, I will."

"Thanks, Chris," Jordan said. "I'll never be able to repay you or Director Dunn for all you've done to help me and my family."

Chris smiled. "Are you kidding? Thanks to you the Director is being reunited with his daughters as we speak. I'd say that makes you even."

Marissa DeSola entered the kitchen, telephone in hand.

"Sorry to disturb you, Jordan," she said. "A Mr. Brian Hartley is calling for you."

"Who?" Jordan asked, not recognizing the name.

Marissa handed her the portable handset. "He's with Farrow Industries. Says he needs to speak with you right away."

Jordan took the call. "How can I help you, Mr. Hartley?"

"Good morning, Mrs. Quest," Hartley began. "Please accept my apologies for calling you at such an early hour. Believe me when I tell you I wish it were under better circumstances. I'm Chief Legal Counsel for Farrow Industries Worldwide. Sitting with me is Stanton Wilder, Executive Vice-President, Worldwide Commercial Business, and Tess Cole, your fathers Executive Assistant. I'm afraid we have a rather urgent request."

"Of course, Mr. Hartley," Jordan replied. "What do you need?"

"We need to meet with you as soon as possible."

"For what reason?"

"I have in my hand a copy of your father's living will and his succession plan for Farrow Industries," Hartley explained. "An emergency meeting of Farrow's Board of Directors convened several hours ago, immediately after we received confirmation of your father's death. I'm very sorry to have to be so direct, but as you can appreciate there are certain decisions that must be made right now to ensure Farrow Industries global operations continue uninterrupted and its stock price remains unaffected. I hate to sound melodramatic but, as they say, time is of the essence."

"I understand, Mr. Hartley" Jordan replied. "How soon do you need to meet with me?"

"Within the hour, if possible."

"Very well," Jordan agreed. "Is there anything I need to do to prepare for this meeting?"

"There is," Hartley replied. "The cover letter to your father's will stipulates it only be opened in your presence, or in the event you have predeceased your father, an assigned representative. Two other parties are mentioned. Your father wished to have his housekeeper, Marissa DeSola, and your godfather, Grant Carnevale, present at the reading of his will. Do you know if they are still alive?"

"They are. Marissa and Uncle Grant are here with me now."

"Good. Please speak with them right away. Can I have your assurance they will join us?"

"Yes."

"Very good," Hartley replied. "Thank you, Mrs. Quest. We're on our way."

60

ONE HOUR LATER, Chris Hanover received notification from the agents stationed at the front gate that the Farrow Industries executives had arrived.

Jordan welcomed her guests in the lobby. Chris introduced himself, then asked for their cooperation as Stanton Wilder, Brian Hartley and Tess Cole were patted down, weapons-checked by members of the protection detail, and their briefcases and personal effects opened and searched. Deemed to be free of weapons and explosive devices, the three were cleared and granted permission to enter the home.

Jordan welcomed the party into her father's home office. Seated at a small conference table in the corner of the room, Marissa DeSola rose nervously from her chair and joined Grant Carnevale in welcoming the members of the Farrow executive team.

"Thank you for meeting with us on such short notice, Mrs. Quest," Brian Hartley said after introducing his colleagues. "On behalf of Farrow Industries Worldwide, please accept our heartfelt condolences on the tragic loss of your loved ones."

"Thank you," Jordan replied.

"Your father was one of the most astute businessmen I've ever worked with," Stanton Wilder added. Jordan had known him as her father's colleague for many years. "Thank you, Mr. Wilder," she replied. "My father spoke of you often. He had a great deal of respect for you and the contributions you have made to his company over the years."

Wilder accepted the compliment. "It was my privilege."

Tess Cole spoke. "I know how difficult a time this must be for you, Jordan. I've been in contact with Farrow's Human Resources department. They've secured the services of a grief counselor who will reach out to you shortly to help you and your family through what I'm sure is a most difficult and challenging time. Funeral arrangements have been taken care of in accordance with your father's wishes. Your parents and husband will be interred at the Farrow family plot at Forest Lawn Cemetery in Hollywood Hills in two days. A Celebration of Life ceremony will follow later at the Los Angeles Convention Center. We've been flooded with inquiries from your father's business acquaintances. Hundreds will be attending the memorial to pay their respects to you and your family. The Mayor has requested LAPD's assistance to control the processional traffic and escort your family to and from the funeral and the ceremony. The President will also be attending. Secret Service is working with our people as well as LAPD and convention center security staff to facilitate his arrival and participation. He's asked if he could say a few words on your father's behalf."

"My family would be honored," Jordan replied.

Tess smiled and nodded. "I'll see to it."

Brian Hartley opened his briefcase, removed several envelopes, and turned to Jordan. "May we begin?" he asked.

"Of course," Jordan said.

Hartley presented the first document to Jordan and his colleagues. "This is a copy of Farrow Industries Emergency Succession Plan. Your father revised it quarterly. As Chief Legal Counsel for Farrow Industries Worldwide, I was required to meet with him to witness any changes made to the document. My signature can be found at the bottom attesting to the fact that it is in order. As Chairman of the Board, your father took his responsibilities to his stake-holders very seriously. He wanted to ensure that in the event of his sudden or unexpected death any interruptions to the operation of the company would be minimal. Unfortunately, we now find ourselves dealing with such an emergency, thus the requirement for the execution of this document." Hartley removed three additional envelopes from his brief-case. "Michael further stipulated I meet with Marissa DeSola and Grant Carnevale, in your presence, and present them with these documents, which we'll deal with in just a minute. Right now, I'd like to turn the floor over to Mr. Wilder."

Stanton Wilder opened his copy of the succession plan. To Jordan, he said, "As a lawyer yourself, I'm sure you understand that when a businessman who is as successful and high-profile as your father dies suddenly there could be immediate and disastrous consequences to the company unless a seamless transition takes place immediately at the C-level of the business. With that in mind, I'm pleased to inform you that your father has stipulated that you are to be his successor. The Executive Committee reviewed the request. It met without objection. As of this moment, you are now Chairperson of Farrow Industries Worldwide. We simply need you to confirm that you accept the position."

Jordan nodded. "I do."

"Very good," Wilder said. "Having you at the helm will maintain investor confidence and stock value. This document further demands that I immediately transition from my current role as Executive Vice President, Worldwide Commercial Business, to that of Chief Executive Officer. Our governance committee has inspected our internal talent pool and selected the executives who will succeed up the ranks. The names of those individuals will be announced tomorrow. We feel comfortable that the future of Farrow Industries is in good hands, just as your father would have wanted it. Your duties and responsibilities as Chairperson will be light. You'll act primarily as a figurehead for the company and liaise with Brian and I from time to time as well as other members of the Board. You'll also be required to attend all mandatory board and shareholder meetings. You'll have a voice on all matters related to the future of Farrow Industries, including our plans for worldwide expansion."

Wilder sat back in his chair. "I know this is a lot to take in right now, Jordan. I hope we haven't thrown too much at you. If we have, I apologize."

"Not at all," Jordan replied. "It's comforting to know that my father has left his company in such capable hands."

"Thank you," Wilder replied. "Please know that we're here for you, day or night."

Brian Hartley spoke. "Now that we've concluded the business of the Board, I'd like to present these documents to Ms. DeSola and Agent Carnevale."

Hartley slid the envelopes across the table to Marissa

and Grant. They had been respectively addressed to them by Michael Farrow. "Please open them," the attorney said.

Marissa and Grant read their letters.

Marissa covered her mouth, let out a small cry. "Oh my," she said. "Oh my!"

Grant Carnevale laughed, then turned to Jordan. "Your old man just had to get in the last word, didn't he?"

Jordan smiled. "What are you talking about?" Jordan asked. "What do your letters say?"

Marissa was speechless. Grant just smiled, continued to laugh, and shook his head.

"Mr. Hartley?" Jordan asked.

Hartley handed her copies of the letters her father had prepared for Marissa and Grant. "For your records, Jordan," he said. "Clearly, your father held Ms. DeSola and Agent Carnevale in the highest regard."

Jordan read her father's letter to Marissa:

Dearest Marissa. You have been a trusted friend all my life. To thank you for your loyalty, I have established a trust in your name in the amount of twenty million dollars as my final gift to you. Payments will be disbursed monthly. Please enjoy the rest of your days knowing how much you were appreciated and loved. Always, Michael Farrow.

As it had for Grant, her father's letter to her godfather made her laugh. It read:

Grant, you old dog! For years I've been trying to lure you away from that damn government job of yours with the FBI and join me at Farrow Industries. Despite my best efforts, you refused. It seems you were more interested in saving the world than you were in working with your old pal. If you're reading this letter now, it's because the Man upstairs has finally called my number. But we can't live forever, can we pal? I can't complain. My life's been one hell of a ride. But I can tell you from my heart it would have been much more fun if you had been at my side to share the journey. With that in mind, I thought I'd leave you with a little parting gift; one you would have earned anyway if you'd had the damn good sense to take me up on my offer back when we graduated from MIT. I've established a trust in your name in the amount of fifty million dollars. Payments will be disbursed monthly. Go buy yourself an island, retire early, or do whatever you want. You deserve it. I love you, my friend. If you would, please do me one last favor. Look in on my family from time to time. With deepest respect and admiration, Mike.

After Marissa had re-read her letter for the fifth time, she asked, "Is this real?"

Hartley smiled. "Yes, ma'am," he said. "Your trust is part of Mr. Farrow's last will and testament. It is one-hundred percent legitimate."

Carnevale looked up. "Thanks, Mikey," he said. "I love you too, buddy."

Jordan turned to Stanton Wilder. "I have an urgent request, Mr. Wilder. I need to visit the families of the crash victims as soon as possible before the funeral for my family takes place. Can you arrange transportation for me?"

"Absolutely," Wilder answered. "When do you wish to leave?"

"First thing in the morning."

"Consider it done."

"If it's all right with you, I'd like to tag along," Hanover said. "Officially, you're still under FBI protection."

"Thanks, Chris," Jordan said. "I'd appreciate that."

61

FOR TWO DAYS, Chris accompanied Jordan as she traveled, paying her respects to the families of Rock Dionne, flight Captain Peter Sanders, First Officer Cameron Brentworth and flight attendants Julie Todd and Gayle Konrath, all of whom perished in the horrific jet crash that claimed the lives of her parents and Keith.

THE FAMILY STOOD inside the Great Mausoleum at Forest Lawn Cemetery in Glendale, listening to Reverend William Harding deliver the committal service, recite prayers and readings, deliver the eulogy, and share stories of the countless acts of generosity and benevolence for which Michael and Mary Farrow had come to be known throughout their lives. He spoke of their boundless love for their grandchildren, Emma and Aiden, and how fortunate they were to be blessed with such a strong, confident and capable daughter in Jordan. The memorial was difficult for young Emma, who cried for her father throughout the brief service, her head buried in her grandmother's dress. Aiden held his own. He stood beside his grandfather, David Quest, listening to the words of the kindly old priest. Marissa DeSola and Grant Carnevale stood at Jordan's side. Positioned throughout the cemetery, FBI agents, including Chris Hanover and Director Andrew Dunn, as well as Farrow Industries shadow security team, kept a close watch on the crowd who, behind the locked gates, appeared to be enjoying their brief glimpse into a private moment in the life of the famous family.

After the service had concluded and final goodbyes were said, Emma and Aiden returned to the limousine with their grandparents and Marissa.

Grant Carnevale rejoined his colleagues. They watched from across the parking lot as Jordan thanked the Reverend and received his blessing.

"Think they'll be all right?" Chris asked.

"Jordan will need a little time," Carnevale answered. "But yeah, they'll be fine."

"You've got one hell of a goddaughter there," Andrew Dunn remarked.

"Thank you, Director," Carnevale replied. "I certainly do."

"She can back me up anytime," Chris said.

"Damn straight," Carnevale agreed. "She's her father's daughter all right, through and through. By the way Chris, how's the shoulder?"

Hanover's wounded arm hung in a sling. He lifted it gingerly. "Hurt's like a sonofabitch."

"And your neck?"

"About the same."

Dunn turned around and saw his daughters and Lily standing inside the front gates of the cemetery. He waved to them to join him.

Jordan walked over to the men and received a hug

from her godfather. "How are you, sweetie?" Carnevale asked.

Jordan smiled. "All things considered, I'm good."

Shannon and Zoe joined their father. Lily stood back, unsure of her place. Shannon took her by the hand. Zoe put her arm around her, pulled her close.

"Jordan," Andrew Dunn said, "I'd like you to meet my daughters, Shannon and Zoe. And this is Lily Maynard. Girls, this is Jordan Quest. Jordan helped us locate you."

"Please accept our condolences on your loss, Mrs. Quest," Zoe added.

"Yes," Shannon added. "Thank you for all you've done to help my father, and us."

"You're most welcome," Jordan answered. She leaned over and shook Lily's hand. The psychic connection with the girl was immediate. In a flash Jordan saw the stables, the bodies buried beneath the ground, the nuclear fallout shelter, the framed pictures of her parents. "They're fine, Lily," she said. "They're with you now, you know."

"I don't understand," Lily said.

"Your parents," Jordan said. "They're here, watching over you, keeping you safe."

Lily's eyes welled. "They are?"

Jordan smiled. "Indeed. Never doubt that. Not even for a minute."

Dunn interjected. "Perhaps I should explain, Lily. Jordan has a very special gift. She's one of the world's foremost psychics."

"I recognize your name," Shannon said.

"Me too," Zoe added. "Shannon and I are both lawyers. We studied a case you were involved with two years ago in Connecticut. The Bamford kidnapping and murders. You helped the police locate the bodies and catch the killers."

"I remember it well," Jordan said. "I understand from your father you both attended Harvard?"

"We did," Shannon said.

"I sailed for Harvard."

"Basketball was my game," Zoe said. "Go Crimson!"

Shannon raised her hands. "Don't look at me. I don't have an athletic bone in my body."

"Me neither," Lily added.

Jordan laughed.

Andrew Dunn's cell phone rang. He checked the display. "Excuse me," he said as he walked away from the group.

Jordan introduced Shannon, Zoe, and Lily to her godfather and Special Agent Hanover. Lily shook Chris' hand and blushed. Zoe noticed her reaction and being Zoe, seized the opportunity to tease her. "Hot, isn't he?"

Carnevale laughed.

Chris smiled, tried to turn away. Jordan grabbed his jacket, saw his face, pulled him back. "Are you blushing, tough guy?" she joked.

Andrew Dunn returned. "That was Commander Reed with Hostage Rescue. CSI found several blister packs of Rohypnol hidden in the wheel well of the Chevy."

"Uncle Emmett's car," Lily said. "Ben and Basil used it all the time."

"Must be what they used to knock us out," Shannon said.

Their father nodded. "Trace amounts of the drug were found in the wine in the condo. CSI also found a manila envelope containing surveillance pics of the two of you on the Harvard campus. The address of the rental condo in L.A. was inside the folder. Prints on the blister pack came back to three subjects: Ben and Basil Maynard, plus a small-time drug dealer by the name of Dwayne Kirby. Agents picked up

Kirby and brought him in for questioning. He rolled on Ben. Said he had accepted the kidnapping contract but got cold feet. He still wanted the payout, or at least part of it, so he sub-contracted it to Ben. The phone you used to call me, Ben's phone, contained audio he recorded of his meeting with Kirby detailing the plan, who was involved, information on your coming and going, the works. Kirby's cooked. And with Ben and Basil dead, he's the one left holding the bag. By the time the Bureau's done with him he won't see the light of day for years to come."

"But why take us in the first place?" Zoe asked.

"The Bureau's been keeping a close eye on me for the past few months," Dunn said. "I can't get into the details. They're classified. All I can say is that the people associated with Kirby wanted to get to me through you."

"There were photos of you on the stable wall," Shannon said.

"So I heard."

"Are you still in danger?" Zoe asked.

"I don't think so, honey. Kirby provided us with enough information to go after the people responsible for this. Arrest warrants have been issued. The raids will take place today. It's over."

"Thank God," Zoe said.

Dunn nodded. "Reed also told me CSI found the remains of a kerosene lamp on the back porch of the house. They lifted finger and palm prints and ran them through RISC, the Repository for Individuals of Special Concern. They came back to Emmett Maynard. Why the old man torched the place is anybody's guess. Maybe he was trying to destroy evidence or cover something up. No matter. CSI's still sifting through the debris and continuing their investigation. With that will come more answers."

"What about the men who tried to kill my family?" Jordan asked. "Have you been able to identify them?"

"We have," Dunn answered. "Their names are James Rigel and Harrison Tasker. Rigel, the man you shot in the house, is the same man who tried to kill you in the hospital. Quantico reviewed the hospital footage we sent them. Biometrics confirms it. We've been looking for him for some time. We found his car parked on a new home construction site down the road from the estate. The site supervisor called it into LAPD. They called us when Rigel's name came up as someone we were interested in talking to. The address on the car's registration was for a condo in Safety Harbor, Florida. Tampa agents searched the residence and found a cache of weapons along with scrapbooks filled with newspaper articles covering a series of unsolved homicides. Some stories had been blown up to poster size, framed, and hung on the wall like pieces of art. They also found a trunk in the bedroom closet containing four wooden cigar boxes. We found a fifth in the trunk of his car. All were filled with miscellaneous women's items: nail files, hairbrushes, scarves, panties... you name it. The box in the car trunk contained a barrette and a tongue-stud, among other items."

Jordan remembered the conference, her conversation with Chief Wayne Ballantyne, and her vision of the final moments in Becky Landry's life when her struggle for survival ended with the barrettes being pulled from her hair.

"They're souvenirs," Jordan said. "Kill trophies."

Dunn nodded. "That's right. Trace DNA on the items matches fifty victims, all unsolved homicides. Most of the names coincided with the articles in the scrapbook or the wall posters. The sick sonofabitch was following the media's coverage of his kills. Trust me, as much as I would have liked to have seen him stand trial for the crimes he committed and the lives he took, you did the world a favor by taking him out."

"My pleasure," Jordan said

"One more thing," Dunn added. "When Quantico ran the hospital surveillance, they got a hit against a photo taken a year ago by our Organized Crime Task Force. The picture showed Rigel meeting with Salvatore Monterra, the boss of New York's Monterra crime family. The Monterra's are into everything from drug trafficking and money laundering to prostitution, kidnapping, extortion, and murder for hire. Various agencies... FBI, Justice, and DEA, had noticed a shift in Monterra's financial activity over the last couple of years. Most notable was the sudden interest he'd taken in the tech sector. A Joint Task Force was established between the agencies to take him down. Investigator's concluded the family was trying to transition away from illegal business activities to legitimate ones. One of Monterra's first investments was a small tech start-up, SerraDyne Terratech, headed by a guy by the name of Allan Marsden. Monterra paid Marsden five-hundred-thousand dollars for the company, then sunk another million into patent filings."

Jordan recalled the book signing. "Allan Marsden showed up at the American Association of Police Chiefs conference I spoke at a few days ago. He told me my father had cost him everything, that somehow he had ruined his life."

Dunn shook his head. "If anyone ruined Marsden's life, it was Marsden himself. There was a back story to his company; one that Marsden conveniently failed to share with Monterra. As you know, Farrow Industries is always on the lookout for up-and-coming tech companies they can acquire to make use of their intellectual properties within one or more of their divisions. SerraDyne Terratech came to Farrow's attention. They offered to buy the company from Monterra for twenty million dollars, including the in-process patent applications. Monterra accepted the deal. But when Farrow's attorneys performed their due diligence on the proposed acquisition, they discovered a problem. One of SerraDyne Terratech's patent applications infringed upon one of their own. They dug a little deeper and looked at the computer files Monterra provided them as part of the deal. The files had been authored by Marsden, who had in fact worked at Farrow Industries for a while. They concluded he'd stolen the technology from Farrow while still in their employ. After leaving the company he waited two years before starting SerraDyne Terratech. Never in a million years could he have imagined that the company that would one day offer to buy SerraDyne Terratech from Monterra would be Farrow Industries."

"At which point Farrow would have cited 'just cause' and walked away from the deal," Jordan said.

"That's precisely what happened. When Farrow pulled out, Monterra was furious. He accused Marsden of costing him twenty-one and a half million dollars. He went after him for the five-hundred grand he paid for the company, plus the million for the patent applications and twenty million he lost on the deal. But Marsden didn't have a dime to his name. He was being sued by Farrow Industries for breach of contract and theft of intellectual property. He figured Monterra would probably have him killed, so he played a card that saved his skin but ultimately concluded with Rigel and Tasker coming after your family. He'd developed another computer technology, one that was worth tens of millions of dollars. That tech was wholly his design. He told Monterra that he could have it, free and clear, to settle the debt, but only under one condition."

"That Monterra authorize a contract to kill my family."

"Exactly. In some twisted way, Marsden wanted your father to pay the ultimate price for ruining him, which he hadn't. There was already bad blood over the twenty million Monterra lost when Farrow Industries pulled out of the SerraDyne Terratech deal, so Monterra agreed. We figure he assigned James Rigel to execute the hit."

"Then where does Harrison Tasker come in?"

"He too is a known associate of the Monterra family. Considering how high-profile a target your father was, Monterra probably wasn't comfortable using just one hitman to fulfil the contract, so he sent Tasker as well."

"There's still the matter of determining the cause of the jet crash," Jordan said.

"We now know what happened," Dunn explained. "Remember I told you that I had a contact at the National Transportation Safety Board? My friend, Bill Parker, is Director of Air Safety Investigation at the NTSB's Los Angeles field office and a plane crash evidence collection expert. I asked him to review the debris collected from the runway and crash site. Bill told me they found pieces of rubber near the end of the runway that smelled like they'd been soaked in jet fuel. The design, structure and composition of those fragments matched the tires on your father's jet. NTSB believes the jet's tires had been wiped down. They found a fuel-soaked towel in a trash can in the hangar and traces of fuel on the tire valve stems and the pressurization equipment used to fill them. I'd sent pictures of both Rigel and Tasker out to the field. Agents working with Bill and his people showed them to the hangar staff. A clerk identified Tasker as a fire chief who had demanded access to the hangars. We think Monterra ordered him to sabotage the aircraft. NTSB believes the jet's tires had been soaked with fuel and overfilled. As soon as the tires came into contact with the hot tarmac during taxi and takeoff, a perfect storm was created. The fuel on the surface of the tires became super-heated. Friction with the runway caused a build-up of static electricity, which ignited the fuel and caused the tires to blow. In his report, the coroner who picked up the bodies of Rigel and Tasker noted the smell of fuel on Taskers clothing. How much do you want to bet that when we swab the tire's valve stem and the pressurization equipment in the hangar for epithelial DNA, we'll get a positive match to Tasker? We found his car parked around the corner from the estate, too. The interior smelled faintly like gasoline."

"We're still not out of the woods," Jordan said. "By now, Monterra knows Rigel and Tasker failed. He'll send another team of assassins after my family to finish the job."

Dunn shook his head. "Agents took Salvatore Monterra into custody yesterday afternoon. He won't be communicating with anyone other than his attorney for quite a while. He won't try anything now. He's too hot. Too many eyes are on him."

"What about Marsden?"

"His landlord found him in his basement apartment yesterday. He'd been shot twice; one bullet to the heart, a second to the head. The contents of a SerraDyne Terratech file were thrown over his body. The message was clear. It was a classic mob hit." Dunn looked around the cemetery. Members of Jordan's protection detail mingled with his agents. "Looks like you're well protected."

Jordan smiled. "Let's hope so."

"So, what happens, now?" Dunn asked. "Will you be taking the helm at Farrow Industries?"

Jordan shrugged her shoulders. "I don't know. The company will continue to run fine, with or without me. My father left good people in charge. In the greater scheme of things, my role would be a minor one, anyway. Besides, I can't just stop what I'm doing."

"You're right," Dunn agreed. "The work you do is too important. Your skills are far too valuable to waste sitting in an office." He paused. "I've been thinking about something," he said. "Are you open to a suggestion?"

"What did you have in mind?" Jordan said.

"Come work for us."

"For the FBI?"

"Yes," Dunn answered. "It will be an unprecedented decision on my behalf and most certainly met with a great deal of criticism. But the Bureau is always looking for new ways and means to stay one step ahead of the bad guys. Maybe the time has come to welcome someone with your unique gift into the organization." Dunn smiled. "Jordan Quest, FBI," he said. "Kind of has a nice ring it, doesn't it?"

Jordan smiled. "Yes, it does."

"You'd have to go through agent training, of course," the Director continued. "But I'm sure in your case special provisions can be made. Besides, you're talking to the guy who'd have to sign off on it and I'm already on board." Dunn extended his hand. "What do you say, Jordan? Will you join us?"

Jordan shook his hand. "It would be my honor, Director."

Dunn smiled. "Good. I think you and the Bureau will make a good team."

"Me too," Jordan said. "I just have one request, if possible."

"Sure," Dunn answered. "Name it."

"If it's all right with you, I'd like to partner with Agent Hanover. We've already established somewhat of a working relationship."

The Director smiled. "Consider it done."

62

___

IN THE WEEKS and months following the tragic events which had affected them all so deeply, Jordan and her family began the long and difficult process of rebuilding their lives.

In memory of her parents, Jordan sold the home she had shared with Keith and moved her family into Farrow mansion, much to Marissa DeSola's delight. Though now a rich woman in her own right, Marissa stayed on at Jordan's request, sharing the grand home with the family she loves so much.

Paula and David Quest stayed with Jordan for a while, spent time with their grandchildren, and helped their daughter-in-law transition to a life without their son and her beloved Keith.

Abe Carmichael was awarded the FBI's *Civilian Award for Bravery* for saving the life of Special Agent Chris Hanover. He continues to work as a mechanical engineer at Angel of Mercy Hospital.

Andrew Dunn petitioned the courts and was granted legal custody of Lily Maynard, who now goes by the name

Lily Maynard-Dunn. She is enjoying her new life with her stepsisters. Shannon reports that, under Zoe's expert tutelage, Lily's swearing vocabulary is now extensive enough to make a trucker blush.

Shannon and Zoe started their law practice, Dunn and Associates, specializing in Human Rights and Humanitarian Law. Lily has shown an interest in following in the footsteps of her stepsisters and stepfather. She plans to attend Harvard Law with a long-term goal of becoming an FBI agent. As a family, they traveled to the site of the home that had once belonged to her parents and become her prison for over a year. The bodies of her parents, Rose and Colton Maynard, were exhumed from the property and laid to rest. Lily was given the closure she needed to move on with her life. She made a vow to visit their graves once a year.

Chris dated Audrey Long, Jordan's nurse at Angel of Mercy Hospital, once. It didn't work out. She is now happily married to Dr. Paul Tremaine.

Under a special program established and overseen by Director Andrew Dunn, Jordan completed her FBI training. Chris Hanover became her partner.

Together they are responsible for investigating the Bureau's most challenging and difficult cases.

ABOUT THE AUTHOR

Gary Winston Brown is a retired practitioner of natural medicine and the author of the Jordan Quest FBI thriller series and other works of fiction. His books feature strong, independent characters pitted against insurmountable odds who are not afraid to stand up for those in need of protection.

On the Author-Reader Relationship

Getting to know my readers and building strong relationships with them is one of the best parts of being a writer. I put a great deal of effort into creating my books. My goal with every novel I write is to make it better than the last, earn your five-star review, and make your reading experience the best it can be.

I'd love to know what you thought of this book (or boxset). What did you like about it? Who was your favorite character? Did I keep you wanting to know what was going to happen next? What do you want to see in an upcoming novel?

Please subscribe to my monthly newsletter. I'll send you the series prequel, *Jordan Quest*, for free as a thank you. Be sure to follow me on Amazon for updates on forthcoming books and new releases.

Follow me on Amazon

Please Post a Review

May I ask for your honest opinion. Did you like this book?

Reviews are the lifeblood to my work as a novelist. They mean the world to me. Long and fancy isn't necessary. What matters is your honest opinion. Did you enjoy this book? Did I deliver a good story to you? Rate it five stars and say a few words about what you most enjoyed about it. Or choose another rating. Your feedback is what matters. It's what makes me a better writer. And the better I can get at writing my books the better the reading experience I'll be able to provide to you.

Why your review is so important

I am a relatively new writer. I don't have a huge marketing machine or advertising department behind me like mainstream authors do to help build a buzz around my books and get them out in front of millions of readers.

But I do have *you*.

I am very grateful to have a growing following of loyal, committed readers who take the time to let me know what they think of my books. If you liked this book (or boxset) I would be extremely grateful if you would take a few seconds to post a review. It can be as long or short as you like. All reviews are appreciated and helpful to me.

Thank you!

Gary

ALSO BY GARY WINSTON BROWN

The Jordan Quest Thriller Series (in order):

Intruders

The Sin Keeper

Mr. Grimm

Nine Lives

Live To Tell

Jordan's next adventure is coming soon!

Follow me on Amazon for the latest updates on new releases.

Coming in 2021:

The Matt Gamble thriller series

(vigilante justice, organized/international crime, assassination, spies, political).

The Vanishing (stand-alone thriller)